Praise for the

Countin.

Counting on Love is a workplace romance story set in an Australian financial firm. Both characters are well developed beyond the bounds of the workplace. The writing and dialogue is well done and the descriptions of sunrise make me want to book a ticket.

-C-Spot Reviews

An amazing workplace and slow-burn romance. This is the first book of this author that I read, and I look forward to the next. I enjoyed the story line. Both the main characters are lovable. And their attraction is obvious. An amazing read!

-Isabelle S., NetGalley

Counting on Love is a book you can count on to love to read. This book has great characters and storyline. It is well written and entertaining.

-Heather B., NetGalley

I liked the main characters as well as the supporting ones. Zoe and Reyna both had backstories that impacted their thoughts and actions. I thought they were both likable and I was rooting for their happiness. There was a nice depth to the story that made me feel invested in how things turned out. It made me cry. So it definitely hit at the heart during a few angsty moments. I recommend this to people who enjoy reading about romance, friendships, the corporate world, unexpected parenting, coping with loss, Alice Springs, and financial improvement.

-Carrie K., NetGalley

Hashtag love

Other Bella Books by RL Burgess

Counting on Love
Match Point

About the Author

Rosie Burgess is a musician, writer, lover, mother, best friend, dog owner, slave to two cats and decaf coffee drinker. She writes mostly when other people are sleeping, spending her days playing music and working with community groups. Rosie lives on the beach side of Melbourne, in Australia.

Hashtag love

RL Burgess

BELLA
BOOKS
2021

Acknowledgments

Thank you to Sam and George. Your hearts inspire me to be the best I can be and your love makes my world go around.

Thank you to Cath for your wonderful positivity in the editing process. You made it feel so easy.

Thank you to Bella Books for giving us all this space.

Thank you to everyone who wants to get lost in a book and chooses this one.

For my darlings: Sam, George, Ruby, Pep and Fred.

CHAPTER ONE

My glasses inched down my nose as if in sympathy with my slowly sinking heart. I checked the time on my phone again. I had been reading this manuscript for an hour, which was now fifty-nine minutes longer than I would have chosen to devote to this project. In total. For some unknown reason my boss was not on the same page. She had given it the green light and this had me flummoxed. Reflexively, I licked my finger and turned the page, sighing heavily as I pushed my glasses back to the bridge of my nose.

A tap at my office door provided a welcome interruption and I raised my head gratefully. Standing in the doorway, in the kind of crisp white shirt I could only ever dream of keeping clean and a pair of flared grey pants, was Cathy Belayme, Publisher in Chief of Red Stone Publishing House. My boss and my best friend. We usually saw entirely eye to eye on the material published by Red Stone. Today we were more like nose to ear.

I peered at her from over the top of my glasses. "Have you come to tell me this is some kind of sick joke?" I asked, eyebrows hopeful, picking up the sheaf of paper and waving it at her.

"I doubt it," she replied, leaning her willowy frame against the door. She feigned innocence saying, "Which one is that?"

I flicked back to the front page and read aloud, "*True Likes.* Hally Arlow.*" I wrinkled my nose as I spoke, not bothering to hide my disdain. What kind of a name was Hally anyway? Had her parents meant to name her after the world's most famous comet and misspelled it?

"Sorry. No such luck, Gin."

"Really? Have you read it? I can't think how it even got past Acquisitions." I sighed again. It had only just gone ten a.m. and I was on a higher sigh count than usual, even for me.

Cathy threw herself into the chair across from me. This was not unusual. Even though she was technically my boss, our long history and close friendship meant she often stopped by for a chat. A telltale line of worry snaked between her eyebrows.

"We can talk about that later. Listen, I've had to move the Round Table up to this afternoon. Mum's had a fall."

"Oh no!" I frowned. "What happened? Is she okay?"

Cathy's soft dark eyes were serious. "Apparently. It looks like she's just bruised her hip but they're doing x-rays and keeping her in for a few days, just in case. I'm flying up to check on her straight after work. I'll let you know more as soon as I know."

"Shit. That's awful. Are you okay?"

"I'm worried. Rachel didn't seem to be overly concerned but maybe she was just trying to downplay things so I wouldn't stress out." She rubbed a hand across her closely cropped dark curls, leaning back in the chair.

"Your sister isn't exactly the downplay kind." I grimaced, thinking about Cathy's extremely sensitive and highly strung sister. If a pin dropped, not only would she hear it, she would make the entire room stop to search for it, just in case someone stepped on it, contracted septicaemia and died. Rachel excelled at imagining worst-case scenarios, all of which seemed to end in painful and protracted death. She and Cathy couldn't have been more opposite. As kids, Rachel had stuck to us like glue, desperate to join our secret societies, pedalling hard to keep up as we coasted off on our big-girl bikes. Mrs. Belayme was so excellent at making us feel ashamed for excluding Rachel that we almost always gave up and grudgingly allowed her to tag along.

Not having a mum of my own, I avoided being the recipient of one of Mrs. Belayme's piercing looks of reproach. She was an affectionate and energetic woman, and I basked in the warmth of her attention. In fact, sometimes I let myself imagine, with my own dark hair and easily tanned skin, that I was a part of their family, that I too had emigrated from Ethiopia. In my childish indulgence, Cathy and I were alternately sisters or cousins. I would pretend that it was my father who had been killed in the war and that was why we had had to come to Australia, Rachel swaddled in a sling on Mrs. Belayme's breast, Cathy and I holding tightly to each of her hands. I even tried to stretch my mouth around the musical tongue I heard when Cathy and I stayed up late pretending to be asleep while Mrs. Belayme chatted with her friends in their native dialect.

And then my dad would call up and hesitantly ask for me to come home. He wouldn't say that he missed me but I would feel insanely guilty for leaving him alone all weekend and pretending he didn't exist. I felt a flash of familiar guilt now, reminding myself that I needed to call him. I filed that thought away for later, focusing now on Cathy's mum.

"What exactly did Rachel say?"

"She said Mum's in the hospital but not to freak out because she's okay and she should be out in a couple of days. But you know how she is. Rachel hates it when I drop everything and rush up to Sydney. Maybe she's just trying to stop me from coming up," Cathy said.

I nodded, aware of the sisters' dynamic.

"How is Rachel doing?"

"She actually seems to be managing incredibly well, all things considered. I don't know if I'd be handling it this well. Apparently Mum had been trying to leave the house every five seconds. Rachel said she thinks she's back in Addis Ababa and is trying to get us out of the country."

"Oh god, how awful."

"I know. She slipped over in the bathroom. She got out of the shower and started trying to pack up her toiletries while she was still dripping wet. Rachel said she'll have to start supervising her showering from now on."

"Is there any medication they can give her? Is it like hallucinating or something?"

"Not really. There are a few drugs that might possibly improve memory, but nothing that reverses the Alzheimer's, and according to Rachel the jury's out on whether anything works. She's done a lot of reading and you know how she is with drugs."

I did know. Rachel's love-hate relationship with her own mental health medication meant many mood swings and difficult days. "Maybe the hospital will be able to help, now that she's there."

Cathy shrugged, dark smudges under her eyes telling the tale of her stress. "Mum's getting even more confused in the hospital, with all the people rushing around and the bright lights and beeping machines. Rachel wants to get her home and back into her normal routine as soon as possible. I told her I was coming up to help out but she totally freaked out. She thinks I'm going to come up to Sydney, declare her unfit to care for Mum and drag them both down to Melbourne to watch over them."

"Yikes. Is there anything I can do?"

"Feed Olive?" Cathy uncrossed her long legs and pushed herself out of the chair. She wandered over to my bookshelf, picking up the snow globe I'd brought back from our trip to the Paris Book Fair last year.

"Of course."

I watched as Cathy shook the snow globe, causing pieces of "snow" to swirl around the Eiffel Tower and the tiny people going about their business underneath it. "I think I'll hang about and work from the Sydney office for the rest of the week while this all pans out."

"No problem. I can pick Olive up on my way home tonight. Asimov will be glad of the company." We had both decided to give a "furrever home" to a pair of rescue cats after attending a donor ball for the RSPCA a few years ago. Thankfully the two cats got along well and we were able to help each other out as needed. Asimov, with his large grey frame and permanently furrowed brow, was not always the most gregarious of cats, but he seemed to enjoy Olive's company. It would be no problem for us to absorb her into our household while Cathy was away.

"Thanks, Gin." Cathy paused in the doorway. "You're the best."

"Keep me posted about your mum. If there's anything else I can do to help, just say the word."

"Of course."

"But don't think you're off the hook with this." I picked up the offending manuscript and with a thud let it drop back to my desk. "This is awful, and you know it."

"Gin." Cathy fixed me with a steely gaze. "We've discussed this already. Red Stone needs to branch out and get with the times. It's do or die in this cut-throat industry. Nonfiction is more than just history and politics, and as the managing editor of this section you need to know that."

"I *do* know that," I said indignantly. "There's also travel and gardening and science and philosophy. But not this. This is... self-help trash." I delivered the words with a curl of my lip.

"Harsh," Cathy replied, shaking her head. "Think of it more as an autobiography."

"Autobiography! It's full of preachy truisms masquerading as advice. Anyway, what has she done to justify an autobiography? She's created an exercise franchise. She won't be the first and she definitely won't be the last. People don't write their own biographies just because they've got a couple of gyms."

"She has more than just a couple, Gin. She's got the whole deal." Cathy ticked things off on her fingers as she listed off, "A national network of gyms, her social media has blown up, her YouTube channel is the most subscribed health channel in Australia, she has her own app, she's all over print media, and she's a special guest on TV every other week. She's a health guru and entrepreneur, and the fact is, that is hot right now. The next step for her is this book and people want to hear from her."

"Seriously." I frowned heavily, conscious of the line starting to imprint itself permanently between my eyebrows. Asimov and me both. I flicked off my glasses and rubbed at it distractedly. "Who cares how many Instagram followers she has? And does anyone seriously want to know how she creates her breakfast Snapchats? Publishing this rot won't help the world, Cathy," I said, aware that I was sounding pompous, but not caring. "And while we're at it, what exactly is latte art?"

"Gin," Cathy said in her soothing voice, "you're fighting a losing battle. People *do* care about this stuff, and Hally Arlow has worked hard to harness the power of social media to build her empire. She's blazing a trail for other women out there to start their own businesses, and lots of people look to her as a mentor. Fair enough, the manuscript might need a bit of work, but that's what you're here for. You're going to help her turn it into something distinguished, something masterful, something we'll be proud to publish."

"Can't be done." I shook my head and ran a hand across the closely cropped back of my head. I could feel the top of my hair standing up in a tousled spiky mess. "You have the wrong girl and the wrong book. Nothing can turn this…this sludge into art."

"I believe in you, Gin."

I snorted. "You shouldn't!"

She glanced at the chunky gold watch dangling loosely on her slender wrist. "I have to get moving. Don't forget, Round Table this afternoon. Two o'clock in the boardroom."

"Cathy!"

"Got to go," she said, holding up her hands as she backed out.

"Shit." I stared at the manuscript, wondering if I should just save us all the trouble and accidentally shred it. Cathy was wrong. There was nothing salvageable in here. Working on this would just get Hally Arlow's hopes up, and worse, it would be a giant waste of my time. But I knew shredding it wasn't the answer. In this digital day and age it was almost impossible to delete something from existence. After last year's unfortunate episode when my laptop had fallen into the bath, the IT department had somehow managed to resurrect all my files, assuring me that I could have run it over with a four-wheel drive and set it on fire and they would still have been able to salvage the contents of the hard drive. I would need to come up with a different plan.

Hally Arlow. What a stupid name. I wondered if it was her real name or if she had made it up. Was anything about her real? Incredibly, given all that Cathy had just listed, I had managed to avoid knowing anything about her. I could just imagine her type—painfully skinny, prancing around in her activewear, swinging her lashings of lustrous hair, probably blond, or maybe brunette if she was trying to project a more serious image. With my spiky black hair and Buddy Holly glasses we were probably exact opposites.

I cursed. Why, oh why had she decided to write a book? Cathy was wrong about this. This work was beneath us and it was a mistake to even consider publishing it. But when Cathy had her heart set on something, there was little anyone could do to shift her. Her slender figure belied an iron will. Unable to think of a way around it, I slipped my glasses back on and continued, forcing myself to take in every painful word as I read on.

At exactly 2:05 p.m., armed with an extra-frothy, double-shot cappuccino, I parked myself at the end of the boardroom table next to Alice from Romance and opened my notebook. I would normally have steered clear of Alice, but unfortunately there were no other seats left. Alice blessed me with a flash of her gleaming white teeth and fluttered her extra-long pale lashes.

"Afternoon, Gin," she breathed, tucking a strand of platinum-blond hair behind a perfect, shell-like ear. Honestly, Alice never just spoke like normal people. She was romance personified. She whispered and simpered and sparkled, where the rest of us just got on with the job of talking to people. I nodded back at her, avoiding eye contact in case she tried to chat, a high possibility given that Cathy had yet to arrive. Her assistant sat at the top of the table, tapping officiously into her laptop, so Cathy wouldn't be far off, but I didn't much fancy being dragged into a pointless exchange of semi-intimate details of the weekend while we waited.

Alice, on the other hand, appeared undeterred in her current pet project, connect-with-Gin. "Jason and I saw the new *Samsara* movie on Saturday night. It was absolutely fabulous. Have you seen it?"

I grunted in the negative, hunching over my notebook.

"Oh, you must see it. It was simply stunning. Apparently it took five years to film because the director wanted everything to be just so."

"Director sounds annoying," I mumbled, in spite of myself.

"The cinematography was astounding," she continued, ignoring my body language. For a romance specialist she certainly didn't excel at reading nonverbal cues. "Did you know the crew actually spent six months living in a yurt in the Himalayas just to get an authentic feel. Apparently the winter temperatures—"

Cathy's opportune entrance spared me the details of a movie I would never see. "Sorry I'm late, people," she said as she swept in and deposited her laptop on the desk. "Let's make up for lost time. Ellen," she signalled her assistant, "are we ready?"

Ellen looked at her pointedly, her hands poised over her own laptop. "Ready and waiting."

"Good." Cathy glanced behind her at the agenda projected on the boardroom's wall-to-ceiling data screen. "I want to skip items one, two and three today. Let's move straight to Round The Table. Frank, can you kick us off?"

Round The Table was the editorial staff's weekly chance to fill each other in on what we were working on and to float any issues for group discussion. Cathy loved it. She lived for the moments when the group cracked a particularly difficult issue through some good old-fashioned brainstorming.

Personally, I could take it or leave it. My style was more go-it-alone. I preferred to put my head down and get cracking, rather than sit around and chat for hours. If I hit an insurmountable snag I could always go to Cathy. Not to say the rest of the team didn't have merit, I've just never really been one for team sports. (Side note: I've never been one for any kind of sports.) And that was why Cathy was the boss and I was just an editor. That, and the fact that she had always dreamed of running her own publishing house and I had always dreamed of being an editor.

Frank cleared his throat and shuffled his notes, then used a thick finger to loosen his tie. His heavy woollen suit hung awkwardly from his lanky frame, making him look like an outdoor adventurer who had somehow found himself in the wrong century giving a boardroom presentation. "Let me see," he said, glancing down at his page. I tried not to squirm in my seat. Frank was not known for being succinct. Thankfully Cathy was excellent at guiding him along without seeming patronising. "Just the dot points, Frank," she said with an encouraging smile. "I've got a flight to catch today so we're a little pushed for time. Where are we up to with Crime this week?"

He rubbed the back of his hand across his greying beard. "Okay, ah." He looked back down at his notes touching the items with his finger as he spoke.

"We're three quarters through editing Gershon's second draft—it's really very good. I particularly think you'll enjoy the inherent tension between the landscape and the subject matter. The artistry with which Gershon crafts his secondary characters is really second to none and something I think many in the genre could learn from—"

Cathy coughed and Frank looked up. "Ah, yes, well, and in other news Patrick is gearing up for his release date and we're working with Marketing on a national campaign so that should be quite the debut. I'm tempted to—" He looked up at Cathy again and managed to redirect himself this time.

"Lastly, Maddie is experiencing writer's block. She says her protagonist is in jail and she can't work out how to get her out without being clichéd." A few members of the team groaned in sympathy. We all liked Maddie Cerwick. She was an eccentric writer, with a lopsided smile and mismatched brown and blue eyes, and she was generous, unfailingly sending the team a

Christmas hamper, remembering birthdays and important anniversaries that most people, myself included, barely remembered themselves. I'd even read a few of her books. For crime novels they were unexpectedly original, full of dry wit and hard-boiled action. It wasn't my genre of choice but I could stretch to it on a beach holiday or a plane.

"Has she tried taking a break?" Lara from Young Adult Fiction asked. "Two weeks off without touching the manuscript can do the trick sometimes."

John, the managing editor of Fiction chimed in, swiping his sandy hair clear of his earnest, bovine-brown eyes. "Maybe she could do a reading. That sometimes helps. Have you set her up with a test group?" John's was the biggest editorial team with three dedicated editors. John and I supposedly had similar responsibilities, but in reality my Nonfiction Department was much smaller. Less of a team, and more of a solo project really. But hey, that was just how I liked it.

Frank nodded and stroked his beard again. "Thank you, yes, both good ideas. I'll check in with her after the meeting."

"Right. Great work. That's Crime. So, John, catch us up on Fiction this week?" Cathy asked, shifting her gaze across the table.

I tuned out as John went through the gamut of projects on the boil. I knew the list would be long and John, for all his enthusiastic conviction, was boring and officious in his delivery. After John, Lara ran us through her happenings, and then Alice lisped and gushed her way through her week's priorities, clasping her hands together passionately as she described the new manuscript she had just reviewed from Acquisitions. "I just know you're all going to love it," she said brightly. "It's my pick for our number-one seller next year. If anyone wants a sneak peek, I'm happy to forward the manuscript."

I tried not to roll my eyes, catching a warning frown from Cathy who was well aware of my low tolerance threshold for Alice from Romance. Honestly, didn't we all have enough on our plates without reading an unedited manuscript? An unedited *romance* manuscript, at that.

"I'd like to take a look, Al," Elsbeth, one of John's Fiction team, said. She had a friendly smile and inviting grey eyes but I immediately struck her off my Christmas list. Encouraging Alice was an unforgivable sin.

"Okay, Gin, lucky last. Your turn," Cathy directed, saving Elsbeth from further exposure to my disparaging frown.

I sat up in my seat, confident in my capacity to be concise. "Right, well. Massimoto's *Brief History of Biology* is in its final edit, Gates has the illustrations ready for *Biodynamic Home Gardening*, I'm mapping out Jess Silverman's *Cooking as Religion* publicity tour and we're going chapter by chapter through the Turnbull biography with Legal at the moment. So far it looks like no one will get sued so everything's pretty much on track," I concluded with a bright smile. More than confident that I had my workload firmly under control, I didn't want to invite commentary or suggestions. I took a sip of my coffee.

"And Hally Arlow," Cathy prompted.

I snorted, nearly expelling the coffee through my nose. "I'm sorry, what?"

"You left off the Arlow manuscript."

"Manuscript?"

"Ginerva," Cathy warned, her eyes shooting laser beams at me across the table. "Please fill the team in on your latest acquisition."

I swallowed slowly, and dabbed my nose, conscious that a small amount of coffee may have trickled out of it. I couldn't believe she was bringing this up in front of the whole team. She couldn't seriously think we would publish this ridiculousness. In deference to her position I said, "Hally Arlow has submitted some...pages for consideration."

"Who is Hally Arlow?" Frank asked, looking with bewilderment between Cathy and me.

"Exactly." I smirked triumphantly at Cathy whose eyes had moved from lasers to bullets. Uh oh. I quickly rearranged my face, trying to look sincere as I explained, "She's a fitness guru lady...woman...person," I corrected myself. "She's built an empire of gymnasiums and menu plans and social-media posts and now she wants to tell everyone how and why she's done it."

"Oh, I love Hally," Alice exclaimed. Of course she did. I ignored her.

"Actually, I'm a member of one of her gyms," John spoke up, startling me. "The premise is pretty cool. They have this deal where you can pay to develop a goal with a fitness instructor, who plans out how you'll get there and you don't pay any more until you've hit it. They do have other regular memberships and stuff, but I like that one because it feels like they're actually invested in helping you achieve your fitness goal—not just taking your cash."

I stared at him, trying to marry his words with what I knew of him. John was the human equivalent of a teddy bear—floppy, hair always falling in front of his eyes, a warm smile hovering in the corners of his mouth, and lots of rounded-off edges. His bulging waistline nudged against his tight shirt and his first chin sat on top of a comfortable-looking second, slightly obscuring his neck. He wasn't drastically overweight, but he certainly did not have the air of a man with a gym membership.

"You go to the gym, John?" was all I could think of in response.

"Not the point, Gin," Cathy said, smirking. "It sounds like we've got a few on staff who might be interested in a Hally Arlow biography. Show of hands around the table please?"

To my surprise, more than half the team complied. In fact, it was only me and Frank who didn't. Darling Frank. I wasn't surprised that he didn't know who Hally Arlow was. If it wasn't detective fiction, he wasn't interested. Most popular culture just passed him right by. I shook my head. "Perhaps if you took a look at it you might change—"

"I don't think so," Cathy cut me off. "We've all received manuscripts that need some work. But it's up to us to find that kernel of excitement, the germ of interest that needs to be fostered, to kindle the spark into a crackling fire. That's what you're all so excellent at. If only every manuscript that came our way was as polished as a Massimoto or a Maddie Cerwick, we'd barely have to lift a finger. But given that they're not, we often have to work a little harder to find the gold in the pan."

"Thank you, Cathy," I replied, my tone undeniably acerbic. "This manuscript is not quite at the stage of kindling a spark. I'd call it more like searching for a forest to cut down a tree in order to start a fire when the wood has dried out next winter."

Despite our argument, Cathy laughed. "I look forward to your weekly reports on the progress of this one."

"Oh, so do I," Alice trilled. "If you need any beta readers, don't hesitate to call me."

"Really? Would you like to take over the manuscript?" I enquired, looking directly at her for the first time since the meeting began.

"I—" She looked confused, eyebrows drawn together over her clear blues, full pink lips parted slightly. She turned to Cathy for guidance.

Cathy banged her laptop lid shut and shook her head in exasperation. "Ignore her, Alice," she directed, gathering up her diary and notebook and piling them on top of her computer. She stood up and addressed the team. "I'll be up in Sydney for the rest of this week. Email me if you need something non-urgent. Call if there's a fire. Ellen will have my schedule. I'll probably be back here Monday. In the meantime, onward and upward," she said with an encouraging smile, which turned into a momentary glare when she met my eyes.

I smiled apologetically. I hadn't meant to cause an issue, I just couldn't bring myself to see a Hally Arlow manuscript as a serious project.

As Cathy left the room Alice put her hand on my arm, startling me into looking at her again. "Gin, if you do need any help with this Hally Arlow manuscript, I really would be happy to."

"Thank you, Alice," I said, looking away from her as I slid my arm out from under her hand. I snapped my notebook closed. "I'm sure I can manage it."

"Oh no doubt," she breathed, "I just know it can be tricky to edit something when you don't really believe in it. So, if you need a second pair of eyes, just swing over to my office."

Ug. She was right. What had my day come to when Alice from Romance was right? It *was* hard to edit a manuscript that you didn't care for. How on earth could I possibly pull this off? I glanced at her again, my eyes shying off with the depth of her sympathetic, azure gaze. "I'll keep that in mind."

"Good." She reached out and squeezed my arm. Once again, I tugged it away, scooping up my notebook and pushing back my chair.

"Got to run," I said and literally jogged out.

I closed my office door firmly, pulled the door blind all the way down and lay on the floor, feeling my back stretch against the hard concrete under my office rug. I pulled one knee up to my chest and held the other straight, rocking slightly from side to side and then slowly released the knee, before swapping legs. The stretch was good and I felt my body relax against the tension of the meeting. Bloody hell. I was going to have to do this Hally Arlow thing or I would have not just Cathy, but now Alice too, breathing down my neck to see if I needed help. And that would be almost as bad as having to edit the manuscript itself. There was nothing for it. I would just have to put on a brave face and get it done as quickly and painlessly as possible.

I brought my knees over to the left side of my body and twisted my head in the opposite direction, enjoying the roll out of my spine, closing my eyes and breathing deeply. I was just about to roll to the other side when my desk phone buzzed and Katie, our receptionist, called through the speaker. "Gin, you there? Phone call."

"I'm here," I called from across the floor, eyes still closed. "Who is it?"

"Hally Arlow for you on line one."

Shit. Already?

"Please tell her I'll call back."

I would at least allow myself a few days' grace before I had to speak with her.

CHAPTER TWO

By Thursday evening I was at war with myself. And the cats.
"Please don't look at me like that," I said to Olive and Asimov, who had both adopted eerily similar expressions of reproach mixed with disinterest, in that way that only cats could pull off. They were perched on different levels of the tree-style cat gym I had jammed into the corner of my tiny living room. They couldn't see each other, but they sure could see me. "I will ring her, first thing tomorrow. I promise. Hey, I just didn't get around to it today."

Asimov looked slowly away, used to my excuses. Olive continued to fix me with an unforgiving gaze. Honestly. Tough crowd.

Hally Arlow's manuscript sat on the coffee table in front of me, my glass of wine resting firmly on top of it. I tucked my bare feet up on the couch, clicking the retractable tip of my favourite red pen. I had meant to return her call today, feeling that two days was an appropriate time to leave her to sweat while I appeared to be very busy and important, but every time

I picked up the telephone I found myself resting it back in its cradle and finding something else "more pressing" to attend to.

I could faintly hear my neighbour, Thomas, talking in the corridor as he entered his apartment. His voice was muffled and I couldn't make out what he was saying, but it reminded me that I needed to return the whisk I had borrowed from him a few days earlier when I had attempted to make pancakes. Perhaps I should go over now. Sure, there was this manuscript I was supposed to be dealing with and a phone call I hadn't made, but he might really need it.

"I think I just need a bit more time to get used to the whole thing," I told Olive, who rolled onto her back and set about vigorously licking her stomach. Conversation over then. Problem was, I knew Cathy was keen for me to get started. Her email this morning had brooked no argument. *Call her back and get on with it*, were her exact words. How she knew I'd dodged the phone call or that I was yet to call Hally back was beyond me. When it came to Red Stone, Cathy was annoyingly omniscient. Thankfully, as a best friend she was much more like a regular person, forgetting birthdays and turning up late to dinner with the best of us.

I sat forward and picked up my wineglass, sliding the manuscript closer with the tip of my index finger. It was thin, probably only fifty thousand words or so. We would have to use large font and lots of pictures to fill it out. Ug. This was becoming a reality. I took a fortifying sip of my wine, shuddering a little at the aftertaste of vinegar. Perhaps this red had been in the cupboard too long after all. When I recorked it at the end of the evening I would transition it to the "cooking wine" shelf.

I flicked open the manuscript for the second time that day and took a deep breath. I had finished reading it, but as soon as I wrote on the manuscript as an editor, I would be invested. The process would have officially begun. Releasing my held breath with a rush, I slashed a thin red line through a large swathe of text and turned the page. More slashes. And again, and again. Off I went, tearing through the text. There would be very little left of it by the time I was done. Oh well, I hoped she had lots of pictures.

"Ha!" I crowed, pausing for a moment to look up and grin manically at the cats. Olive looked startled and leapt off the cat tree, stalking away into the bedroom. Asimov licked himself in annoyance, clearly not happy with my behaviour.

"Sorry," I said, "but of course she will have lots of pictures. Isn't she some kind of social-media queen?" Asimov didn't answer.

I nodded, and smiled again, a little less intensely this time, allowing my red pen another ruthless sweep over the text before me. This would be a doddle. Sure, it might end up looking like more of a photo album than a book, but Hally would probably enjoy that. Just like Instagram in hard format.

An hour later I was done. Hally's manuscript was so covered in red ink it looked like a casualty patient in need of an urgent transfusion, but it wasn't just all cuts and slashes. I had also added some helpful little pointers, like "Do we really need this?" and "Could replace this with picture." I was pleased with myself for my restraint, refraining from writing comments like "This section is crap" and "Who cares?"

Good. I was keen to get a move on now. The quicker we could spit this drivel out, the sooner it would be off my desk. In fact, if I sent it through to her now, I could even avoid looking like the arsehole who hadn't returned her call. I had simply been too busy with her work to call her. And, of course, Cathy would be impressed with my speedy response.

I picked up the wodge of paper, now looking a little scuffed from its multiple trips to the office and apartment, and the couple of times I had pushed it off my desk in frustration, and crossed to the corner of my lounge where I had my desk set up. A functional, slightly weathered card table, picked up from a neighbour's hard rubbish pile when I first moved into the apartment, served as my desk and I had purchased a cute set of fat little wooden drawers from an office sale, which sat snugly under it.

The apartment was tiny and had been advertised as "Capturing the bespoke essence of Melbourne." I supposed they got that from the garish blue and gold carpet that ran through the living room into the bedroom, with a paisley pattern that jumped out at you in strange shifts of perspective if you stared at it for too long while drunk. The kitchen suffered from a brown and white checked linoleum flooring that would be perfect for a game of chess if I ever felt so inclined.

My apartment, though small, was sparsely furnished, giving the impression of space. There was no general colour scheme— the landlord had whitewashed the walls many tenants before me, and I hadn't bothered much with decorating, as I was only renting while I saved for a deposit for my own place. For me, the blue carpet was feature enough, and the marks on the walls seemed like a story of the room's past, almost like cave paintings.

I tapped the edge of the manuscript on the desk a few times to align the pages and then set the lot onto the feeder tray of the wireless whizz-bang printer-scanner. I stood back and watched it drag each page into its belly and spit them out the other side. The manuscript was thin, but this would still take a while.

Feeling much more relaxed now that the manuscript was done, I popped my laptop on a cushion and navigated to BestReads, a book-review website to which I enjoyed contributing. I had seven new notifications. I clicked on the first, *Joh728 has responded to your review*. I wriggled my nose in anticipation. I prided myself on my ability to write a fair but pithy review and doing so was one of my favourite pastimes.

"Thanks for your thoughts on this, GBreads01. I'm not sure the writer would revel in your characterisation of his writing as pleonastic, but I happen to agree. He seems a little too in love with the idea of himself as a writer."

I chuckled, clicking the thumbs up button under Joh728's comment. I enjoyed writing reviews, but I also loved thrill of the fierce debate that followed as other readers chimed in with their two cents' worth and sometimes more.

I clicked and scrolled through the remaining comments, pausing to sneer acidly at Easy_Reads_Jeff who questioned if I had even read the book or just the blurb. I shook my head in disbelief. As if.

BestReads was also a good place to check out what people were saying about my authors. Even though we were a boutique publishing house, Red Stone's authors still drew quite a lot of traction online. I put it down to the quality. We could never match the volume of the big publishers, but we definitely gave them a run for their money on quality. Hence my big beef with publishing a work like Hally Arlow's. It would never live up to the standard our readers expected. I only hoped I could drag it over the line into the not-great-but-acceptable territory.

I spent the rest of the evening surfing BestReads, making lists of books that caught my eye and reading strings of review fights. At ten thirty I stretched and yawned, reaching out a hand to scratch Olive, snuggled up next to me on the couch, under the chin.

"We should go to bed," I advised, as she opened her mouth wide and gave a fishy yawn of her own.

A flashing light on the printer-scanner caught my eye and I remembered the manuscript. I located the file on my laptop and composed a new message to the email address I had been given for Hally.

Hi Hally, I tapped out. *Finished a first pass on your draft tonight. Edits attached. Why don't you flick through and I'll get the digital document updated to reflect changes. We can go from there. Feel free to call when you're done. Ginerva Blake*

I signed off, pressed the little aeroplane and watched as my message winged its way out of my inbox. With a sense of satisfaction I snapped my laptop shut and gave Olive one last scratch. Even though this was just the beginning, I was already getting a sense of the finishing line and could see how it would all play out from here. After Hally approved my edits, with perhaps a few changes of her own, and chose a bunch of pictures for the book, I would mock-up the digital document, she would approve it and I'd send it to Marketing. We could be done here with very little sweat. Sure, the book was a bit wishy-washy, but I could see now I'd made a mountain out of a molehill. With all the crap cut out it was no masterpiece, but it was much more palatable. I still thought the premise was ridiculous, but I would sleep well tonight knowing I was moving it along.

When I walked into my office the following morning the message light was flashing on my telephone. I made myself a coffee and settled in at my desk, switching on my computer and reading through a couple of emails. What with overseas distributors and international marketing campaigns, the publishing game had become a twenty-four-hour business. I reached for the telephone and dialled my message bank.

Five new messages. Weird. It had just gone nine a.m. I rarely received five messages in a day, let alone this early. I flashed to Cathy, worried that there had been an issue with her mum. We had spoken after work yesterday and all had been well. Her mum had been given the all-clear and was being discharged from the hospital that afternoon, but maybe something had gone wrong. Surely she would have called my mobile.

Message one, the robotic voice told me, had come in at eleven last night.

"This is Hally Arlow." A confident, well-modulated voice came down the line. "I have just received your email and was hoping to catch you at your desk. Please give me a call as soon as you hear this. I'll be up. Late."

She must have tried to call me at the office after I had sent her the draft last night. I pressed five to delete the message, making a mental note to call her later today. I really would this time.

According to the robotic voice, I had received message two shortly after the first, at eleven thirty.

"Hello, Ginerva, this is Hally again. Just in case you don't have my number, you can get me on my mobile." And she proceeded to inform me carefully, with enunciation that would have given my high-school debating team teacher a hot flush. I didn't write it down. It would be in our system. I hit five again and listened for the next message.

Hally had left message three this morning just after seven, her morning voice sounding a little huskier than the evening before as she let me know she was still trying to get a hold of me and would appreciate a call back at my earliest convenience. An early riser I surmised, sending the message to trash. I scribbled her name in my notebook and drew a little squiggly line under it, moving from mental to actual note.

Messages four and five had occurred in the last hour, as Hally Arlow again tried to touch base and left me the number of her landline, where she could also be reached. Sheesh. She was keen. At this rate we'd have the book done and dusted by the end of the week. I replaced the handset and stared at her number on my notebook, then I lifted the receiver again. Let's get this over with.

Strangely there was no dial tone. I jiggled the switch hook a couple of times, trying to get a tone. Nothing. I was just about to hang up the phone and go to find help when a voice came down the line. "Hello?"

"Hello," I replied, feeling confused. Did I have a crossed line?

"Is that Ginerva?"

Ah. The voice from the messages. "Yes, this is she. Hally, I presume?"

"Yes. That was strange." She gave a short, soft laugh. "The phone didn't even ring. Look, I've been trying to call you."

"You certainly have," I said, feeling vaguely annoyed that she had beaten me to it. Somehow I felt more in control of the call if I was the one making it.

The laugh again. It was pleasantly musical and I wondered if it had always been that way or if she had had to work at it. "Yes, well, I wanted to make sure I caught you this morning. I have a crazy day and this is my only chance to talk."

I brushed off a flash of irritation. Sure, she was busy. Weren't we all? "You got the edits then?"

"Yes, look, I don't think you've quite got the feel of what I'm going for."

I wasn't entirely surprised. The fact was, I did have the *feel* for what she was going for, I just didn't like it. "And how is that?"

"My manuscript. There's basically nothing left. You've crossed it all out."

I gave a laugh of my own, trying for busy, but important, and understanding, all in one. It came out as more of a strangled gurgle. Note to self: keep laughs simpler in future.

"Actually, I feel it reads a lot better now. There's an easier flow, if you like. I was going to discuss adding in some photographic material to support the text. I assume you have a bank of visuals to choose from?"

She hesitated and clicked her tongue. "Of course. I have heaps of photos, but that's not really the point. People can get those from my social media. I wanted to give them something special, something more substantial. I don't just want this to be a regurgitation of my Instagram account. I want this to be more like a degustation, titbits of background for entrée, chew on the gristle of the journey for mains, sip the sweet successes for dessert. I want to serve up a three-course meal of my life and the lessons I've learnt, if you like."

I didn't like. "But is that what the public really wants, Hally? It sounds…dense." I allowed a note of superiority to creep into my voice. "As a matter of fact, there's a real upswell of people choosing to publish their Instagram posts in book form at the moment. Have you heard of the Instagram poets?" I had only just discovered this phenomenon last night through a review on BestReads, but Hally Arlow did not know that.

"Yes, yes, of course I've heard of them. Ruzil Komo and I sat on the Arts and Social Media panel together last year at the Entrepreneurs' Conference."

"Right." I tried to stay upbeat. I had come across that name the previous evening. "So, then you know that's totally hot right now. A great way to boost profile."

Hally sighed so heavily into her end of the receiver I almost felt it on my ear. "Is that why you think I'm doing this?"

I was confused. "Doing what?"

"Putting out a book."

"Um. Yes?"

"Well, you're wrong. I want to tell my story so that others, especially women, can learn from it. I want to give advice on how to navigate the treacherous world of social media and building a brand in a man's world. I want people to see how possible it is to carve out a niche for yourself even when the big boys are telling you the pool is full."

"You had that line in your introduction."

"And you crossed it out."

"Yes, I thought it was a little…" I paused, searching for the right words. It wasn't my style to criticize or put down my authors, but then Hally wasn't a typical one. "I thought it was a little mixed. As in mixed metaphor, which is poor writing. Not to mention overly familiar as a premise."

"I'm sorry, what?"

She was pushing. "It's the kind of language others have used before you, many times over."

"They have?"

"Perhaps not in those exact words, but a similar vein, yes."

"You're saying it's clichéd?"

"That's it," I replied brightly, glad she was catching on.

"Well, isn't that what you're here for?"

Now it was my turn to be confused. "Er, I'm not following."

"You're here to help me fix up things like that so that it reads well. You're the editor. I thought that was the whole point. Instead you've just gone along and crossed it all out."

"There is a limit to how much I can fix."

More breathing down the line. When she finally spoke again her voice sounded tight. "It's that bad is it?"

I had a flash of guilt. This wasn't how things were supposed to go. Whilst I had little respect for Hally and the gym-junkie, hashtagging world she operated in, I wasn't lining up to be the one to take her down a notch. I reached for my coffee and swirled the dregs around a few times, before gulping the last mouthful. Bloody Cathy. This was all her fault. How could I possibly get around this without seeming like a total arsehole, yet keep my integrity?

"The thing is, it's not that it's bad, I just thought it could be better in a slightly different format. Go for what's trending right now, you know? Yes, my job as an editor is to help you massage the writing, but it's also to look at the bigger picture. I need to consider the commercial viability, the marketing, and the target audience, so that you're heading out the door with a piece that says what you want it to say, to the people you want it to speak to. And I think, given how oriented your audience is to social media, it makes sense to give them what they know: a feast of photos, bite-size titbits, chewable chunks. See, it can still be a meal!"

"Sounds like you want to give them chicken nuggets."

"Not exactly." I considered her health-conscious audience. "More like protein balls. They're all the rage at the moment aren't they?"

"Jesus, Ginerva, is that all you care about? What's *all the rage?*" Her tone mocked mine.

"Huh?" I was stung. "Me? I'm thinking about what's best for your work. Don't you want to sell books?"

"Of course I do, but that's secondary. The most important thing is that I tell the story. Look, I don't want to be rude, and I hope you're not offended, but perhaps it's better if I work with a different editor."

I didn't know whether to laugh or cry. This was exactly what I wanted. But who else could she work with at Red Stone? Nonfiction was entirely my domain and as a rule, we never crossed over into each other's genres.

"While that does sound like it could work for you," I eventually replied, "unfortunately I'm the only nonfiction editor at Red Stone, so it is me that you're stuck with."

"Unless I go with a different publisher."

"Oh, well, yes you could do that."

"I think I will. This just doesn't sound like it will work. Will you let Cathy know or shall I?"

"I can do that."

"Right, well. Thanks anyway, and goodbye."

Hally rang off with a soft click and I replaced the handset in the receiver slowly, chewing on the inside of my cheek. I scrunched up my nose and flared my nostrils a couple of times, feeling twitchy. I should have been relieved to have dodged the Hally Arlow bullet, but I couldn't help feeling that Cathy would not be pleased. I sniffed and pushed my glasses up my nose, telling myself it would all be okay. At the end of the day, Hally had not been a great fit for us and it was probably for the best that she had decided to find a more appropriate publisher. Cathy would be a little tetchy but deep down I knew she would understand. And perhaps one of those Instagram poetry publishers would like to pick Hally up. I mentally kicked myself for not suggesting it to her, momentarily considering calling her back to share the thought, but no, I didn't want her to get the wrong idea. If I attempted to help her now she might start calling on me every time something went wrong with the publishing process and the last thing I wanted to be doing was babysitting Hally Arlow.

I pushed my chair out from behind my desk and stood up for a stretch, trying to shift the uncomfortable feeling tugging at my insides. Should I call Cathy or wait to tell her when she returned next week? I decided not to disturb her while she was in Sydney.

I settled back into my chair and turned back to my computer screen, ready to focus now on the tasks of the day ahead. There was plenty of work begging for my attention and it wasn't long before I was pleasantly absorbed in Massimoto's final proof. Now, here was a woman who could write. The words sang from the page, an opera of the trials and tribulations of organic life, transporting me back three and a half billion years from the little black chair and thin cream walls of my office to a world of rusty, red oceans and life-breathing stromatolites.

When Frank paused on his way down the corridor to stick his head into my office, saying "Have a great weekend, Gin," I was only marginally closer to the present time, riding a shifting continental plate through the end of the Cretaceous Period and an explosion of plants and concupiscent insects.

"You too," I replied, my eyes still locked on my screen as I tied up a punctuation point that had somehow slipped through the net.

He coughed. "It's six o'clock."

"Uh-huh."

"Gin?" He said my name loudly and I finally looked up, blinking over the top of my glasses as my eyes adjusted their focus.

"Yes?"

"Just checking you're okay to lock up? You're the last in tonight."

I glanced at my watch. "Oh, it's six o'clock!"

"I just said that."

"Sorry, Frank, I was miles away. Final proofing," I said by way of explanation. I pushed back my chair and stretched, yawning widely.

"You won't forget the alarm?"

"Frank!" I pouted at him. "That was one time. Now go, enjoy your evening. I'll head off in a minute. The cats will stage a mutiny if I don't get going."

His smile pulled at the lines on his face, accentuating some of the deeper crevices. He looked as if a child had drawn him, scrunched up the paper and tried to smooth it back out again.

"Want me to wait and walk out with you?"

"You don't trust me with the alarm?" If I was honest, the alarm had slipped my mind more than once before and we both knew it. I had been on the receiving end of a number of terse emails from HR over the years, and if it wasn't for my personal friendship with Cathy I would surely have had my after-hours access revoked.

"Not really."

I laughed at his honesty. "Fine, just give me a sec to switch everything off."

We walked out together, Frank hovering at my shoulder as I punched in the alarm code and locked the front door.

"See ya, Frank," I said, giving him a wave.

He tipped an imaginary hat at me and tapped the side of his nose. I had no idea what that meant but I nodded and smiled and made a beeline for my car. I hadn't been joking about the cats. The last time I had lost track of time at work and slid in the door after eight, Asimov had shown his displeasure by knocking over a vase of flowers in the living room and making a nest for himself in a pile of important papers on my desk. I dreaded to think what the two of them would get up to.

As I pulled out of the car park my mobile blasted its ring tone through the stereo speakers. Seeing Cathy's name flash up on the display I hit the answer button on the steering wheel.

"You still in Sydney?" I said, by way of greeting.

"No." Cathy's voice sounded tense. "I'm in a taxi on my way home from the airport. Where are you?"

"On my way home from the office. Is everything okay?"

"Actually no. I don't want to talk about it in the taxi but things are not okay. I need to see you."

My pulse quickened. "Shit, what's happened? I thought your mum was doing well."

"It's not Mum. It's about work. Let's just say I heard we lost a certain manuscript."

I wrinkled my brow. "That's very cryptic. Any more clues?"

"Gin!" she admonished. "You know what I'm talking about."

I checked my rearview mirror and slid in behind the line of cars waiting to turn at the lights. "Me?"

"You."

A light flashed in the back of my brain. "You're talking about Hally? I'm sorry, it slipped my mind. I was going to call you but I got caught up in the Massimoto final proofing today. Oh, Cathy, you're going to love this book. I can't wait for you to read it. I'm telling you, she writes biology like it's Mozart."

"And while that sounds lovely, that is not my major concern right now. I can't believe you let this go."

"I didn't, Cathy, I swear. I even started the first edit but she decided we weren't the right fit for her and told me she wanted to move on. There was really nothing I could do."

"We need to talk. I'm coming over."

I shook my head, moving with the flow of traffic to take the turn. "Fine by me. I'll be home in ten. Pizza?"

"Yes. I'll be half an hour. And, Gin?"

"Yes?"

"We're going to need wine."

CHAPTER THREE

Thomas, my next-door neighbour, stuck his head out of his apartment across the corridor, intercepting me as I was putting the key into my door.

"Ginny," he exclaimed, popping out and swooping down from his great, gangly height to kiss me enthusiastically on both cheeks. He was pretty much the only person in the world I allowed to bastardise my name in such a way. "I've been waiting for you!"

"Thomas," I said, as I submitted to his kissing. "What's up?"

"Two things. Mrs. Roarshark is at me to organise a tenants' meeting for the building. She's convinced someone is stealing her mail and wants us to install a camera system over the mail slots."

I rolled my eyes. Mrs. Roarshark was always convinced that something untoward was happening in the building. "Fine, it doesn't bother me. I'd prefer it if someone stole my mail, all I ever get are bills."

"I know right. In other news..." Looking coy and leaning against my doorway, he paused and bit his lip. His cheeks were grazed with a gorgeous five-o'clock shadow, accentuating the strong lines of his chiselled jaw and high cheek bones. "Drum roll please." He looked at me expectantly.

"Yes?"

"I said, drum roll please."

"Er, da da da dum," I supplied.

He clasped his hands together and squeaked, "Kevin is moving in."

"Oh wow, that *is* great news." I was genuinely happy for him. He and Kevin had been dating for over a year and they were still completely doe-eyed and lovey-dovey. They were sweet together and I always enjoyed spending time with them.

"Anyway, I just wanted to tell you, and let you know if you hear any banging going on, it's just Kevin moving in." He wiggled his eyebrows at me suggestively and I laughed.

"Got it."

"You should come out with us tonight to celebrate."

"Can't tonight, I've got work to do and Cathy's coming around in a sec, but another time, for sure."

He leaned down and kissed my cheek again, his stubble prickling my skin. "I'll hold you to that. Ooo, that's my phone, got to go," he said as the sound of "I Will Survive" filtered out from his apartment.

I watched him gallop inside and then let myself into my own apartment. I was relieved to see things were pretty much as I had left them. Two mildly offended cats were perched on the cat tree, studiously ignoring me as I threw my handbag and keys on the table. They perked up immediately, jumping down gracefully to join me in the kitchen when I opened the fridge door and got out the food tub. They snaked around my legs, purring and rubbing up against me as I forked a good-sized chunk of raw meat onto each of their plates and set it before them on the little rubber mat next to their water. I watched for a moment as they both chewed daintily, Asimov leaning over to sniff Olive's food before returning to his own. They were like a pair of strange little aliens, munching away in my kitchen, and I enjoyed the sight of them together.

Pizza, I thought, tuning in to my own hunger. If I ordered now it would probably arrive at the same time as Cathy. I pushed away the uncomfortable feeling gnawing at my stomach at the thought of Cathy. Was it guilt? I hadn't lied to her, but I hadn't tried exceptionally hard to keep Hally Arlow in our stable. I would need to be honest with her about that. I hated to disappoint Cathy, but hopefully with a good heart-to-heart she would come to see, as I did, that we were better off not shackling ourselves to such a low-grade project.

I fished my laptop from my bag and jumped online. I knew what Cathy would have—she always had a small vegetarian, minus the onion, add pineapple and chilli. I hummed and hawed for a moment trying to choose between an old favourite and something new for myself, my tired brain eventually going for the tried-and-true comfort of a small Hawaiian and a garlic bread. That done, I flicked on the kettle, opened a bottle of wine and kicked off my shoes, then headed into the bedroom to change into a comfy pair of trackpants and an old T-shirt. Friday night, here I come.

When the doorbell rang I was sipping from a large glass of red wine, talking quietly with Asimov and Olive about the downfall of the trilobites in the Devonian Period, the world Massimoto had so skilfully and elegantly laid before me still engrossing my thoughts. It was hard to envisage a world without humans, something the cats didn't seem as interested in as I was. I buzzed open the entry, unsure if I would find the pizza or Cathy, only to find both at my front door.

"I bumped into the girl with the pizzas," she said, holding the boxes aloft.

"Hi," I greeted her, stepping away from the door to let her enter. "How are you? I'm starving."

"Same." She took a deep sniff, her nose grazing the top of the pizza box. "This smells amazing. I'm so hungry I could eat the box."

I poured Cathy a glass of wine while she said hello to Olive, who was conducting a complicated maypole dance between Cathy's legs. Plates and napkins in hand, we settled on the couch.

"How's your mum?" I asked, wrangling a steaming piece of pizza from the box onto my plate.

"Actually, she's doing pretty well," Cathy replied, taking a slice of her own. "The scans came up clear and there's just a little bruising which is already beginning to fade. She's in good spirits." She took a large bite and closed her eyes as she chewed. "Heaven," she mumbled.

"And Rachel?"

She swallowed her mouthful. "Also in good spirits. I think she was pleased to be able to show me just how well she's managing with Mum, and I have to take my hat off to her. She really has a handle on everything." She took a sip of her wine, cradling the glass to her chest as she leaned back on the couch. "And let's face it, if it wasn't for Rach being with her twenty-four-seven I'd probably have to look at putting her into care. Or quit my job."

"Thankfully you don't have to make that choice."

Cathy sighed deeply and stared into her wine. "Some days I feel like it might be a better option."

I frowned, returning my pizza slice to my plate. "What's that supposed to mean?"

"It means, Gin, that sometimes this Red Stone shit is hard and I have to do things I don't want to do." She regarded me, her dark brown eyes boring into mine.

"Like what?"

"Like telling my best friend that if she doesn't fix her attitude she's going to find herself on the receiving end of disciplinary action at work."

I reeled back, her words a slap on the face. "Excuse me?"

Cathy sucked in her bottom lip and shook her head. "This can't be news to you."

My stomach twisted and I was suddenly aware of the hard lump of pizza sitting in my otherwise empty belly. I couldn't believe this. I had always prided myself on being the one person at work Cathy didn't need to worry about. I turned up on time, I met every deadline and my work was flawless. I personally produced a stable of what I felt were some of the finest authors in Australia, ensuring their work hit the shelves in full glory after a rigorous process of squeezing, stretching and pummelling into the greatest manifestation of the author's initial idea. "I actually have no clue what you're talking about," I said stiffly, my throat tight with disbelief.

"Gin." Her voice was kind. "You're like an island at work. You act as if you're surrounded by sharks when you couldn't possibly be working with a nicer team. You shut yourself away from everyone and do an excellent job of scaring off anyone who tries to connect with you."

"Not true! Frank and I are…" I trailed off, trying to think of the most appropriate word to describe our modest camaraderie. I couldn't say we were friends, but I didn't mind chatting with him every now and then. "We're pals," I finished, feeling like the word was a bit lame. If it had been written by one of my authors I would have underlined it in red pen and suggested a replacement.

"Pals?"

"We often leave work at the same time."

"Well that's nice, but it's not enough. It's like you alienate people on purpose. Poor Alice—"

"Alice! Surely you're not going to tell me I have be friends with simpering, fluffy *Alice*?"

"You don't have to be friends with anyone. But you do have to be friendly. You practically tie Alice up in knots every time you speak to her. When you deign to speak to her at all, that is."

"I'm not at work to make friends. I don't need more friends. I thought I was covered in that department," I said, glaring at her pointedly.

Cathy said nothing, tapping her finger against her wineglass as she watched me. I shifted to edge of the couch, straightening my pizza box in line with the edge of the coffee table. Staring straight ahead I said, "I'm sorry you feel this way."

"That's just it. It's not actually me that feels this way. You're the perfect friend to me. It's everyone else who bears the brunt of your ice-queen facade. And now, to top it off, your authors are voting with their feet."

"What?" I spun around to look at her. "Which authors?"

"Hally Arlow, for one."

"Hally!" I choked out the word. "Cathy, she is not one of my authors."

"She was supposed to be."

"So, you win some you lose some. I know we don't see eye to eye on this but trust me, she really wasn't up to our standard."

"Actually, this was when you were supposed to trust me. I wanted Red Stone to have this manuscript because we must have some commercial hits to stay viable. You know how cut-throat it is out there. Slimming margins, shorter print runs, digital piracy, self-publishing." She ticked the items off on her fingers as she spoke, her pizza forgotten in her lap. "You know the drill. We can have all the standards in the world, but if we don't charge up the coffers every now and then with something that's commercially appealing, that's all we'll have. And you can't eat standards. I thought this would be a win for nonfiction. Do you know what percentage of our profit comes from nonfiction?"

I racked my brain but she didn't wait for me to answer.

"Eight percent. Not a large chunk of the pie. There are those who say we shouldn't even bother with nonfiction at Red Stone—it's costly, it's difficult to market and we don't move much copy."

"But you—"

"But I love it. I want to keep running nonfiction, Gin, and I share your passion for releasing high-quality work, but you have to cut me some slack. I have a CFO and an HR manager who are breathing down my neck to move you on, so I need you to step up. You can't just chase away the authors you don't like, and you have to try harder with the team. Be nice. Be polite at the very least."

My neck felt creaky as I attempted to shake my head. My mouth was pursed so tightly I could barely bite out, "I am polite."

"You're prickly. And sometimes downright rude. This Hally Arlow mess is a perfect example."

"Oh my god, Cathy, I wasn't rude to her at all! I never even mentioned how substandard her work was."

"She forwarded me the draft you sent her. You crossed everything out."

"I thought it might work better as a picture book."

Cathy snorted. "That's called being an arsehole. You insulted her to the core. She made a point of emailing me to let me know how disappointed she was with Red Stone. She felt it was grounds to be released from her contract. You made us look bad and I'm upset about it. It's not good enough. The thing is, I just can't keep covering for you, Gin. Rory and Vanessa wanted me to put you on immediate probation when they heard about the Hally Arlow manuscript."

I grimaced. I had little to do with the officious Rory from HR, and his just-as-officious colleague and Red Stone's CFO, Vanessa, and that was the way I liked it. As far as I was concerned, we needed to put up with each other to get the job done and that was as far as the relationship went.

"Did you tell them to get lost?"

"I told them I'd talk to you, but I agreed that this would be your last chance before an official warning. You're my best friend and this is the last thing I would ever want to have to do, but consider this an unofficial warning, Gin. You're on very thin ice here."

I set my pizza plate on the coffee table and stood up from the couch, my mind a whirling dervish. I tilted my head in the direction of the bathroom and mumbled, "Loo," scooting down the hallway to the toilet, just to get away from our conversation.

I closed the door and sat on the toilet lid, staring at the Escher print taped to the door as tears stung my eyes. Two hands, drawing each other. A symbiosis. In many ways, I had always felt like that about my friendship and work relationship with Cathy. We were a flawless team. She set high standards and I felt we shared them. Sure, I knew I was reserved with other people, but I wasn't there to make friends. I had all the friends I needed. I had Cathy, and Asimov, and Thomas from across the hall and...my dad. Did he count? Probably not, but we did speak on the phone fairly regularly, so it was a friendship of sorts. There was Mark, my mechanic who sometimes shared a beer with me when I picked my car up from its biannual service, and the lady from the library who liked to chat with me about what books we had coming up. And what about the BestReads community? Some of the people on that site logged in almost every night. Sure, I only knew them as things like Joh728 and Crackmyspine, but it was like a virtual book club and in a funny way I guess I counted them as friends.

I put my head in my hands and drew a shaky breath. My emotions ricocheted like a pinball. Embarrassed and ashamed to have upset Cathy, furious with Hally Arlow for causing all this mess in the first place, stubborn defiance holding back the tears. And to top it all off I felt guilty.

I had never really considered the privilege of my position, choosing works I considered to be of high value to publish, in a world that favoured fast, instantly digestible, pulp. I had taken for granted that because Cathy shared my love of nonfiction I was somehow above the humdrum of profits and sales targets, not stopping to consider the risky financial aspect of the genre. I adhered carefully to my budget and worked diligently with the marketing team to ensure my authors had the best possible chance of success, but we weren't in the same league as Crime or General Fiction, or dare I even say it, Romance, so I didn't invest too much thought into that side of things. I knew they were the bread and butter of Red Stone, but I had allowed myself to think of Nonfiction as a select, fine red wine.

I could see now, with a painful flash, that my snobbery would never have been tolerated at another publishing house. I had confused my elevated and protected position at work as Cathy's best friend with a general sense of superiority and as I stared at the back of the bathroom door I felt everything suddenly slide away as if a skin had peeled off me. I had been a complete idiot.

I heard footsteps in the hallway and Cathy tapped on the bathroom door. "Gin?"

Shame held back my tongue.

"You okay? Talk to me," she insisted.

"Just a sec." I flushed the toilet, for show, rubbed a washcloth across my face, and washed my trembling hands.

I opened the door and Cathy immediately grabbed me in a hard hug. I let her squeeze me for a moment and then ducked clear.

I met her eyes and then shied away like a twitchy horse. "I'm sorry. I'm going to fix it with Hally. And with everyone at work. You won't have to make excuses for me again."

"Gin, I—"

"I'll fix it," I repeated.

She hugged me again and this time I hugged her back, tears wetting her shoulder as we stood in my small hallway. A loud crash and a muffled yowl broke us apart and we jogged back into the living room to find an overturned pizza box on the floor and Asimov vigorously washing red sauce and cheese from his whiskers. Olive was sniffing delicately at a slice of my pizza, bouncing her nose off it in that way that cats did when they weren't sure.

"Hey," Cathy cried, righting the box and returning my pizza to it. She shooed Olive away. "Naughty girl! Since when did cats like pizza?"

"Actually, I think they do quite like it," I said, easing back onto the couch. I folded my napkin and blew my nose into it heartily. "I think they like cheese."

"You can't feed cats cheese."

"Okay," I acquiesced, feeling submissive after my show of emotion.

"Have you been? Oh, never mind." Cathy shook her head. "I'm sorry I hurt your feelings," she said quietly. "I did need to say it though."

I sniffed. "I guess I needed to hear it. I'll call Hally first thing tomorrow."

"I think it's too late for Hally. She has another publisher lined up and she hadn't signed our contract yet. Anyway, tomorrow is Saturday."

"No harm in trying," I said, giving her a wan smile.

Cathy returned my smile, but I could tell she wasn't entirely convinced.

The next morning, I perched on a stool at my kitchen bench and flicked through my notebook until I found Hally's number. Asimov was at my feet, nosily crunching his way through a bowl of cat biscuits while I nursed a coffee and a head full of red-wine regret. Cathy and I had finished off the bottle and opened another, getting increasingly sentimental as the evening wore on. By the time she had tucked Olive into her carry box and stumbled down the stairwell into an Uber we had both pledged undying friendship and renewed our commitment to a life of high ideals, reminding me of the first time we had gotten drunk together as fifteen-year-olds. Bleary-eyed and achy from a fitful sleep, I felt far older and much less inspired almost twenty years later.

"Shh," I told Asimov as I dialled, pausing over the call button. "Keep the crunching down please." He ignored me and if anything, attacked his food more vigorously. I wasn't looking forward to this conversation. Worst-case scenario, I hoped it would be short. She would thank me for my call but tell me she had signed with someone else. I would let Cathy know I had done my best and resolve not to make the same mistakes again in the future. We would put this incident behind us and hopefully never speak of it again. Best-case scenario she would agree to bring her book back to Red Stone.

I inhaled slowly through my nose and stabbed at the green button. I listened to the soft purr of the ringing signal. After six rings I breathed a sigh of relief, readying myself to leave a professional-sounding voice message when Hally's musical baritone suddenly broke through saying, "Hello?"

I screwed up my face at Asimov who had thankfully stopped crunching but was scrutinising me with an impenetrable look.

"Hello?" she said again, sounding impatient.

"Hally, it's Gin, Ginerva from Red Stone," I clarified. "Have I caught you at a bad time?"

"It's nine a.m. on a Saturday," she replied.

I couldn't tell from her voice whether she was suggesting that nine a.m. on a Saturday was wide open and she had all the time in the world for me, or if it was an entirely inappropriate time to call, so I ploughed on, hoping for the former. "Good. Listen I wanted to talk to you about your book."

"I can't imagine why." Her tone was so acerbic she could have bottled it and sold it as a salad dressing.

"Yes, well, it's come to my attention that I was less than... generous with my handling of your material, and I would like to apologise for any offense I may have caused you."

"Less than generous?"

"Yes. It's possible I was a bit of, well..." I searched for the most appropriate word. "An arsehole."

"You were," she confirmed.

I grimaced, forcing a smile at Asimov who shrunk away in response. I tried to keep my tone light. "The thing is, I've had a bit of a chat with Cathy, and well, we really would like the opportunity to publish your book. Would you consider letting us have another crack at it?"

"I can't see why. I've got another publisher lined up and I am confident I will receive far better treatment in their hands."

"Would you mind telling me which publisher? Which editor?" I asked, my curiosity piqued.

"I can't see it's really any of your business."

"You're right, it's not, but I do have some knowledge of this industry and I could potentially give you a little heads-up, some titbits of knowledge to help smooth the way for you with one of my associates."

"I can't imagine I could possibly need your help to smooth the way with anything."

"Fair point," I conceded. It was becoming clear that I was unlikely to succeed in my efforts to bring her back to Red Stone, but for Cathy's sake I gave it one last attempt. "Look, I really am sorry for being such a..."

"A shit?"

"Okay, yes, a shit."

"You made me feel really small."

I winced, guilt and shame mixing with last night's red wine to create a wave of nausea. "I'm sorry," I said again, regretting making the call. I stuck the tip of my index finger into my coffee and swirled it around, unsure how to continue. What could I offer this woman that would make her change her mind?

"I suppose you thought you were just being honest."

A flash illuminated my thoughts and I removed my finger, sucking it clean. "Exactly. And that is what I can offer you, Hally. Absolute honesty. You can go to another publishing house and they'll pander to you because you're sort of famous, and you'll get a mediocre book published that you'll be vaguely proud of. But if you work with me, I will be absolutely honest with you. I'll challenge your writing and your premise. I'll push you to try harder and dig deeper and you will be proud of the end result in a way that you can only dream of right now." Was I laying it on too thick? She hadn't hung up on me so I took that as a cue to open my cannons and fire away. "The fact is, I have no idea why you've written what you've written, or why you do what you do. I loathe social media, and I never exercise, but if you can convince *me* with your writing, then you'll know you have a truly great product. I don't mean to blow my own horn, but I'm just saying that if you can win over a sceptic then you're a step ahead of the game."

She didn't answer for so long that I had to check she was still there. "Hello?" I asked, feeling stupid. Had she hung up after all?

"I'm here," she replied curtly. "I'm thinking. I don't know if I really want your brand of absolute honesty."

"I understand," I said quickly, trying to fan the glimmer of hope she was offering me. "But I can be diplomatic, I promise."

She snorted down the phone and I allowed myself a little smile.

"Would you like to meet for a coffee to discuss things further?" I asked, trying hard to sound friendly and light.

"I need to think it over."

"Of course, take your time. Shall I check in with you later in the week?"

"No, I'll let you know if I change my mind. Thank you for calling. I'm sure you're only calling because Cathy is annoyed with you for losing the deal, but I can tell you're trying hard and I do appreciate that."

"No problem," I said, the glimmer fading. "Well, you have my number. I'll be here if you change your mind."

I hung up feeling humble and raw. I had never meant to be hurtful, but it seemed Cathy was right. I had some work to do on my manner.

CHAPTER FOUR

I spent a quiet weekend at home with Asimov. We did a little tidying and sorting out, making a small pile of clothes and books to take to the Op Shop on my way to the office on Monday. Mostly I made piles and Asimov sat on them. I signed myself up for an online music account so that I could broaden my musical horizons and spent Saturday night streaming an eclectic mix of funk and soul and Sunday morning with the latest Martha Wainright album. I didn't often gravitate toward music with lyrics, finding myself irritated by trite lines and eye-rolling clichés, but Martha was music and poetry all in one tangy package. I admired her combination of grit and beauty. Her music was like a freshly manured rose garden.

Asimov didn't say much and I tried to keep busy, avoiding thinking about the mess at work. He especially didn't say anything when I spent Sunday evening doing a deep dive on Hally Arlow, checking out her Facebook, Instagram and Twitter handles. I couldn't bring myself to look at her Snapchat account because I didn't even have the app, but what I did see confirmed my worst fears about her. Her feeds were full of inspirational quotes (#youcandoit), pictures of Hally with other people (#love, #bestiesforlife, #youandmeforever), some of whom I recognised as other Australian celebrities, videos of Hally giving workout advice (#more #youcandoit, #pumpit, #liiiiiiiffffft), photos of epicurean delights (#yum, #numnum, #latteart) and hashtag after hashtag after hashtag.

No doubt, she was next-level beautiful, with her very symmetrical face and slightly kinked chestnut hair that always seemed to be kicking out in just the right place. Her smiles were wide, in that Julia Roberts kind of way, with just the perfect amount of straight white teeth on display. And her eyes, well what colour did you call that, anyway? They appeared to be a tawny-gold, with flecks of russetty copper. Were amber eyes a real thing? Perhaps she wore coloured contact lenses. Whatever the case, I couldn't deny she was arresting to look at, but all those hashtags kept my feet firmly on the ground. Hashtags and inspirational messages were my definition of an absolute nightmare.

So, while a strong part of me hoped like hell she'd never call me again, I had promised Cathy I would do what I could to get this book back to Red Stone. If she did call I would have to suck it up and give it my all. I just had to hope that her attitude to #secondchances extended to unintentionally rude editors at boutique publishing houses.

I felt pretty low, but I was committed to turning over a new leaf on Monday, and as I went to bed on Sunday night I reminded myself and Asimov of my promise.

"I will say hello nicely to Alice," I told him, as he settled himself against my leg and purred gently. "And I will ask John about what he does at the gym." I stroked Asimov's head and tried to remember what else I had resolved to do. I would probably need to make a list, but I could do that in the morning over coffee. I plumped up my pillow and grabbed my book from the bedside table, allowing myself half an hour with Margaret Atwood before I turned out the light.

I headed out early, deciding to take advantage of Melbourne's cool autumn morning and walk to work. It was only an hour's stroll, and with my coffee in my KeepCup and my new streaming music service I thoroughly enjoyed the leg stretch. Who needed the gym when you could get a perfectly good cardio workout on the way to work? Hally may have made a lot of money from her SweatHard brand but as far as I was concerned it was a bit of a farce.

I cut through a park where the trees were ablaze with flaming cherry-red, orange and golden leaves, bright against the crisp blue sky. Trams clattered past me, passengers packed tightly into carriages, most probably going to work just like I was. The streets of my inner-city suburb were already busy with bike riders and joggers getting their workouts in early before work. I enjoyed the weight of my backpack as I made my way, houses gradually petering out in exchange for city blocks and skyscrapers. I tried smiling at people I passed and was rewarded with a few in return. I could be friendly, Cathy would see.

I left my bag of items in the op-shop collection bin and strolled the remaining few blocks to work. As I entered the building, my mobile rang and I stopped in the reception area to retrieve it from my bag.

"Hi, Katie," I said, favouring our receptionist with a wide smile. She looked startled.

"Morning, Gin."

I rummaged through my bag for the phone, still smiling diligently at Katie. Just another day at the office with Friendly Gin, I thought to myself.

"Are you okay?" Katie asked, her brow furrowed. "Are you in pain?"

"No." I dug deeper in my backpack, finally breaking eye contact to look for my phone. "I'm fine, fine," I said as I grabbed at it, anxious to answer it before the call ended. I waved the phone at her. "Excuse me while I take this."

"Of course." She narrowed her eyes suspiciously.

I answered the call, not a number I recognised. "Hello?" I mouthed "Bye" to Katie who frowned in response and continued to my office.

"Ginerva. It's Hally."

Shit. I rushed down the hallway and closed my door, ignoring John and pushing past Alice in my hurry. Friendliness would have to wait.

"Ginerva? Are you there?"

"Yep, yep, sorry." I tried not to sound breathless. "What can I do for you? How are you? Did you have a happy weekend?"

"Er, yes, thank you. Quite a…happy weekend."

"Good. That's excellent, I'm glad to hear it."

"Look, I've decided to give you another chance."

My heart leapt and plummeted like a bungee jumper. "Thank you," I said carefully, trying to sound professional while my insides warred. Cathy would be rapt, and what with my newfound friendliness, there'd be no more talk of me losing my job, but oh hell, this book was my ultimate idea of pain. I hated the thought that my intellectual haven would devolve into a cesspool of superficiality and all I felt was wrong with the world. But I took a deep breath and said, "That is wonderful news for Red Stone. Fantastic, Hally, thank you so much."

"Yes well, I thought about what you said, and I actually think you're right."

"You do?"

"Yes. If I can get *you* on board with the project then my book really will benefit. I don't just want some yes-person who won't strive for excellence. So, whilst—I'll be frank—I don't really like you, and I can tell you're not really sold on me, I think we could possibly create something worthwhile together. You're honest and I appreciate that quality in someone I'm doing business with."

She didn't like me? Well, I guess that wasn't exactly a surprise but it still stung a little. "Um, okay. Right."

"So, where to from here?"

I snapped to focus, moving on from the not-liking-each-other business. She was right, we certainly didn't need to like each other to work together. As it turned out I did like most of the authors with whom I worked, and I assumed they enjoyed my company within the bounds of our professional relationships, but what did it matter at the end of the day? We didn't need to be best friends to get her book moving along.

"Why don't we make a time for you to come in and discuss your vision for the book? If you're happy with how everything looks I can have the contract ready for you to sign."

"Okay. I have a couple of hours this Wednesday afternoon. Are you free then?"

"I should be, just hang on and I'll double check my schedule." I took the phone away from my ear and navigated to my calendar, thankful for the first time that Cathy had forced me to set up a calendar synced between all my devices. "Wednesday afternoon is clear for me," I told Hally.

"Great. I'll come in at three p.m."

"Perfect, see you then."

I sat back in my chair, staring at my blank computer screen. This was really happening and I had to get my head around it. It was essentially great news and I forced myself to focus on that, thinking of how happy Cathy would be. In fact...I put through a call to her. She answered first ring and I launched right in.

"We've got the Hally contract back," I crowed.

"What? Oh, Gin, that's bloody excellent. How on earth did you manage that?"

I smiled smugly, even though she couldn't see me. "I guess I just said the right things. She's keen to get started as soon as possible. We're meeting on Wednesday."

"Right." Cathy's voice held suspicion. "Is there anything you're not telling me? Something I should know?"

"No, really, I convinced her Red Stone was the best place for her book. I'm going to get this nailed, Cathy. I won't pretend I'm excited about having to do it, but if it's good for Red Stone, it's good for me. You don't have to worry, okay?"

"Thanks, I appreciate that. Just please let me know if you think things are going pear-shaped. I don't want to lose her again."

"Absolutely," I promised. "Do you have her contract? I told her I'd have it for her to sign on Wednesday."

"Sure. Email Legal. They'll send it to you. And, Gin?"

"Yeah?"

"Nice one." I could hear the smile in her voice down the line.

"Thanks," I said. "Now, I'd better go, I'm very busy and important and have a new author to prepare for."

Cathy laughed and said goodbye.

I smiled to myself. I didn't like this, but at least I got to keep my job, and Red Stone would continue to flourish. And for those two things, I could put my principles on ice temporarily.

I fired up my computer and pounded out an email to Legal, requesting the contract for Hally Arlow pronto, marking it "IMPORTANT" with the little red exclamation mark in my email program. That done, I decided I deserved another coffee and headed off to the tearoom.

"Good morning, Alice," I said brightly. She had her back to me, putting on the kettle. Friendly Gin strikes again.

She started and turned around, eyes wide. "Hi, Gin. Are you okay?"

"Why does everyone keep asking me that today? I'm excellent, thank you. And how are you?"

Alice gaped at me, her little pink mouth an almost perfect circle. "Good, thank you," she stammered.

"Do you mind?" I asked as I indicated the kettle and waved my cup. "Can I get in on that?"

"Of course. There's plenty to go around."

I smiled at her brightly and set about spooning pre-ground coffee into the office plunger. I could feel her eyes on me as I moved about the kitchen. When the kettle clicked off, Alice stood back and waved me forward.

"Oh no, you go, you were here first, Alice."

"It's okay, I'm not in a rush. Please."

Dipping my head in acknowledgement I said, "Thank you," and filled the plunger with boiling water. While I waited for the coffee to brew I watched Alice make her cup of tea.

"Hey, you still interested in looking over that Hally Arlow manuscript?"

Alice's eyebrows shot up. "Um, me?"

"Yes. If you're still up for it, I'd appreciate your help. Hally's coming in on Wednesday, so perhaps we can make a time to catch up about it after that. I'll email you a copy. I'd appreciate your thoughts."

Alice seemed stuck for words, her eyebrows almost crawling off her forehead into her hairline. Maybe I was overplaying it but what the hell? I needed to show these people that they had nothing to complain about where I was concerned.

"That'll be okay?" I asked.

"Of course," she answered in a rush of breath. "I'd be more than happy to help."

"That's great, Alice. Thanks." I pushed down the plunger and poured a full cup of black brew into my mug. "You were right. This book is going to be a challenge for me and I'd really appreciate your perspective. Let me know when you're free, after Wednesday." And part of me meant what I said. This was alien territory to me, and it was possible that Alice could really help.

"I will," she squeaked, eyes wide.

I waved goodbye at her and took my coffee back to my desk where I could savour it slowly while I devised a plan for the next few weeks. I had a number of projects on the go and I would need to make sure they progressed while I devoted time to pummelling Hally's manuscript into publishable shape.

I took a final longing look at the Massimoto file and forced myself to open Hally's manuscript instead. I decided to read the whole thing again, making notes as I went. I could share these with Hally at our meeting and show her I was taking the project seriously. With my phone silenced and my email closed, I took a deep breath, settled my glasses back up on my nose, and dove in.

This time I read the work critically, but with the intention to publish, forcing my natural cynicism to take a back seat while I looked for any positives. I had to admit that it wasn't entirely without merit. Her writing lacked imagination and flow, coming across as "and then I did this, and then I did that," but if I looked carefully I could see glimpses of a story trying to be told. I made a note to talk to Hally about the "show" rather than "tell" aspect of writing, the power of painting a picture with words. I sipped my coffee slowly and forced myself to highlight paragraphs I thought could be expanded, rather than my previous slash-and-burn approach.

Where I had skimmed and skipped before, I nitpicked and dissected, going through each paragraph with a fine-tooth comb, mining for gems. It was slow going, and by the time lunch rolled around I had only covered half the manuscript. I gave myself a quick break, stretching my legs and grabbing a yoghurt and an apple from my stash in the tearoom. On the way back to my desk, I poked my head into John's office where he was sitting at his desk, engrossed in paperwork. His sandy hair was tousled, as if he had been tugging at it while he worked.

"G'day, John."

John's head whipped up. "Gin. Everything okay?"

"Yep. And with you?"

"Er, yes, all fine, thanks."

"Good, good." I hovered in the doorway, trying to think of something else to say to show off my friendliness. "How's the gym stuff going?"

He tilted his head, eyes narrowing slightly. "It's all right. Feels like I'm making progress slowly but surely."

"Excellent. Well, I'm sure you are." I backed out of the doorway. "Have a good one."

"You too."

I retreated to the sanctity of my office and shut the door, not entirely sure I had nailed that conversation. I would have to think up some better talking points if I was going to continue with this newfound sociability, but for now I could get back to work feeling more than a little self-satisfied with my morning's efforts.

With renewed vigour, and anxious to finish, I ploughed back into Hally's manuscript. When five o'clock finally rolled around I had learnt that Hally had one divorce in the bag (her ex-Husband, Xi, was an Olympic silver-medal marathon runner), she had saved her deposit for her first gym by working three jobs (one as a cleaner, one as a waitress, one as a bike courier), and she'd grown up poor as the proverbial church mouse. All the ins and outs of how she had built up her SweatHard Gym brand and media empire on the back of the social media wave were there, along with lashings of advice and tips on how to manage the constantly changing landscape of the digital world, health, fitness and entrepreneurism.

But by the end I found myself wondering if I really knew her. Where was the deep reveal? There were plenty of anecdotes and snapshots of her life, but who was the real Hally Arlow? How did she *feel* about things? She would need to dig a lot deeper if we were going to have a book to publish.

CHAPTER FIVE

On Wednesday afternoon at exactly three p.m. my desk phone buzzed. "Gin?" Katie's voice piped over the speaker.

"That's me."

"Ms. Arlow is in reception for you."

"Right, I'll be there in a sec."

I paused for a second in front of the small mirror on my bookshelf to straighten my hair and check my teeth. The last thing I wanted to do was sit through a meeting with the glamorous Hally Arlow and afterward find I had spinach in my teeth. Not that I was a big spinach eater but left-over pizza would be just as bad. Worse, probably, given Hally's likely attitude toward pizza. There was little I could do to tame the black spikes, but I patted them into reasonable shape, adjusted my glasses and headed out to reception.

I had seen the pictures of Hally, but I wasn't quite prepared for the real-life version laughing at something a pink-cheeked and fawny-eyed Katie had said.

Of course, she was long and shapely, a perfectly toned-looking body sporting a well-fitting olive-green shirt, open at the neck in a tasteful V, and fashionably flared black slacks. But it was her face that stopped me in my tracks. She had looked glamorous online, always beautiful and smiling, long, shining chestnut hair flicked behind her or swept up in a ponytail, but here in the flesh as she turned to greet me, there was a strength and poise in her features that didn't come across in the pictures. There was a boldness in her wide mouth and straight, Grecian nose, her dark eyebrows perfectly framing those amber eyes, so bright they were almost golden. I swear, as I stepped toward her, I could smell the freshness of her glossy hair as if she had just stepped out of the shower.

"Hally, I'm Gin, Ginerva, call me Gin," I said, suddenly feeling stupidly tongue-tied. I offered her my hand and she took it in a warm, firm grip, capturing my eyes with hers. Wow. I wanted to lean in toward her, feeling like an asteroid that had stumbled into Earth's gravitational field.

She let go of my hand and smiled, releasing me from our connection. "Nice to meet you."

I took a deep breath, forcing my mouth to return the smile, with a breezy, "And you, and you. Come through to my office."

Hally turned back to Katie and said, "See you, Katie. It was nice to meet you in person."

Katie practically fell over her tongue trying to express her own joy. "I'm such a fan, Ms. Arlow, I'm a SweatHard's member and I can't wait to read your book. This is so great. Usually Gin does such boring stuff, so it's going to be a real treat having you around. I just know—"

"All right, Katie, thanks for that," I said, cutting her off, not keen to hear what it was she just knew.

I led the way down the corridor, conscious of a pair of heels tapping on the linoleum behind me.

"Please, take a seat." I waved at the chair in front of my desk and scooted quickly around to mine, adjusting it slightly down with a pneumatic hiss. I felt strange, and it was throwing me for a six. I had had plenty of authors in my office before, but for some reason I was nervous. *Get it together, Gin.*

I adjusted my glasses and offered her another perfunctory smile. "Thanks for coming in. Can I offer you a tea or coffee? Biscuits?"

"I'm fine with just water, thank you. I have my own." She retrieved a fancy water bottle from her briefcase and set it on the desk, her voice even richer and more melodious now that it wasn't coming down the telephone at me.

"Great. Shall we get started then?"

"Absolutely."

I suddenly realised I didn't quite know where to start our conversation. I had read through her manuscript, made copious notes, and dissected the hell out of it, but I wasn't entirely sure how to begin without being rude. I'd never edited a manuscript I found so flawed before. With all my other authors, we started with the good bits, pow-wowing about all there was to love about the manuscript before broaching any weak points that would require changes. I couldn't do that with Hally, because whilst I had committed to the project, I hadn't revised my initial opinion on the subject matter.

I pushed at my glasses which were already high on my nose and wriggled slightly in my chair.

"I guess I don't really know how all this works," Hally said, relieving me from being the first to speak and I realised she thought I was waiting for her.

"That's what I'm here for," I said, magnanimously.

She fixed her clear eyes on me and asked, "Can you talk me through the process?"

"Sure. Good idea," I said, relieved to be on firmer ground. I knew process. "Actually, it's pretty simple. We start by going through your manuscript. We'll discuss edits and you'll make revisions, after which I'll read through it again, and potentially we'll have further discussion. Once we've settled on a final version we proof it, print it and publish it. Along the way we'll meet with Marketing to talk strategies and come up with a release plan. You'll most likely need to do a bunch of media spots to support the launch. I have a copy of your contract here. Please feel free to look it over. When you're happy with everything we've talked about you can sign it." I slid the document across the desk to her and she picked it up, carefully reading through each page.

"Shall I sign it now?"

My heart leapt. I hadn't expected it to be this easy. I'd pictured myself diving through hoops and working hard to get back on board with us. "Sure, that makes it easy for everyone."

I watched as she dashed her name across the page and then pushed it back to me.

"Thank you," I said. I signed my name in the space provided for me. "I'll get you a copy of this before you leave today."

"So, about the actual book."

"Yes?"

"You said we'll talk about edits?"

"Yes, that's something we can start on now if you have time?"

"I've got a couple of hours before my next appointment."

"Perfect." I decided honesty was not only the best, but really the only policy in this situation. "I think we've got quite a bit of work to do."

"I got that feeling from our phone conversation."

I smiled, trying to put her at ease and make up for any discomfort our previous conversation had caused her. "All first drafts need editing."

"Yes, but you think mine is particularly bad."

"I think yours…doesn't represent you as well as it could."

"How diplomatic."

"Thank you."

"So, what's wrong with it?"

I wanted to say "Everything," but instead I said, "There's a few things. For starters, I think it needs crafting. Right now it's like a book that can't decide if it's an autobiography or a self-help book, but we can sort that out with some mapping and structure. The bigger problem is that it's missing something deeper, Hally. I can't work out why you've written it."

"What do you mean? I wanted to tell my story, to inspire others, especially women, to overcome obstacles and roadblocks to live out their dreams. I wanted to help others make their way out there."

"A noble premise. But why do you think people will want to you read *your* story? Why do they want *your* advice?"

She fixed me with a blank look. "I don't know. Because it's mine, I suppose. Because they want to know about me."

"Exactly." I smacked the back of my right hand into my left palm, feeling more at ease now. "And I think that's what's missing. We can tinker with a structural overhaul and the writing could use some work, but the main thing missing is you."

"Jesus." Hally sat back in her chair and crossed a leg over. "You don't mince words, do you."

Shit. Was she going to quit again because I had been too harsh? I couldn't bring myself to butter her up with lies. It was bad enough that I was having to do this work in the first place.

My expression must have given me away because she waved a hand in front of her and said, "By all means, go on. What do you mean it's missing me? It's all about me."

I leaned forward. "Your book doesn't tell me how you *feel* about anything." I tapped my chest with my fist for emphasis. "You tell me what happened to you and what you did about it, but never how you felt while it was happening. Take, for instance, that bit where you describe telling your dad how you want to open your own gym, and he blows you out of the water and says a woman can't do that. Clearly you must have felt something about the lack of faith he showed in you, not to mention the misogynistic attitude, but you just describe it as an obstacle to be overcome, which is a bit trite really, and you never tell us how it made you *feel*. Feelings are what make people read to the end. People need to care about your plight to connect with it, otherwise it's just a load of factoids sitting on a page for people to take or leave." I took a deep breath and held up a copy of her manuscript, reprinted with all my comments tagged into the margins. "I've been through the manuscript and written notes for you. They'll highlight what I'm talking about."

Hally reached for the manuscript and I handed it over, watching as she thumbed through it and then looked up at me with an unreadable expression. "At least this version doesn't have everything crossed out."

"That it doesn't."

She thumbed some more and sighed. "Looks like there's a lot of work to do here."

"Writing a book is a huge effort," I said. "A good book that is."

Hally narrowed her eyes.

Too close to the bone? I rushed to reassure her, in case she felt like backing out again. "But you've done the hardest part, and that's getting out the first draft. The rest is downhill skiing from here."

"Have you ever been skiing?"

"Ah, no. Have you?"

"Yes. It's bloody hard."

"But fun? I'm guessing people wouldn't do it if it wasn't fun."

"Sure. But will this be fun?"

I shrugged. "As fun as you make it, I suppose. Shall we dive in? Kick off? Hockey one, hockey two and all that?"

Hally contemplated me for a moment, her full lips pursed and her eyebrows drawn. "Do you always make so many sporting references?"

I felt myself blush. "No."

She smirked. "Good."

We spent the next two hours deep in discussion. Hally was articulate and expressive, making me wonder why she was such a stilted writer. She wanted to let the story unfold in a free-flowing way. I expounded on the importance of structure, even if mostly imperceptible to the reader, to drive things along and keep the reader engaged. The conversation came easily now that we were on familiar turf.

"You'll need to decide which primary premise you're going for, self-help or autobiography. That will make a big difference to how we structure the book."

"Can't it be both?"

"It can, but it's better to have one dominant, wrapping around the other so people know what they're getting and we can market it appropriately. For instance, is it 'read the heart-warming tale of one woman's battle to overcome adversity and make her vision of the future a reality, where along the way you will also happen learn a lot about how to manage your own social media and take your business to the next level'? Or is it 'learn how to use social media and become an entrepreneur, and along the way you will happen to find out lots about Hally Arlow'? See what I mean?"

"I do. I need to think about that." She chewed her lip, momentarily distracting me. Her lips looked like perfect little plump cushions. And those teeth. Such brilliant white teeth. Guaranteed she used whitening toothpaste.

"Take your time," I said, waving my hand, forcing my mind back to business. "There's lots to think about here. Have you written much before?" I asked.

"Do you count Instagram posts and loan applications? Business reports? Presentations?"

"Not exactly."

She laughed, the same deep, throaty laugh I remembered from our first telephone call. "Then, no. Nothing."

"Right. What about reading? Do you do much of it?"

"I love reading, but I just never seem to have the time anymore."

"Have you read many autobiographies?"

She scrunched up her nose, creating a little set of wrinkles in her otherwise perfectly smooth skin. "I don't think so. Oh, wait, I think I read Flea's autobiography ages ago."

I looked at her blankly.

"You know, the bass player from Red Hot Chili Peppers?"

"Okay."

"Have you read it?"

"Not that one, no. But I have read plenty of other autobiographies and I think it would help you to read some too. Give you a bit of an idea if that's the kind of thing you're going for."

"I'm open to the idea. I don't have heaps of time, but if you think it will help I'm willing to do it."

"How about I make you a list? You definitely need to read some Maya Angelou, and there are a number of great musician autobiographies out there, if you're into that kind of thing. Bob Dylan's *Chronicles* is a fantastic read. I also think you could benefit from some books about writing, just to get a basic understanding of structure and composition."

Hally puffed out her cheeks and blew out a stream of air. "Books about writing as well? I don't mean to sound whingy, but isn't all this what you're here for?"

"I think it'll make the difference, Hally. I'll certainly give you guidance and talk you through the changes we need to make, but reading it for yourself is the best kind of learning." I leaned back in my chair. "You're trying to make a point with this book. Whichever way you go, you want to show people that you're a trailblazer, and others can follow in your footsteps, correct?"

Hally nodded.

"Then you need to give them a book that's accessible, that flows, that makes your point with clarity and grace. You said yourself you don't just want to regurgitate your social-media accounts, so you'll need to craft your writing for best effect. You don't want to sign off on something mediocre, and if I'm being perfectly honest, neither do I."

She worried the paper clip on the edge of the manuscript stack for a moment and then said, "And you'll guide me through this process?"

"I will."

"Okay then. Email me the list."

"Consider it done," I said, writing a note to remind me. "Now, why don't we go over some of the comments I've made so you can see, more clearly, what I'm talking about. Then when you leave here today you'll have a solid idea of what to do next. Also, you've got seventeen chapters here, which is a nice way to break up the book, but I'd like to go through and map out what it is you're trying to say in each chapter. Some of them might be better off rearranged. And some of them might need to be lengthened or shortened."

Hally checked her watch. "I've got a meeting at five thirty. I've probably only got another forty minutes tops."

"That's okay. We can get started and see what we get done."

I moved to my electronic whiteboard and divided it up into sections. "I can print you a copy of this when we're done."

"I'd prefer it if you emailed it. I'm not big on wasting paper."

"Of course." I had no idea how to make that happen but surely someone else in the office would.

"We've got a start, a middle and an end. We know where you're starting, so I'll put teenage years in this box." I paused to write *Teenage Hally* in the first section. "And the end is obviously *Now Hally*, with your franchises and your Internet bizzo."

"You mean social media?"

"Yeah, all that stuff."

"You know every time you refer to 'all that stuff,' as you put it, your lip curls." Her eyes flashed as she spoke and I rolled my traitorous lips in. "I get that you think it's beneath you, but it is actually an amazingly profitable customer-acquisition tool, not to mention an incredible avenue for product promotion and brand awareness, and you'd do well to engage with it to promote my book. My business has grown one hundredfold as a result of Instagram and Facebook."

"Snapchat a cappuccino, earn yourself a new gym junkie?"

Hally narrowed her eyes. "You can be as dismissive as you like, but I wouldn't be sitting here today if it wasn't for the power of digital platforms to bring together like-minded people and disseminate information quickly. It actually creates community."

"It doesn't really bring them together though, does it?" I challenged. I knew I was stepping on shaky ground but I was irritated by her Pollyanna view of what I saw to be a very two-sided coin. "Mostly it just makes people feel bad for not looking as good as you. Social media guilts them into going to the gym and drinking kale smoothies, even though they feel stupid and hate every minute of it, but at some point they realise it's all a big lie. No matter what they do, no matter how many smoothies they do or don't drink, they'll never actually look like you because you're different, you're not like an average person, so they give up and feel like a crap. And then every time they log on to social media they feel bad about themselves because, not only are they not you, now they're also a failure."

Hally stared at me, her immaculate eyebrows raised. Determined not to be intimidated by her glamorous looks, I stared back. Until I remembered that glaring at the client was probably not the best way to keep them on side, and I offered a half smile. "If you know what I mean?"

She cleared her throat and crossed a leg, brushing some invisible lint from her trousers. Finally, she said, "SweatHard Gyms are about bringing people together and promoting a sustainable body image. I believe in long-term health and wellbeing and I never promote anything unrealistic or unachievable on my social media."

"But looking the way you do, you can't really help but do that."

"Looking the way I do?" She eyeballed me and I flushed.

"You don't look like the rest of us," I stammered. "Like most normal people."

She raised her eyebrows. "A compliment?"

I shrugged. "A fact."

"Regardless," she went on. "I truly believe everyone can change their lives for the better and I employ that philosophy in my gyms as well as through my community work. My foundation has recently set up a schools' program which will roll out next year, to educate kids about healthy eating and realistic bodies, and every day we work with our clients at the gym to create body positivity and real success, not just short-term hope." Her eyes were serious as she spoke. "You should come to the gym and see for yourself."

"Maybe I will." I fiddled with the whiteboard marker and leaned against the board. "If I may ask, how many of your members pay without actually showing up?"

"Less than five percent. I know that because it's a statistic that's super important to me. More than half our client base are women and the last thing I want is an already financially disadvantaged cohort paying for something they don't use. It's our policy to work proactively to re-engage with people or cancel their membership if they don't use the gym for more than two months. Most of our memberships are structured differently to a normal gym anyway. We work on a goal-operated system where the customer pays for the development and instigation of a program, and further payment depends on results."

I vaguely recalled John waxing lyrical about something along those lines. "Pay as you go?"

"Basically. You come in, we set you up with a trainer and a plan and you pay upfront for the package. We check in with you and see if you're hitting your goals and adjust things if you're not. When that goal has been met, you develop a new plan. You don't pay for something you're not getting. I've never had any interest in setting people up to fail or taking their money for nothing."

"Right, well, that all sounds very honourable." I looked up at the wall clock and realised we had all but run out of time. "I guess we've gotten a little sidetracked."

"As I said, Gin, you should come in and check it out some time." Her eyes swept over me and I resisted the urge to hug my arms around myself. What did she see? The navy suit I'd chosen today was functional, one of my more slimming outfits, but I was certainly no model. And I most definitely didn't have any muscles to speak of. "The results speak for themselves."

"Fine. I'll come in some time. Listen, I know your time is short and I'd like to address this before you have to go. It's here in the middle that we are having some trouble." I tapped the whiteboard with my pen to bring our focus back to the issue at hand.

"Like most of the people who come to our gyms," she said with a smile.

I couldn't help but laugh. "Yes, I imagine so. If it helps to put this into gym terms, the middle of your book is flabby, it lacks definition."

She raised her eyebrows.

"This is the part where you tell us about your struggle to get the bank loan, to convince them that a woman can set up a business on her own, to get backers and attract customers, to set yourself up as a trusted brand. This is the part where doors close in your face and you realise you're going to have to tar your own road and get creative to achieve your goals. But this is also the part where you get married, then you divorce, you learn how to run a business, and you're dishing out advice left right and centre. There's a lot going on here Hally."

She flipped the lid off her water bottle, and tipped her head back, her throat working as she swallowed. My eyes were drawn to the long line of her neck, the curve of her collarbone as it disappeared behind her shirt. "It was a big time," she said, recapping her bottle and pushing back her chair. She strolled over to my bookshelf and picked up my snow globe, giving it a little shake.

"If it's going to be an autobiography, we can address that by creating a timeline and presenting everything more logically. But if you're going to focus more on the self-help side of things you'll need to pare that back, and that's not me trying to cut things out of your book, I promise." I held up my hands.

She peered into the snow globe, the curved glass magnifying her eye comically.

"Paris?"

I nodded, feeling like I had lost my audience. "Look, why don't we stop here. I think that's enough for today and you've got a lot to digest. Take all this away and we can regroup when you're free next and see what progress you've made."

Without thinking I hit print on my whiteboard and what I'd written on the board slid out smoothly on an A4 piece of paper.

"Email," Hally said, with a frown. Jesus, even with a grumpy look on her face she was ridiculously beautiful. Her lips were the perfect shade, almost a pink-grapefruit colour, and I wondered if she was wearing lipstick or if they were just naturally like that. If she was, it was expertly applied. I never wore make up. If I did, it inevitably ended up smudged and streaked from a day of scrunching and rubbing my face while I thought about things, and I looked like a clown. I bet Hally couldn't look like a clown if she tried.

"Gin?"

"Huh?"

"I prefer, next time, if you don't print all this stuff out. I really don't have room in my life for a whole load of paper, and I'd prefer not to waste the planet's precious resources."

"Shit, sorry, I forgot."

"You're forgiven. Just this once." She winked to soften her words, which, if I was being completely honest with myself, gave me a strange little fizz in my stomach. I put it down to being unused to being winked at by glamorous women. Actually, I couldn't remember the last time I'd been winked at full stop. Then she took the piece of paper from me and folded it in half, sliding it into her briefcase with the hard copy of her edited manuscript.

"I'll have my PA call you to arrange another time. I'm flat-chat the rest of this week."

"No problem. We're not in any rush."

"I'll see myself out," she said and reached over to shake my hand. As our hands connected I felt myself tumble into her orbit again. "Thanks for meeting with me. I know this isn't your cup of tea but I appreciate your opinion, even if it is a bit brutal, and I think you're right. It will be better in the end."

And with that she strode out of my office, closing the door quietly behind her.

I stood for a moment longer at the whiteboard, holding the duster, feeling off kilter. There was a power to this woman, a magnetism for which I had been entirely unprepared. Even I, who prided myself on valuing intellect over the superficiality of looks, wasn't immune to her beauty. I supposed this must be the power of celebrity. Their stars burned brighter than those of us average people.

I set to work rubbing off the board. I didn't really know what to make of Hally. She was so articulate, clearly intelligent and capable, strong-willed. She was driven and successful, and she had sunk all those valuable attributes into things I thought unworthy. Exercise and food were fine, but it was the obsession with body image and food fads that drove me bananas, not to mention all the ridiculous social-media stuff. I wiped harder as I thought of her irritatingly perfect features and sculpted body. I mean, who actually looked like that? Most people, myself included, couldn't look half as good as that if we truly gave it our all. John was an excellent example of this, and I resolved to bring him up with Hally at our next meeting. There he was, slaving away at one of her gyms, and he still looked like a pudgy Paddington bear. No, the proof was in the pudding, or in this case, the protein shake.

CHAPTER SIX

"I want it out by the summer quarter," Cathy said, sitting in the chair that Hally had recently vacated.

"What? That's ridiculous. The first draft is barely finished and it's basically terrible. We'd need to have a final draft completed in the next few months to get it out by summer."

"That's the time frame, Gin. A December release."

"But why?" I stared across at Cathy, frowning deeply, not caring to hide my displeasure. "Isn't it enough that we're getting it out? What's the big rush?"

"Because she's hot right now and I want to capitalise on that. I don't want to miss this boat and things change pretty rapidly in this world."

"You know you're literally saying this book is the fast food of literature."

"How's that?"

"People are going to gobble it up and move on. This is so off-brand for us." I thumped the desk as I spoke. "We're supposed to be producing quality literature that people will want to read and read again, to share with their friends and book clubs, to pass on to their children and keep in their bookshelves. This... this book is nothing more than a cheeseburger."

Cathy sighed and ran a hand through her hair, shaking out her curls. "Gin, can you retire the sanctimonious preaching for ten seconds, please? I'm tired of it. Red Stone needs this release. It's going to be a big hit and that is good for our bottom line. Everyone's looking for a good easy read over summer, and what better to give them than a rags-to-riches tale about an exercise queen who has taken the country by storm? They'll give it to each other for Christmas, they'll snap it up for their beach hols. It's a no brainer."

"Doesn't Alice have some smash hit romance coming out? Can't we use that instead?"

"I've slated that for autumn."

"So, she gets a full year cycle." I counted off on my fingers. "and I get eight months to get this off the table and into stores. That leaves me two months to finish editing and get to final copy, Cathy. Two months!"

"That's about the sum of it. Come on, Gin, it's not like you don't have time. Your workload is absolutely manageable. You need to jump on this. I want you meeting with Marketing right from word go so they can be prepared. They can start booking in a tour as soon as Art locks in the cover."

I sighed and swivelled around in my chair, swinging from side to side. Cathy was right. My current projects were ticking along nicely and there was nothing that required my attention on the scale of Hally's book. I could afford to take on this project timewise, I just didn't want to. But I had promised myself and Cathy that I would turn over a new leaf so I stopped swivelling and sat up.

"If Hally's up for it, I'll do all that I can to get the book up to scratch and into stores by December. She did say she's pretty busy at the moment, so I suppose I'll need to talk to her and make sure she's on board, but otherwise, you can go ahead and put it in the calendar."

Cathy smiled at me approvingly. "Good work. Now, what am I going to do about Rachel?"

I shifted gears mentally. "Your sister? What's up? I thought things had calmed down now that your mum's back home."

"Mum seems stable, but Rachel is spinning off the dial. She's caring for Mum around the clock and barely getting out to see the light of day. She's getting thinner by the second and I don't think I've ever seen her so uptight."

I grimaced. "That sounds bad. Have you tried convincing her to accept some help?"

"I told her I'd pay for a carer to come in every morning to give her a break but she wouldn't even hear me out. Just screamed that I never thought she was good enough and locked herself in her room. I honestly don't know what to do."

"Does she still have that friend? Andrew? Adam? Alfonoso? What's his name?"

"Aidan," Cathy supplied. "I don't know. Why?"

"You could call him and see if he could convince her to take some time for herself."

"Shit. She'd just about come down here and kill me with her bare hands if I interfered like that. No, I think I need to go back up and spend a bit more time in Sydney. I think the only way to give her a break is to sub in myself. She'll hate it but she can't really argue with it—she's both our mum at the end of the day."

"True. It's bummer you have to go back to Sydney though."

"I don't mind it so much up there. The beaches are excellent."

"Since when did you have time to go to the beach?"

"I don't," Cathy acknowledged with a dip of her head, "but I drive past Bondi on my way to the office and it always looks so sublime. Maybe I'll try to make time for it."

"When will you go?"

"I actually think I'll head up on the weekend. If I drive up I can take Olive with me."

"Woah, driving up takes ages. And taking Olive? She'll hate that! How long are you thinking of going for? Asimov and I are happy to look after her."

"I can't ask you to do that. I might be there for a month. Longer. Who knows?"

"Duh, of course you can. I'm your best friend and it's no skin off my nose. I think Asimov likes the company. Why don't you leave her with me for now and if things change you haven't had to haul her all the way up to Sydney for no reason. You might find you're back in two weeks."

Cathy looked doubtful and scrunched up her nose. "I don't know about that, Gin, but I guess we'll see."

She rose from the chair, groaned and stretched her arms over her head. "I've got to get going. I've got a Zoom meeting I could live without right now and a pile of paperwork sky high. Call Hally, okay? Lock in that release date."

"I will, I will." I stood up and yawned. "Tomorrow though. I need to get out of here now. Just let me know when you want to drop Olive over."

"Thanks. I'll probably bring her Friday night after work. With pizza."

"Deal."

The next morning as I walked to work through the tree-lined streets of Fitzroy, I plugged in my handsfree headphones and called Hally, filling her in on Cathy's plans for the summer release date.

"So, basically, it's up to you Hally. We'd need to spend quite a bit of time editing over the next two months, and then from November on you'd be gearing up for the release."

"Hmm, it's a little...ner th...I was exp...ing." Hally's voice crackled, the connection breaking up.

"Sorry, I missed that. Can you say again? I think we have a bad line."

"I'm...st drop...ff...phews."

"Um, nope, still can't hear you."

"I'm just dropping off my nephews, I'll call you back," Hally shouted, her voice suddenly crystal clear.

"Ow." I grabbed my ear. "Yep okay, got it this time."

We rang off and I continued my walk, thinking about Hally and all that she had to juggle. Running a large business was demanding. Add in all the publicity stuff, life in the public eye, as well as family commitments and I felt tired just thinking about it all. I found it hard enough to make time for my dad, and all

I had to manage was a nine-to-five job, a small dull apartment and a cat. I couldn't imagine how she did it all.

I stopped to pick up a coffee at my favourite little hole-in-the-wall café. It was literally just a window in a brick wall with a counter for ordering, run by a couple who prided themselves on good coffee and fast and friendly service. Planter boxes of vermillion geraniums sat under the window and the brick was covered with a cool spray-painted piece that looked like a sailor's tattoo. They had a few small tables and chairs set up on the street but most people, myself included, handed over their KeepCups for takeaway.

"Morning, Gin. The usual?" Con, with his bushy bohemian beard and friendly brown eyes, was at the window taking orders this morning while Graham, a slightly shorter and fatter version of Con, manned the machine. They swapped roles regularly, I supposed to keep it interesting for themselves.

I moved aside to lean against the wall while I waited. My phone buzzed and I saw Hally's name pop up on my screen.

"Can you hear me okay now?" she said, skipping the pleasantries.

"Yep, loud and clear."

"Great. Sorry about that. I was dropping my nephews to school and there's always a patch of shitty reception just before we get there. Some kind of technology vortex. My GPS always flips out around there too."

"Weird."

"Yes. Anyway, we're talking about the possibility of a December release, huh? How do you feel about that?"

Con called my name and I went to the window, mouthing "Thank you" to him. "I guess it's more about how you feel than me. You said you're pretty busy. Do you think you'd have the time for some intense work on the book over the next month? If we go with Cathy's timeline we'd need to have the structural edits completed in a month and then we have a month to proof, make changes and lock in the final copy."

"I do have a lot on, but then, when don't I? I feel like we might as well strike while the iron's hot."

"Okay. And you'd be happy to do some touring for the book in November and January? We'd probably have you getting around to the capital cities at the end of November, just before the book comes out, and maybe even a few regional centres as well to promo it with radio. Then in January, we could send you on a signing run to some of the stores we have relationships with."

"Actually, I think that would be perfect. I was planning to do some travel for SweatHard in November anyway. I like to get around and eyeball my gyms at least a few times a year. We communicate electronically the rest of the time but it's just not the same."

"So, I'll tell Cathy we're good to go?"

"Woah, watch it arsehole," Hally suddenly shouted into the phone, stopping me in my tracks. "Not you, Gin, sorry, some idiot just cut me off. Yes, tell Cathy it's all systems go," she said and gave a little whoop.

"Right." I breathed out, taking a fortifying sip of my coffee. "Get your PA to call me as soon as she can and I'll set up a weekly meeting for us. If you can fit that into your schedule?"

"Natalie's a genius with that kind of thing. I'm sure she'll manage something."

"I'll wait to hear from her."

The blips of another call interrupted her sentence. "I've got to take this. Talk to you later, Gin."

She rang off and I left my headphones in, choosing Verdi's *Aida* as the soundtrack for the remainder of my walk. I let myself float away on a cloud of soaring trumpets and sweeping strings, like a boat let loose from its mooring. I figured I had at least four days or so, maybe even longer if I was lucky, before Hally would be able to come in and we'd have to knuckle down to get her book underway. As a gift to myself, I would spend my time indulging in all the highbrow work I could get my hands on. I would finish the final Massimoto edit and continue with my other manuscripts and authors. I would put Hally Arlow and her book as far from my mind as possible. I wasn't looking forward to this book taking up all my time.

CHAPTER SEVEN

I spent my next two days at work deeply immersed in the ancient history of the earth's biological development, Australian politics, and the fundamentals of biodynamic soil propagation. It was invigorating and I felt strangely emotional, as if I knew somehow I would be saying goodbye to this kind of thing for a while. The expected call from Hally's personal assistant, Natalie the genius, had set the next meeting date for Tuesday morning, which only gave me a few more Snapchat-free days. I was doing my best to make the most of the time.

"Hey you, I've got two tickets to Sarah Ruzden's new play, *I Am Woman Or Am I?* tonight," Cathy announced, poking her head around my office door as I was drifting gloriously through the last chapter of Massimoto's manuscript. "Want them?"

"I thought you were going to Sydney straight after work."

"I am, but you can go. Take someone else."

"Aren't you coming to drop off Olive?"

"I can let myself in if you're not there. I still have your spare key."

I thought about my options. Dad would be free, but he pretty much never left the house. And extreme feminist politics in play form didn't really seem like his bag. Thomas and I sometimes went out together, but this also wasn't his kind of thing. He was more into Ru Paul-esque drag shows and late-night cocktails, and with Kevin moving in I could hardly invite one without the other. Cathy was my usual go-to for these kinds of things, I'd either have to miss it or go by myself.

"Or you can go by yourself," Cathy continued, as if reading my thoughts.

"I could."

"I'll email them to you. If you decide to go, just let me know and I'll let myself in to drop off Olive."

"Okay, thanks. I might need to do something like this, all things considered."

"What things?"

"As of next week, my life is pretty much over."

"What? Why?"

"The Hally Arlow thing," I said, leaning back in my chair and stretching out the kinks in my neck. "She's coming in on Tuesday and then it's all systems go. I'll be up to my ears in this social media and all-hail-the-body-beautiful crap for the next few months."

Cathy grinned. "Melodramatic much? Come on, Gin. It's not going to be that bad."

"Says you. If you're so into it, why don't you take it on?"

"This *is* me taking it on. You're the editor from *my* business and I've chosen to make this happen."

I gave Cathy a pleading look. "No chance you can un-choose me? Make this un-happen."

"Nope, not a chance."

I huffed and sat forward again, pushing my glasses up my nose. "Well, in that case, I've got to get back to work. I'm very busy and important you know."

"How could I forget." Cathy blew me a kiss. "I'll call you from Sydney."

"I might not answer."

"I might need to FaceTime with Olive."

"Fine, whatever, damn you." We grinned at each other and Cathy left me to my reading.

I ended up going to the play on my own and woke up on Saturday morning feeling invigorated by the subject matter and the intellectually piquant conversations of the trendy thirty-somethings surrounding me at interval.

After a lazy morning I drove around to see Dad and shared a beer with him in his workshop. He showed me the bedside table he was putting together, his talent as a carpenter evident in the perfect lines and smooth operation of the drawer.

"This is amazing, I need something like this. My bedside table is very wobbly."

"I could show you how to make one," he offered.

"As if. How come I never got any of this practical talent, Dad?" I asked as I perched on his workbench, watching him sand a small piece of wood that he called a dowel pin.

"Guess you take after your mum," he replied with a grunt as he held the pin up to the light and examined it, blowing it free of sawdust.

"She wasn't practical?"

"Not a scratch. Something didn't work, she chucked it straight out."

"Most people don't fix things when they break though, Dad."

He looked up at me with surprise, peering over the top of his multifocals. "I suppose they don't." He went back to his sanding.

"She was lucky she had you around."

"I was the lucky one," he said, without missing a beat. "I'll always be sorry you never knew her."

"Me too." My heart ached a little at that. Not so much for myself. I'd been through the prerequisite angst and sadness as a teenager, berating the world for taking my mother from me soon after I was born, and leaving me to grow up with a monosyllabic father and no siblings. It had been replaced instead with a sadness for my dad, left alone with no desire to reach out beyond his current circumstances. But I could hardly judge—it wasn't as if I was out there trying to partner up and settle down. I, too, was happy enough with the *status quo*, content with my own little world. I supposed in some ways we were very alike, my dad and I, even if I wasn't practical.

On Saturday night Thomas and Kevin invited me around for drinks and celebratory board games. In amongst a rigorous round of Trivial Pursuit I told them about my woes at work, knocking back a glass of red wine that deserved to be drunk far more slowly.

"Hally Arlow is hot," Kevin declared, rolling the dice and moving his circle three paces forward. "Fuck, Art and Literature. I'm so shit at that. Go on, Tommy, read me the question."

"It doesn't matter what she looks like," I expounded, shaking my wineglass at him precariously. "It's the fact that her book is awful that is the point here. And I have to put my professional name to it and edit it. I'll be laughed out of town."

"Which town is that? 'Cos most people I know think she's hot," Kevin repeated.

"Okay here you go," Thomas said, picking up a card. "Who is credited as the designer for the many statues that surround the Parthenon?"

"Oh, fuck me." Kevin took a swig of his beer. He turned to me and asked, "Who could possibly know that? Do you know that?"

I nodded miserably. "And I also know that until this book is finished I'm going to be in all kinds of purgatory."

"Come on, babe, it can't be that bad," Thomas said, throwing his arm around me and squeezing my shoulder.

"It is. It's the worst. It's all about using Facebook and Instagram to get ahead and going to the gym." My voice sounded hollow.

"You can meet cute chicks at the gym," Thomas said.

"I'm not going to the gym. I'm just having to read about it. I don't know which is worse."

"How do you know that?" Kevin asked.

"What? Which is worse? I suppose—"

"No, the answer to the question. Who made all the statues in the Parthenon? How could you possibly know that?"

"I guess I've read it somewhere."

"Well I give up, what's the answer then?"

"Phidias," I supplied.

"Is that right?" Kevin asked, turning to Thomas.

He grinned and nodded.

"Jesus, Gin. You've got to get out more. Maybe spending a bit of time with a hot, socially active health nut isn't the worst thing for you."

"As if," I said, draining my glass and setting it down with a forceful thud.

"She's not Gin's type," Thomas said, picking up the dice and giving them a shake before he tossed them on the board. "Gin is looking for a meeting of the minds, an intellectual polymath to challenge her on the nature of existence and thrill her to her core, isn't that right, babe?"

He wasn't wrong. It wasn't that I didn't appreciate good looks and lovely bodies, it just wasn't what I was after in a girlfriend. My last partner, Pam, had been a scientist of unparalleled genius. Unfortunately she had spent so much time delving into the secrets of the universe, she had all but forgotten about me, and we had eventually drifted apart. I still held a soft spot for her though, with her serious face and permanent rings around her eyes from peering down a microscope. "Right," I replied, taking the next card to ask his question.

"But you must have at least noticed Hally is smashingly good-looking," Kevin probed, studying me carefully. "What about her eyes? I met her once and I couldn't believe they were real. Do you think they're real or contacts?"

"Who knows. That's the thing though, isn't it? Beauty is so artificial these days no one knows what's real anymore. Anyway, I think real beauty is in the stretch of the mind, the art of conversation, the poetry of nature and connection."

Kevin stared at me for a moment and then grinned. "You're one of a kind, Ginerva Blake."

"Thank you," I said. "I think."

If my brain hadn't been suffering the ill effects of too much red wine I wouldn't have answered my phone on Sunday morning, but as it was, I reflexively reached for it when it woke me with its irritating bleep. I had forgotten to put it on silent when I had eventually stumbled across the corridor to my apartment and into bed. I fumbled blindly, my eyes blurry without my glasses, knocking a disgruntled Asimov off my pillow.

"Hello?" I croaked as I managed to answer the call.

"Gin?"

My brain creaked into gear, confusion clouding my thoughts as I recognised the voice. "Hally?" Had I skipped a day? Was it somehow Monday?

"Not waking you am I?"

"Er…" I sat up and grabbed my glasses from the bedside table, blinking as I tried to make sense of my bedside clock. It seemed to be saying it was 8:30 a.m. "No, of course not. Is everything okay?"

"Yes, I just have some questions about your notes. I've been at it most of the weekend and I think I need to clarify a few things before I go any further."

"You do? We're meeting on Tuesday, right?"

"I was hoping we could make it earlier."

My heart sank as I thought of my last Hally-free workday. "Okay, I'm sure I can fit you in tomorrow if you want to come in then."

"What are you doing today?"

"Today? As in, it's Sunday today?"

"Yes. I'm absolutely flat-chat on Monday. Any chance you can meet me this morning?"

"I…" I couldn't think of what to say. I had no plans and no excuse was coming into my struggling brain.

"Sorry if it's an imposition. I'm just keen to get the ball rolling. Now that it's happening I want to seize the momentum and run with it."

"Unfortunately the office is closed today, Hally."

"We could meet in a café? Are you anywhere near Northcote? We could grab a table at the Penny Kettle, or I could come to where you are if that's easier."

Irritatingly, my apartment was only a short drive from Northcote and I knew the café well. It was famous for its artisan coffees and mouth-watering pastries, the thought of which led me to say, "What time?"

"You name it. I'm free this morning until midday."

"Give me an hour," I said and tipped myself out of bed.

CHAPTER EIGHT

Hally was waiting for me in the back corner of the garden, seated at a little table hidden amongst a nook of ferns and a small willowy tree. The courtyard caught the morning autumn sun and Hally looked more casual in a soft black tank top with a high neckline and tight-fitting cargo pants. She wore a peaked NY Yankees cap, pulled down low and was sporting a pair of dark sunglasses. With the angle of her cap and her hair tied up, she looked exactly like a celebrity in disguise. Which I suppose in some ways she was.

"Hi," I said as I took a seat at the table.

Hally slipped her sunglasses off and dealt me a practised smile, the kind I bet she trotted out for journalists and the like. She reached for a large colourful teapot and held it up, the muscles rippling in her tanned forearm. "Tea?" I wondered how much she had to work out to get that effect. It was nice and all but seemed like such a waste of time. As long as my muscles were strong enough to hold up a large cappuccino and a good book, that was enough for me.

I shook my head. "I ordered a coffee and a croissant on the way past the register. Are you eating?"

She rested the pot back on its coaster. "No, I've had breakfast already." She regarded me across the table for a moment, her eyes sharp and steady and I felt slightly unnerved, wishing my head was clearer and my eyes didn't feel like I'd given them a going over with sandpaper the previous evening.

"So, what's up?" I asked, trying to get off the back foot. "You had some queries for me?"

"Yes, thanks so much for meeting with me. I hope I haven't put you out on your day off."

The correct answer would have been "Of course not." Not quite able to bring myself to say that, I merely dipped my head in acknowledgement.

"I've decided I want the book to be more autobiography than self-help," Hally said, pulling the manuscript out of her handbag and making room for it on the table in front of her. "But I'd still like to keep in some of the helpful advice on social media and entrepreneurism."

"That shouldn't be a problem," I replied, wondering why this couldn't have waited until Tuesday. "You could create little boxed sections at the end of each chapter with pieces of advice," I suggested. "That format could work well for you. Almost like, here's how I experienced life and now here's how you can learn from my experience."

"I like that," she said, nodding seriously.

"Here you go, lovely." A waitress in a long half-apron, with tattoos covering both her forearms, slid my croissant and cappuccino onto the table in front of me. She snapped her gum and looked at Hally appreciatively. "Get you guys anything else?"

"Not for me thanks," Hally said, and I declined with a shake of my head. The waitress shimmied away from our table. I lifted my cup to take a sip as Hally cried, "No, wait!"

I froze, the cup hovering near my lips. "What's the matter?"

"Look what the barista has done with your coffee."

I lowered my cup and glanced at the coffee, surprised to see what looked to be an eighteenth century bust of a woman, Jane Austen style, dusting the top of my coffee.

"Impressive," I said. "I wonder how they do that."

I raised the cup again to take a sip as Hally threw out her hand and again cried, "Wait."

"What now?" I asked, pausing.

She pulled her phone out of her pocket. "This is really awesome. We should get a photo of it."

I sighed and put the cup down, desperate to take a sip. "You want to take a photo of my coffee."

"Sure, why not?"

"To which I might reply, why?"

"To share it, Gin," she said, emphasizing my name. "To let other people see something really great so they can enjoy what we're enjoying and experience some of our experience. This is the whole point of the community."

"The community? You mean your followers."

"I don't like to think of them as followers. It demeans them and takes away their autonomy. The people I interact with have the power to influence each other and share and disseminate information. We're a community. And if we put this up on Instagram, the barista gets kudos for their art."

"Can't we just thank the barista on the way out? Do we need to tell everyone what we're doing every step of the way? Maybe not everything needs to be shared. Maybe it's okay to have experiences that don't involve your thousands of Internet followers, sorry I mean, *community*."

She put her phone down carefully on the table and leaned forward, a strand of hair working loose from her ponytail. "This here. This right here is the problem."

I sat back. "What problem is that?"

"You look down on me for what I do."

"What? That's ridiculous." She was right, but it seemed mean to say so.

"I was pretty sure it was the case and I wanted to meet you today to confirm it. You're so high and mighty about social media, and it's clear that you think going to the gym is a waste of time. You basically think me and my life are inferior and I don't know how the hell I can do what needs to be done here with you when you're so uppity. Putting aside the fact that it feels like shit to have someone think like that, you said you want me to put more of myself into this book to draw people in and engage them with my story, but the first person who is going to be critiquing my work is someone who I already know looks down their snooty nose at me and it's hard to move past that and get writing."

I didn't know what to say. I felt paralysed, unable to drink my coffee, head beating painfully. My nose wasn't snooty. But I also hadn't changed my mind and signed up for a gym membership and Facebook in the last few days. I wasn't #changed and I certainly wasn't #turningoveranewleaf. By the same token, I didn't like the picture she was drawing of me. "Look, Hally." I tried my best to sound reassuring. "I'm sorry if I've come across as a bit...pompous."

"A bit!"

"Okay." I held up my hands and took a deep breath. "A lot. You're right, it's not fair on you and it's something I'm trying to work on, so I apologise. Please, take a photo of my coffee. And my croissant." I pushed it toward her. "I'm on board with this. I want you to write your story and I will do my best to support you in the process."

"And you're not going to try and cross it all out again?"

I felt my face heat for a second and took a quick sip of water. "That was a mistake and I'm sorry. I think we've established that I'm all in on the project now."

She stared at me for a moment longer, her face shaded by her cap making her eyes unreadable.

"Please, Hally. Take the photo. I really want you to, and I also really want to drink my coffee. I actually have the tiniest bit of a hangover and if I'm going to be of any assistance to you at all this morning, I need to drink this now."

She laughed and her eyes softened, accentuating the glow of her tanned skin and perfect features. "At least you're honest," she said and took her time to position the shot. She tapped and swiped her screen and then showed me the photo uploaded to her Instagram page. There were all the prerequisite hashtags of #latteart and #coffeeaddict, but she was right, it really did look quite cool.

"So, shall we get down to it?" I said, getting stuck into my coffee before she could stop me again.

We spent the next hour trawling through my notes, discussing ways she could expand on the parts I felt held the most merit.

"I've checked out those books you recommended. I've listened right through the Maya Angelou book, *I Know Why the Caged Bird Sings*, and you're right, it was very helpful," Hally said, taking a sip of her tea. "What a powerful book."

"You listened?"

"Yeah. I like to listen to books while I'm working out."

I was impressed. I hadn't expected her to follow up on my advice. "She's an incredible writer. And I'm not saying you need to sound like her, because her experience is what makes her unique, but you do need to sound more like you. Imagine you're just writing it for your personal journal. You can tell it how you feel without fear of judgement."

"So, like the opposite of you."

I smiled. "Ah. Touché."

"It's actually hard to shut off the idea of being judged. I know when I put myself out there people will judge me, and I know plenty of people think of me the way you do, but I'm not as shallow and vacuous as you assume. My image, what people see of me, it's not just a free-for-all. I choose carefully what I reveal and what I don't and it's easy to do that with little bite-sized chunks of social media. I'm finding it hard to get past that in long-form writing."

I nodded. It made sense. No wonder her writing sounded stilted. She wasn't used to having so many words to say her piece. "I get that. I can't imagine giving out half as much of myself as you do on a daily basis, so I'm sure the idea of digging deeper is unsettling, but I suppose you need to keep the bigger picture in mind. Remind yourself of why you're telling your story, why it's important that you do this."

"You said it was trite."

"Well…I was possibly still in my resistance phase of the project when I said that."

"And what do you call this phase?"

"Being supportive, of course," I said and finished the last crumbs of my croissant.

"Right. They don't seem super different."

I dipped my head in acknowledgement. "Maybe it's just about the way you expressed it, but it does feel like every thirty-something-year-old woman with a thriving social-media account wants to tell all the other thirty-something-year-old women out there that they can do it too. The fact is, they can't. It's not possible for everyone to be an influencer. Some people have to follow or the whole system falls apart."

"I'm not trying to say everyone can do exactly what I've done. I'm trying to say that people can follow *their* dreams, blaze their own trails."

"But can they? Isn't that just providing false hope? Do you really think everyone can do whatever they want?"

"Why not?"

"It's not realistic, for one. And for two, because not everyone has the opportunities you've had."

She scoffed, brushing a hand in front of her face. "Which opportunities are those, exactly? My mother worked as a cleaner and I got a job working with her at fourteen. I had to give her all the money I earned because my father kept throwing away everything we had on the pokies. And when I say everything, I mean everything. He even sold our dog one day. Is that the kind of opportunity you're talking about?"

"I didn't know that. You mentioned in the book that you grew up poor, but you didn't really say why. Or what it was like. This is good, Hally. This is the kind of thing that needs to go in."

"You want me to tell people that my dad was a loser gambler and he sold our dog?"

"Would that be a problem?"

"It would feel disloyal."

"I hate to say it, but your dad doesn't exactly come across in the greatest light already. Even from the small amount you've put in there, he sounds, at best, like a bit of a misogynist. He's part of the adversity you had to overcome. People have to be able to relate to you. They have to understand where you've come from and why you've made the choices you did."

She took a sip of her tea, gazing down at the manuscript. "I should talk to my mum and my sister."

"Not your dad?"

"Dad died a few years ago."

"Oh, okay, I'm sorry to hear that." The words felt inadequate but I didn't have anything better to offer.

She turned her honey-coloured eyes on me, a tight smile on her face. "Don't be."

I had a strange urge to reach out and touch her arm, to soothe her in some way. It was painful to see her so obviously unsettled. Instead, I folded my napkin over into little squares, unsure what to say.

"It's okay. My dad was a pretty big arsehole. I was trying to be polite by not mentioning that, but I guess I'll have to get to it in some way. I just need to clear it with my family first."

"You're close to your family?"

"Yes. It's just Mum and Delphi, my sister. And her two boys, Cameron and Scott."

"They're the boys you were taking to school the other day?"

"That's right." Her face lit up. "God, they're a handful but I love them. We have so much fun together. They're teaching me to skateboard at the moment. It's awful and I'm terrified of falling off, but they love it."

I shuddered. "I've never tried a skateboard. We used to bike ride a lot as kids, but that's about as adventurous as I get."

"Who's we?" Hally asked, taking a sip of her tea.

"Cathy and I."

"Wait, as in Cathy from Red Stone?"

"That's the one. We've been friends since we were in primary school."

A knowing look passed over her face. "Huh."

"What?"

"That'll be why she urged me so strongly to give you another chance."

For the second time in ten minutes I felt my face flush. Damn, I'd never been much of a blusher, and here I was, blooming like The Rose of Tralee twice in a single conversation.

"That's probably less about me and more about what's good for Red Stone. She's very excited to be publishing your book."

"And you're not."

I decided that honesty was the best policy. We were going to be working together, closely for the next six months and there was no way I could keep up a charade for that long. "The topic isn't my cup of tea, but that doesn't mean I won't do my absolute best with your work, Hally. I pride myself on my high standards and I apply them to everything I commit to, and I've committed to bringing out your book."

She pursed her lips. "Why have you?"

"Because Cathy asked me to," I said simply. "It's important to Cathy and Red Stone, and Cathy and Red Stone are important to me."

"Fair enough."

"So, do you have enough to go on with from here, until we meet again on Tuesday?"

"I do." She hefted the manuscript between her hands. "It feels like there's a lot here already."

"There is. You just need to flesh it out. Tease out the strands and weave them into stories. I guess you could think of it as turning poetry into prose."

She wrinkled her nose. "What do you mean?"

"Your Instagram and Facebook posts, they're short-form, like poetry. Your book is just a long-form version of them, like prose."

She tilted her head at me, a hint of a smile hovering around her lips. "You know you just called my social-media posts poetry."

I rolled my eyes. "It was an example."

"No, it's okay. I'm glad to know that you're secretly a big fan of what I do."

We stopped to pay at the counter on our way out. In true Northcote fashion, the café staff were having an impromptu dance off to Janet Jackson's "Rhythm Nation," and we waited as behind the counter a tall, androgynous-looking twenty-something twirled a guy with a beard that would have made Ned Kelly jealous.

"My shout," Hally said. "I did drag you out of bed with a hangover on a Sunday morning."

I thanked her and stepped back, watching as the staff, suddenly aware of our presence, made eyes at each other behind the cappuccino machine. Did they recognise Hally?

"Ms. Arlow," the twenty-something said, a little out of breath as they confirmed my suspicions. They released their dancing companion and come around to the register. "Sorry about that."

"No problem. I love that song," Hally said, giving her shoulders a little shimmy. On anyone else it would have looked ridiculous. On Hally it simply looked glamorous.

"Thanks so much for tagging us in your post. Our page has gone off this morning. Totally viral. Coffee's on us."

"No, no," Hally protested. "It's important to me to support local businesses. We're happy to pay and it's my pleasure to share cool stuff. That really was an amazing decoration in the coffee. By far the best I've seen."

At this there was so much blushing and grinning and fluttering of eyelashes that I was worried for a moment they might be having some kind of a seizure. Hally handed over her card and the server finally took it, tapping it on the electronic card reader before handing it back.

"Are you local?" they asked Hally.

"Sort of, I'm not far from here," Hally answered, striking the perfect balance between not giving too much away and answering the question. It was very smooth.

"Come back and see us any time. We love to have you here," they said, holding Hally's gaze with such a meaningful look I almost felt like blushing.

Hally laughed kindly and tucked her card away. "I'm sure we'll be back."

Before we left I tucked a ten-dollar note into the tip jar and offered up my own smile. I hadn't always had my dream job. I knew how hard café work could be, on your feet all day, and I liked to show my appreciation. Hally raised an eyebrow at me and I shrugged.

Out on the street I said, "I suppose that kind of thing happens all the time?"

"What's that?" Hally asked, putting her handbag over her shoulder.

"People trying to give you stuff for free because you have so many Internet fans."

She shrugged. "I guess. I try not to take it. You don't want to be rude but you also don't want to walk around taking freebies all the time. It feels wrong and it also undermines your authenticity."

"Admirable. I'm guessing not everyone in your position holds themselves to such high moral values."

"Possibly not," she acknowledged. "I'll see you Tuesday. Thanks again for this morning. It was very helpful."

She held out her hand and I took it, feeling conspicuous shaking hands on the busy streets of Northcote with someone as beautiful as Hally. Her hand felt smooth and strong in mine, the touch of her skin was warm and I had an overwhelming desire to keep hold. She broke the contact and I shoved my hands in my pockets.

"Tuesday," I said and watched as she headed away from me down the street. With her lithe frame she walked with the poise of which I could only dream and I noticed people turning to look at her as she passed. It was a funny thing, beauty. As a society we held it in such high esteem, but thankfully I could count myself as one of the few who wasn't distracted by it. The hand-holding thing was just a physical response, an irritating and brief treachery of my biochemistry, and that was okay. Not a big deal. The physical was the physical. It was the metaphysical that interested me, the space where minds met beyond the mere biology of our beings. That said, as I made my way to my car, the morning's conversation running around in my brain, I found I was thinking of Hally in a more favourable light.

That evening I hummed as I made dinner, absentmindedly singing the words, or at least my best guess at the words, to "Rhythm Nation" as I chopped mushrooms for me and dropped crunchies in a bowl for the cats.

My mobile bleeped and flashed Cathy's name. I answered it with a broad swipe, tucking it under my ear as I continued my work in the kitchen. "How's your mum?" I asked, even though she had texted me an update that morning. "Everything okay?"

"She seems to be making a full recovery, thankfully," Cathy replied and I could hear I was on speaker phone.

"That's bloody excellent. Are you driving?"

"I'm on my way back to the hotel from Rachel's. How are you?"

"I'm great," I said, pouring a bowl of beaten egg into a sizzling pan. I wasn't usually much of a cook, but every now and then I felt mildly inspired to prepare something slightly more elaborate than pasta. Tonight would be vegetable omelette. The egg spluttered and spat in the pan.

"You're cooking?"

"I am."

There was a moment's silence on Cathy's end. "Weird."

"Why?"

"You never really cook."

I stirred the pan vigorously. "Well, I felt like it tonight. Is that a crime?"

"No," Cathy said slowly. "No crime. What did you get up to today?"

"Nothing much, I bummed around with the cats. Oh, and I met up with Hally this morning."

Cathy squeaked incredulously. "You did? What for?"

I paused to flip the omelette carefully, cursing as it broke in half. "Damn. We just met up to talk a bit more about her book. She had some questions about the notes I'd put together for her."

"On a Sunday?"

"It's cool, I didn't really mind. We met at that hipster café, the Penny Kettle. We should go there sometime. The coffee was really good."

"Sounds like someone is beginning to enjoy working on this book."

I froze, and put the spatula down on the bench, carefully turning the heat down. "Please don't get the wrong idea, Cathy. I'm doing this for Red Stone and for you, because you are my best friend, and I don't want to lose my friend or my job. There's nothing to *enjoy* about this for me. I loathe the fact that we are sinking the earth's resources into such a puff piece, but I am doing my best to bring it home because that's what needs to happen. Okay?"

Cathy guffawed in my ear. "Remind me why you haven't written a book, Gin? You have such a way with words."

CHAPTER NINE

"Delivery," a voice said, and an arm jiggled a brown paper bag through my office door. Following the arm came Hally's face, with her trademark wide smile, and I felt myself follow suit. "I brought snacks," Hally said as she parked herself in the chair opposite mine.

I pushed aside the stack of documents in front of me and stretched, covering my mouth as I yawned. This was Hally's third visit to my office in the last two weeks and I felt we were finally beginning to make real headway.

"Gosh, sorry," I said. "It's been a long morning. Snacks are most welcome. Shall I grab us a coffee to go with them?"

"Yes, I'm dying for one."

I left her in my office and ducked down the hallway to the tearoom. When I returned, Alice was standing in my doorway, animatedly simpering as she chatted with Hally.

"I loved Suzanna's take on the bento box," I heard Hally say as I squeezed past Alice into my office.

"Oh, I know. How divine. We should all eat like that every day. If only I had five more hours in the day."

They both tinkled with laughter and I sat back in my chair, watching them beam and sparkle at each other. There had been a disturbing increase in foot traffic to my office since Hally and I had begun working together. Somehow most of the office needed to borrow a stapler or drop off something for me when she was around and our meetings had begun to blow out.

"Close the door for me on your way out, thanks, Alice," I said, interrupting Alice mid-flow. "Hally and I really need to knuckle down this morning. Deadlines, you know."

With a guilty look, Alice raised her hand to her mouth. "Of course, sorry," she said, backing out of the doorway. "Nice to see you, Hally." She shut the door behind her quietly.

"Jeeze, Gin," Hally said, as I pushed her coffee toward her. "Subtle much?"

I frowned. "What?"

"That was a bit mean."

"It was?" I was genuinely puzzled. "But I really wanted her to close the door. All these interruptions make it hard to concentrate and we've got work to do."

"I know, it's just..." Hally trailed off. "I think you made her feel bad."

Oh. This was what Cathy had been talking about. I sighed and ran a hand through my hair. I couldn't win. I was doing Hally's book and going out of my way to be nice to people, but somehow I still just wasn't nailing it. Did I need to send people chocolates and teddy bears to get some work done around here?

"What is it?" Hally asked, her brow creased with touching concern.

"Nothing," I grumbled, nearly stabbing myself in the eye as I pushed my glasses roughly up my nose.

"You might as well tell me. We won't get anything done until you clear the air."

I glared at her, irritated because she was right, annoyed with myself for getting it all wrong again. "Cathy may have mentioned that I could be nicer to people, that people in the office find me too..."

"Abrasive?" Hally supplied.

"I was going to say gruff. And I've been trying, but I keep tripping up. I'm a functional person. I don't wrap things in rainbows and cotton wool. What you see with me is what you get and it's frustrating to constantly have to be careful about what I say."

"I can understand that."

I snorted. "You're the last person on Earth who can understand that. Everyone loves you."

"Not everyone. Lots of people would be quite happy to see me fall, to push me down. But also, I'm in the public eye. I have to watch everything I post. I say something stupid and it's all over the Internet. It comes with the territory and you just have to suck it up."

"It doesn't come with *my* territory," I said, knowing I sounded petulant. "I'm not some famous person who has to watch what they say. I'm just a regular person with a regular job who needs…I don't even know what I need." I rubbed my brow in frustration.

"You just need to employ a bit more tact. It's not that hard. Just think about how you'd like people to speak to you and do it back."

"I just want people to be honest. The world would be a much easier place to navigate if people dropped all the bullshit pretence and spoke the truth."

"Maybe." Hally chewed her lip for a moment. "But I don't agree with you. I think it's easier when we're kind to each other."

"You don't think telling the truth is ultimately kinder? White lies just give people false hope. Like all these people slaving away at your gyms, hoping if they push hard enough they'll look just like you. You think it's kinder to tell them they can do it if they just keep pushing themselves? Surely it's better to just be honest and say hey, some people are going to get there and some people aren't and that's okay."

Hally raised her eyebrows. "I'm surprised by you."

"Why?"

"You think there's a particular end result, that we're trying to get everyone to look the same, but it's not like that. Going to the gym is just one aspect of finding the best version of yourself. It helps you get fit and strong and puts you in a mindset to make better choices for your life, but it's not supposed to be the end of the story. Exercise causes endorphin release, lifts the spirits— there's ample scientific data on it all. And there's no one-size-fits-all, cookie-cutter outcome. I keep trying to tell you that. Honestly, Gin, you should just come and check it out."

I shuddered. "I really don't think you'd want that."

"What would be so bad about it?"

"Me in Lycra, for one."

Hally smirked and gave me an appraising look, which for some reason made me blush. "I wouldn't mind seeing you in Lycra. But don't worry, regular tracksuits are fine. I dare you to come with me. Let me show you what's really going on behind the closed doors you're making so many assumptions about."

Now it was my turn to laugh. "You dare me? What are we, twelve?"

"Whatever. I don't know what you're so afraid of," Hally said, fixing me with a challenging stare.

"I'm not afraid."

"Good. Tonight after work then."

"Tonight's no good, I'm afraid. I'm..." I cast about trying to think of a good excuse. "Worming the cats."

She wrinkled her nose. "Tomorrow then. I'll pick you up from here at six."

Damn. My mind was as blank as the whiteboard. I floundered in the face of her inviting smile, wondering if it would be that bad after all. An hour at the gym couldn't hurt me, and it was almost my duty to get a firsthand look at what she was talking about in her book. "Fine." I blew out a sigh. "So, what's in that paper bag then? If I'm going to the gym I'll need to get my strength up."

I felt weird standing outside the office in my tracksuit pants. I had changed upstairs, and caught the lift downstairs in my casual clothes. The closest thing I had to sportswear was a black tank top, some tennis shoes I had never played tennis in, and the comfy green tracksuit pants I usually reserved for sitting on the couch watching weekend movies. I pulled on my hoodie against the afternoon chill and looked for a place to hide on the street while I waited for Hally, but there really wasn't anywhere. The city streets were teeming with the after-work rush of people leaving offices, heading home or to the pub, or in some cases I noticed, like me in their workout gear, possibly to the gym. Even though no one gave me a second glance, I leaned against the wall of our building, trying my best to blend in with the concrete tower.

Why had I agreed to do this? This was so unlike me. God forbid if Cathy ever found out, I would never live it down. Something about Hally had me saying yes to things I would previously have laughed out of town, but with her easy smile and the amused challenge in her eyes, here I was.

A black VW pulled up in front of me, double parking with a blast of its horn.

"Jump in," Hally called through the open window and I dashed out, calling apologies to the cars behind whose horn blasts were expressing their disapproval at her illegal move.

"Sorry, sorry," I called out as I slid onto the leather seat and slammed the door shut.

"Nice outfit," Hally said as she hit the accelerator.

I looked her over, taking in the dip of her figure-hugging, V-necked workout shirt and skin-tight black short leggings. She looked every bit the part and the part really suited her. "And to you," I said.

Hally navigated the city traffic expertly, twisting and turning her way through the side streets with practised skill.

"You know your way around the city pretty well."

"I have three gyms within ten blocks of your office. I'm in here quite a bit."

"Are we going to one of those?"

"No, I want to take you to one nearer to my place. It's my first gym and it still feels like my baby."

She flicked on the radio and drummed her fingers on the steering wheel to the beat as we waited at the traffic lights. I noticed her hands were very pretty: long tanned fingers with well-kept nails, and delicate wrists. She wore no rings and her nails were merely varnished, not hideously long and covered in the garish polish favoured by most people of her ilk. Sitting next to her, in her short little shorts, was causing me to have the kind of physiological reaction I normally experienced with people I was attracted to, which was strange. I supposed she really was very beautiful, with all her smooth skin, so much of which was exposed right now. Being alone with her in the car was affecting my heart rate. Suddenly she turned to look at me, catching me in her gaze. "I'm pretty impressed that you're doing this."

I tried to sound casual, ignoring my pulse as it skidded in my throat. "Call it part of the research."

"I don't suppose you've had to get out in the field too much with the other books you've worked on."

"Sometimes. It depends." With a squeal of tyres, she took off from the lights and I found myself gripping the side of my seat.

"On what?"

What with Hally's driving and my sudden urge to reach out and put a hand on her knee I was having trouble ordering my thoughts. I forced myself to pull it together. "On what the book needs. Every book is different, every author unique. I've been out to a few archaeological digs in my time, quite a number of private gardens, and I'm over at the university fairly often. We need to fact check and confirm sources and sometimes it can't be done satisfactorily over the telephone or email. Although that does make it a hell of a lot easier."

"So, this is really like a fact-checking mission then, for my book."

"I could probably have just taken your word for it, but then, you did dare me," I said, with a grin.

"That I did."

I tried not to, but I couldn't resist stealing another look at her as she drove. Her hair was pulled back in a low ponytail, tendrils of chestnut escaping around her ears, and she had minimal make up on as far as I could tell, just a little mascara and eye shadow. I was struck by the strength of her profile, the straight line of her nose, the perfect curl of her ears and the purse of her lips. We were close, sitting side by side in her little sports car, her hand grazing my leg when she changed gears.

Not wanting to be caught staring again, I forced myself to look away, gazing out my window at familiar streets which seemed different now, almost new with Hally sitting next to me making my pulse jitter. Houses butted up against each other, trees bumped shoulders and elbows, people dragged their wheelie bins to the curb in time for the following morning's rubbish pick up—just Melbourne going about its regular business and yet it all felt imbued with a new sense of aliveness.

"Did you always want to do this?" I asked. "You haven't mentioned in the book if this was your big dream."

She took so long to answer I almost wondered if I'd asked my question out loud. Then she suddenly said, "In a way, yes. In a way, no. I wanted to run my own business. I wanted to be my own boss. I wanted to be out from under the thumb of living with someone who constantly took everything away from me, from my sister and my mother. I wanted to be free and I wanted to live a healthy, happy life. So, it wasn't so much that I always wanted to start up a chain of gyms, but that just fitted the brief so I ran with it."

Her voice was edgy and I had a surge of protectiveness, surprising myself with a wish to have been there to shield her from the past, which had clearly scarred her. If I hadn't been in the car with Hally I would have laughed out loud at myself. Clearly, stepping so far outside of my comfort zone like this had me in some kind of cerebral and hormonal melt down.

"It was Xi who got me into the gym."

"Your ex-husband."

"That's the one. We're still friends, by the way. He trains at one of my gyms and runs a builders' club from there."

"What's a builders' club?"

"As in body builders. Anyway, he was majorly into fitness when we met and I got inspired. The rest is history."

"And you met at high school. Seems so young to have gotten into such a serious relationship."

"Tell me about it. It was all part of the getting away from my dad thing. When Xi asked me to marry him we'd had half a bottle of the cheapest champagne two seventeen-year-olds could get their hands on. I married him the day I turned eighteen and moved out of home the same day. Delphi had already left and I was just dying to get out of there. I did feel bad about leaving my mum though. Parents have that way of making you feel so guilty for living your life, do you know what I mean?"

There was a hint of sadness in her voice and I wondered if she was so open with everyone. We barely knew each other and yet here she was telling me about her life so freely, seeming to expect that I would reciprocate. But it wasn't that easy for me. I knew exactly what it was like to feel guilty for living my life. I felt that way about my dad all the time, but I wasn't a fan of the heart-to-heart, the let's-drag-up-all-the-things-from-our-past-that-hurt-us-and-bring-them-out-in-the-open-to-examine-them-together kind of talk. That kind of thing was just too painful and I didn't go in for it.

"Hey, um speaking of your parents," I said, dodging the question. "Have you told your mum about the book yet? You were going to talk to her about writing about your dad."

"I know, I haven't done it yet. It's on my list for this weekend. We're all getting together for dinner and I'll talk to her and Delphi then. You know how it is with family. Serious conversations can be awkward."

I did know. As small as my family of two was, trying to talk to my dad about anything much felt like pulling blood from a stone. He wasn't a talker and I had never really known how to get past that. Interestingly, Hally and my experiences of family were very different but they seemed to have evoked very similar emotions in us.

"So, you and Xi are still friends then," I said, changing the subject. I wasn't in the mood to get caught up in thoughts of my dad. "That's rare these days."

"We married so young, it was inevitable that it wouldn't work out. The fact that we kept it together for so long still kind of blows me away. Looking back, I was just a child playing an adult."

"And yet you managed to build up a gym empire during that time."

"Well, I definitely got started on the path. The empire came a bit later. And what about you?" She glanced at me as she changed lanes. "Do you have a permanent someone in your life?"

"Er, no," I said, feeling thrown by the personal question. This was even worse than talking about family. "Anyway, I think you should expand your initial chapter to give some of this background. If you get the green light from your family of course. It will give so much more authenticity to your story and the advice you give if people can see where you've come from."

"Mmm. We'll see."

The gym was crowded, but everyone was falling over themselves to be of assistance to Hally, and by association, me. I assumed it would not be like this if I had walked in sans the boss, but I couldn't help but enjoy the sedulous attention.

"All right, let's put our bags away and get started," Hally said, handing me a fresh towel that smelled like lavender. "Keep this with you, you'll need it."

I doubted that. I wasn't a break-a-sweat kind of girl, but I threw it over my shoulder as I noted others were doing.

"I'm going to treat you as I would any other client who had come to see me for the first time," Hally announced, putting her hand under my elbow and leading me to a little room with a desk and two chairs. "When I first started this business I was on the floor, doing the personal training, you know." I did know. I'd read it in her book.

She opened the desk drawer, pulled out a clipboard and pen and motioned me to sit, taking the chair opposite me. "First we get to know you, then we give you a personalised training plan."

"Is that really necessary? It seems like a lot of work for a one-off thing."

"Just let me do this. I want you to have the full SweatHard experience."

I sighed, glad I had had the forethought to have a banana before I left work. This was obviously going to take some time, but I had said I would do it so I needed to surrender to the experience. "Of course, let's go."

"Great. We start with your vital statistics, date of birth, height, weight, any pre-existing illnesses, etc."

"Shoot," I said.

We made our way down her list, Hally taking careful notes of my answers, me being as succinct as possible. I prided myself on my capacity to answer questions like this efficiently.

"Pregnant?" Hally asked, and I raised my eyebrows. "It's an important question. There are exercises we wouldn't do if you were."

"Well, no, I'm not."

"Right. Now for the fun part. Your fitness history and goals."

"Hally," I said, interrupting her. "Could we possibly skip that bit? I'm averagely fit and I really don't have any fitness goals. I'm not like the other people here. I'm just coming as a one-off because you invited me. I'm not intending to come again."

She paused for a moment, her hand hovering over the clipboard and then laughed and put down her pen. "The ever-tactful Gin strikes again."

"Oh, I didn't mean—"

"It's okay, I'm not offended. Just tell me, is there anything at all you'd be interested in getting out of this session?"

"Not really," I said, offering her a weak smile. I tried to soften the blow. "I mean, not really in particular. It would be good to try a few different things out."

"Okay, well what is your favourite kind of exercise?"

I blinked at her. "Er…"

"Do you do anything to maintain fitness?"

"Does walking to work count?"

"Sure, walking is great for fitness." She smiled at me. "Let's face it. You're in great shape for someone who doesn't seem to do much to take care of themselves. So shall we see if we can make some muscles for you?"

"We can try."

"Right, well, come with me, Ms. Blake," she said, standing with a flourish of her hand as she indicated the door. "First stop, chest press."

We made our way through the gym, Hally greeting people with warm smiles and high fives. They seemed to know her and she them, if the little snippets of personalised encouragement she gave each of them were anything to go by. The atmosphere was almost party-like, dance music pumping from the speakers, everybody moving around us. There were small groups sharing each machine, and I couldn't see how we were going to get anything done.

"Looks like we've come at rush hour," I said.

"This is definitely peak time. Shouldn't be a problem though."

As we approached the machine Hally was angling for, the group miraculously melted away and she turned to me and smiled. "Some perks come with being the boss. Take a seat."

The machine looked like a giant metal lobster and it took me a moment to work out where I was supposed to sit.

Hally shook her head. "Chair's not high enough, you'll need to put it up a couple of notches."

I stepped out of the machine and bent down, trying to work out how to raise the chair. There was a blue metal knob sticking out under the seat which I tried pushing, and then pulling. When neither of those worked I gave it a twist but still nothing. I looked up at Hally for help.

"Give it a pull," she instructed.

I pulled but still nothing happened. "I think this is broken."

"Let me try." I stepped out of the way and Hally bent down to examine it. She gave it a sharp tug and the knob popped out, allowing her to raise the chair. "You just need to give it a little more force."

Embarrassing. I wasn't even strong enough to raise the chair. I felt like an idiot and slid back onto the now appropriately raised chair.

"I guess weakened it for you," I said.

"No doubt," she replied with a grin. "I'm going to start you off on a low weight with higher reps, and then from there we'll raise the weight and lower the reps, okay?"

"Sure," I said, agreeing with no idea what she was talking about.

Hally flicked a pin in the machine and instructed me to put my hands on the bars in front of me. "Not like that," she said, taking my hands in hers and turning them over. "Like this. Now push upward."

I pushed against the bar but nothing happened.

"A bit harder," she encouraged.

I gave it a strong shove but still nothing moved. "Broken?" She grinned. "Let's take the weight down a little."

She adjusted the pin and this time when I pushed, the bar shifted slightly in front of me.

"Good," she cried. "Now push all the way through until your arms are straight out in front of you."

I strained and concentrated and managed to get the bar out in front of me and then let it go. The bar contracted with a great clank and I jumped with fright, as did most of the people around us. "Sorry," I said, grimacing at Hally. "I didn't realise that would happen."

"Don't worry about it. Now, we're going to try to control the movement," she said. "Let me just bring the weight back down a little and we'll do nine more of those."

"Nine more!" I exclaimed. "I don't think I can do nine more."

"Sure you can," she encouraged. "Okay, from the top. Push out and bring it back slowly."

What followed was an hour of the most physical exertion I had experienced since my high-school sports teacher had insisted I participate in the cross country. Except this was worse. My muscles trembled and spasmed. I felt like I was going to die. I groaned out loud and made effort noises as Hally guided me through a specialised torture routine. The only breaks were when she demonstrated on the machine herself, expertly, gracefully lifting, pulling, twisting. Her muscles sprang to attention, rippling under her tanned skin, accentuating the supple lines of her body. Even in my compromised state I couldn't help but admire her, as did the rest of the gym from the attention she received.

"Now you do it," she said, swinging a sculpted leg off the bench and gesturing for me to sit down.

I gritted my teeth, desperately wishing the experience to be over, but not wanting to give in. "Is this the last one?" I asked, unable to keep the hopeful note out of my voice as I sat down.

"Do you want it to be?"

"Yes." I looked up at her. I wouldn't beg. But then maybe I would. "Please?"

She laughed. "Okay. Reach up and grip the bar, then pull it down to your chest. It needs to touch just here," she said and lightly tapped me just under my collarbone. Her touch tingled.

I reached up and grabbed the bar, willing it to come down as I tugged hard on it. It came down with much less resistance than I was expecting and I all but punched myself in the chest with the bar, letting it go with another surprised clang.

"Easy, tiger," Hally said, a laugh in her voice. "You're not vying for a spot in the Olympics here."

I growled and reached back up for the bar, this time ready for its weight. I pulled it down, touching it carefully to my chest and let it back up, repeating the movement as she had shown me.

"Good." She rested a cool hand on my shoulder. "That's it, Gin. You've done the first circuit."

"Just the first one?" I asked, confusion and despair warring with in me. Surely there wasn't more of this to come.

"That's it for today. But if you did want to come back, you could have one of the staff take you through circuit two sometime."

Relief flooded through me. Endorphins from the pain must have been winging their way through my system because I actually giggled, putting a hand over my mouth in confusion.

"Want to take a shower?"

I stared at her, forcing myself to understand that this was not an invitation, but a friendly suggestion to relieve me of the workout-induced sweat. I stammered, "Sure."

Hally pointed me in the direction of the change rooms. I grabbed my bag from the lockers and shut myself into a free cubicle. It was a mini private bathroom, with a shower and toilet and mirror, complete with complimentary cans of deodorant and little soaps.

I stepped under the shower, muscles trembling as I washed myself off. I could barely lift my arms to turn off the taps and when it came to drying myself I almost cried. What had she done to me?

I struggled back into my work clothes, tucking my tracksuit away in the bag and made my way back out to the gym floor, where Hally was talking intently with one of the trainers. The young woman appeared to be upset, her long hair hiding her face and Hally put her hand on her arm as they talked. Not wanting to interrupt I took a seat in the waiting area near the front door and watched. The woman finally laughed at something Hally said and they hugged. There was so much touching in these places, and so much exposed skin. It was definitely a different world to mine. Publishing never showed any skin and we certainly never touched each other at work, although I suspected if Cathy encouraged us to hug each other Alice would be first in line to dish them out.

"Ready to go?" Hally asked when she joined me.

I stood up, feeling my muscles scream. "Please."

CHAPTER TEN

I gave Hally directions back to my place and she took the short drive at a clip.

"That trainer you were speaking with," I said as she pulled up at the lights. "She seemed a bit upset."

Hally nodded, watching the lights as she said, "Kerry. She's having a hard time. She puts a lot of pressure on herself to get the best results, for herself and her clients. Sometimes she pushes too hard and it doesn't end well."

"Complaints?"

The light went green and Hally put her foot down. "Thankfully, no. But she's had a couple of injuries and she won't rest, just keeps trying to soldier on when she really needs to take a break. Her supervisor had to bench her last week and put her on desk duty. She wasn't pleased but I was just checking in with her and she seemed to understand."

I thought of Hally hugging the woman and making her laugh. She clearly cared about her staff. Not too many CEOs would know the general staff well enough to pull off that kind of exchange.

"You did really well tonight," she said as we pulled up outside my apartment block.

"I think I'm dying," I croaked.

"Just eat lots of protein tonight, okay? It will help with muscle repair."

Protein. Right. I could manage that. I would order a double Aussie pizza with two eggs and extra everything. That should cut it.

"And some people have a tendency to binge on junk food after a gym session, but it's not a great idea. Try for something fresh and rejuvenating for your body."

Hmm, perhaps a vegetarian pizza would be better.

"You okay?" she asked, peering at me with concern.

"I honestly don't know," I replied. "I've never experienced anything like that."

"Which floor are you? Need me to help you up the stairs?"

I gave her a weak smile. "We've got a lift. But thanks."

I thanked her for the gym experience, bid her good night and hauled my spent body out of the car. I couldn't believe that people did this more than once in their lives, let alone more than once a week.

Back in my apartment the cats and I agreed that fried eggs with salad and toast ticked off both the fresh and protein requirements and I settled on the couch with my laptop. I had loads of BestReads reviews to catch up on, and some personal email, but by the time I'd finished eating it was all I could do to crawl off the couch, brush my teeth and flop into bed. The cats settled themselves around me, setting up a rolling purr. I had read somewhere that cats had the power to heal with their purr and I hoped fervently that it was true, drifting off to sleep to their rumbly chorus.

Groaning loudly, I rolled out of bed the next morning, feeling like I had been trampled by a herd of wild elephants. I hadn't felt this bad since I'd had glandular fever as a teenager and ended up in hospital on a drip. I considered calling in sick but decided the distraction of work was probably better than moping around at home in pain, focusing on muscles I didn't know I had. And besides, I was hoping to put in a bit of time on some manuscripts other than Hally's, now that hers was coming along so well.

I struggled into the office, hoping that the walk in would stretch out my tight muscles but I was still cramped up and limping when I arrived. There was a hamper on my desk, which surprised me. Inside the basket was a container of effervescent Muscle-Eaze tabs, a jar of bath salts, a protein-powder sachet, and a bunch of bananas. The card read, "To help you with your recovery. Thanks for checking out my world. Hope you don't regret it this morning, Hally."

I did regret it, but there wasn't much I could do about it now other than grin and bear it. I ate one of the bananas and washed a couple of pain killers down with the protein shake, already looking forward to trying out the bath salts later that evening. Hally had absolutely caned me at the gym, but the hamper was a sweet and thoughtful gesture and fitted with the picture of her I was beginning to build. Sure, all the social-media stuff was shallow and boring, but I was starting to see there was more to her than just a bunch of Snapchats and hashtags, and spending time with her definitely wasn't as bad as I had imagined. We'd had quite a few laughs throughout the editing process so far. I was doodling on my pad, thinking about how she had asked me if I was seeing anyone when my computer blipped with a video call from Cathy.

"Hi, stranger," I said.

"And to you. How's my cat?"

"She's a darling. I swear she and Asimov are having a love affair. He gave her his spot on the big couch pillow last night. You know that's his special possie."

Cathy widened her eyes. "Wow. What a gentleman."

"I know right. Hey, where are you? That doesn't look like the Sydney office."

"I'm at Rachel's. I stayed here last night and decided to work from here today. Just in case they need me. Mum's recovering but she's still very confused." She leaned into the computer and whispered, "I know Rach doesn't want me here but it's too bad. It's too much for one person to handle on their own."

"Good for you," I said. "Let me know if you want me to come up and help too."

"I need you at home to look after the cats. And to do your job, which I understand is coming along pretty well."

I frowned. "Which bit?"

"Heath from Graphic Design showed me a mock-up of the front cover for Hally's book. Apparently you told him you're ahead of schedule with the editing. Bravo, I'm proud of you."

I did my best to look modest but I was also pretty impressed with myself. "Thanks. Hally's been working on it around the clock. I don't know how she fits it all in but she's smashing out the edits and it is coming together. We'll have it ready on schedule at the latest, if not a bit before."

"That's great news, Gin. So, you're loving it after all."

I snorted. "Whatever. I suppose I'm not hating it as much as I thought I would. Hally is actually all right and the book isn't as terribly bad as I thought it would be."

"I'm sorry, what did you say?" Cathy raised her eyebrows comically high. "I think the line must be scrambled. I heard you say Hally is all right, but that can't be correct. I seem to remember someone telling me this was just self-help trash. You've certainly changed your tune."

"She's done a lot of work on it. Let's just say I wouldn't read it by choice but I won't die inside if other people do."

"*When* other people do, Gin. It needs to be a *when*."

"Fine. So *when* are you coming home? Any thoughts on that?"

"I don't know, at least few more weeks, maybe a month. Is that okay? Can you handle having Olive that long?"

"Of course. You don't even need to ask. She's not the greatest best-friend substitute though. I do find her a little self-centred."

Cathy chuckled. "I'm going to pop back for the Wine and Spines gala. We can hang out then."

"Oh god. I'd forgotten about that."

"Well, un-forget. I expect everyone to be there. It's—"

"A horrible hobnob affair where all the big publishing houses gloat about their massive budgets and their blockbusters and the little guys try not to get caught stuffing dinner rolls into their backpacks at the end of the night. It's so boring. Do I really need to be there? You'll have Alice and John and Frank. Frank always goes."

"Everyone, Gin. Red Stone has three tables booked and I expect them to be full. Invite some of your authors. I've asked the other managing editors to do the same. You can invite two people each."

"Why don't I invite three and then not come myself."

"Why don't you stop complaining and just embrace this. You know, this is the perfect place for you to meet someone."

"And why is that?"

"Because it will be full of intellectual snobs, just like you, who love nothing more than talking about books."

"I actually don't know whether to be insulted or pleased, but I'm not really looking to meet anyone right now."

"And why is that?"

"I don't know. I've got a fair bit on my plate, and after Pam, well, I just think I'm doing pretty well on my own. Besides, I've got the cats and they wouldn't be happy if I tried to squeeze someone else into the bed."

"You're ridiculous."

"I'm not. Anyway, why don't you look for someone at Wine and Spines. Why do I have to meet someone?"

"Oh sure. Hi, I'm Cathy, I spend all my time trying to sell books very few people apparently want to read and dashing up to Sydney to look after my chronically ill mother and my unstable sister. I'm a real catch."

I sighed and groaned as I shifted in my chair. "We're a pair."

Cathy pulled a face at me. "Why are you groaning? What's wrong with you?"

I felt myself blush and hoped the webcam would hide it. Just to be sure I momentarily ducked out of sight. "Just a sec," I called. "Dropped something."

"Gin. Get back here," Cathy commanded.

I raised my head. "Yes?" I said, as innocently as I could manage.

"What's happened?"

"Nothing, everything's fine."

"I'm not hanging up until you tell me, and that's going to be a problem because we're all supposed to be on a conference call for Round The Table in fifteen minutes. Why are you in pain? I'm worried about you."

Shit. I would have to tell her and withstand her ribbing. "I went to the gym with Hally last night. As part for the research for her book," I quickly added. "I've pulled up a bit sore today."

"You went to the gym?" Cathy's eyebrows drew together in confusion.

"Yes, as I said, I thought I should get a firsthand look at what she's created. Just so we know what we're promoting and all that."

Cathy didn't say anything for a moment and I wondered if the screen had frozen.

"Cathy?"

"Yes, I'm here. I'm just processing."

"Okay."

She grinned at me slyly and said, "Well, that's good work. You do always go above and beyond and I knew I could count on you to get this book done. Thanks, Gin."

"You're welcome," I said, wondering how I had gotten off so lightly.

"I'd better go. I've got a few things to organise before the conference call, but I'll see you all over the interwebs in fifteen."

"See you then." And the call clicked off.

I was surprised Cathy hadn't teased me about going to the gym, but also relieved. She really did best-friend very well.

Realising I didn't have long before Round The Table, I quickly fired off an email to Hally, thanking her for the hamper and attaching the mock-up of the front cover Heath had sent through to me. I let her know it was just a first draft and welcomed her thoughts. We would be meeting with Heath later that week to discuss the launch plan and could address any issues with the design then.

With Cathy's words in mind, I also sent out a quick invitation to Wines and Spines to a couple of my favourite authors, hopeful that they would be able to make it. An evening with Massimoto and Jess Silverman wasn't the worst thing.

I gathered up my diary and laptop and headed to the conference room. With the progress we were making with Hally's book, and the rest of my portfolio, I would have a lot to report to the team this week.

When my mobile phone rang at five o'clock that evening I was deep in conversation with Melbourne University about adding Massimoto's *Brief History of Biology* to their required-reading list for first-year Biology. It would be a real coup for Red Stone and I was doing my best to be charming and persuasive without being pushy. Marketing wasn't usually in the managing editor's wheelhouse, but sometimes, due to the very specialised nature of my books, I did get involved. It was unlikely anyone in our marketing department would have enough knowledge of the subject matter, let alone read the book from cover to cover. Having immersed myself in the project, I was truly the best amongst us to sing its praises.

Hally's number flashed on my screen, momentarily knocking me off my train of thought. I silenced the call but, as the professor on the other line waffled on, found myself wondering what she wanted.

"If you can get me some advance copies for my teaching staff by the beginning of next month we'll be able to make a decision," he said finally.

"Done," I replied, trying not to look at my mobile phone vibrating with a message, probably from Hally.

We finally wound up the call and I high-fived myself before I picked up my mobile. I was really kicking goals here. I didn't bother checking my messages and returned Hally's call straight away.

"That was quick," she said by way of answer. "Thanks for getting back to me."

"No problem, what's up?"

"I just wanted to let you know that I spoke with my mum and sister last night and they're not super keen about the whole thing but they've given me the green light to talk about Dad."

"That's great, Hally. That will make a real difference to the book."

"I know. So, thanks for pushing me to do that."

"That's what us pushy editors are here for," I quipped.

"Oh and Cathy invited me to the publishing wine and books thing that's coming up, I forget what it's called. Just wanted to let you guys know I can make it."

I was puzzled. Why hadn't Cathy mentioned that to me this morning? "She invited you to Wine and Spines?"

"Yes, that's it. Is that a problem?" she asked, obviously picking up my hesitation.

"Oh no, I just wouldn't have thought it was your kind of thing."

"Why, what is it?"

"It's just a bunch of book-industry people getting together to talk about books and parade their achievements."

"Do authors go?"

"Yes, some."

"But you don't think I'm a proper author, so I shouldn't go?"

"Hey," I protested. "I didn't say that. I just wouldn't have thought you'd want to spend your evening surrounded by a whole load of intellectual waffle. It's probably not the greatest fit for you."

"Because I'm not smart enough?"

"Hally! That's not what I'm saying." What was I saying? The conversation was really getting away from me.

"Try not to underestimate me quite so obviously, Gin. Or at least, don't be such a snob to my face, okay? I may not be a university graduate, but I have read a book or two, and as much as you clearly don't think of it as such, I have now written one too, so I think I'll be just fine at this wine and whatever it's called thing. Anyways, I'd better run, I've got a Chomsky to finish." And with that, she cut the call.

I was surprised that she knew about Chomsky, but she was wrong. I wasn't judging her because she didn't have a university degree. I just couldn't see her sitting at a table with the likes of Massimoto and Silverman telling them about how she used Snapchat and Instagram to take over the world. I cringed just thinking about it.

As much as I thought I was right, I didn't like the idea that I'd offended her. Should I call her back? Try to explain further? No, even I could tell that she probably needed time to cool down and a call from me might not be well received right now. I sent her a text to explain that I hadn't meant to be hurtful. She could call me back if she liked.

That evening, as I curled up on my couch with the cats, my apartment felt strangely small. I felt hemmed in and I couldn't relax. Outside, autumn was doing its best to turn into winter, blowing a steady smatter of rain against the window. I got up to press my nose against the glass and watch the storm blow by. The street below was empty of pedestrians, just the occasional streak of red taillights as people drove through the rain.

I couldn't shake off the guilty feeling that had stuck with me since speaking with Hally. The fact was, Cathy had also called me an intellectual snob, and I was starting to question myself. What I had always thought of as my cerebral standards suddenly seemed exclusive and mean. I did look down on Hally because I considered her interests beneath me. I had built a little fortress around myself and only those who qualified as my kind of people were allowed entry. Thinking of Hally, with her warm smile and her enthusiasm for everything and everyone around her, I couldn't recall why I had done that.

Before I went to sleep my phone finally beeped with a response from Hally. It simply said, *All good.* But was it?

CHAPTER ELEVEN

"I love the size of the hashtag key on the typewriter," Hally said, pointing at Heath's computer screen. They sat together behind his desk, looking at the cover mock-up. I knew she would love it. "It's really clever."

Heath puffed out his chest, obviously pleased, a satisfied smile on his handsome face. It was a big chest and I could see it was well-sculpted through the tight fit of his soft grey T-shirt. Perhaps he too went to one of Hally's gyms. He rubbed at the dark stubble of his five-o'clock shadow and I wondered how weird it would be to start out the day with a freshly shaven face only to find it had grown hair again by the end of the day.

"I enlarged the hashtag key in Photoshop," Heath said. "And then I overlayed the original image so it makes it look like this typewriter just has a really big hashtag key."

"Huh." Hally nodded at him encouragingly. She turned to look at me standing across the room, leaning against the wall. It had been a long day and I was tired of sitting. Our eyes caught and I smiled encouragingly, but she merely nodded. She had been cool today, to say the least. I found myself missing the warmth of her smile, unsure what to do to fix my previous week's gaff.

Contrite, I had sent her a hamper with a bottle of wine and an anthology of poems featuring modern and contemporary female and gender-diverse poets, and a note that simply said *We'll be lucky to have you at Wine and Spines.*

She had texted me to thank me for the package, but the coolness persisted.

"Anything you'd like to change here?" Heath asked, a lock of his well-oiled dark hair falling in front of his charcoal eyes. He brushed it away carefully. He really was exceptionally good-looking, a sort of muscular Cary Grant. Did Hally find him attractive? I had seen pictures of her ex-husband, Xi, on the Internet and he was also the tall-dark-and-handsome type. Nothing I'd seen online gave any indication of who she was dating now, though. There were no hints on any of her social media, and a quick Google search brought up thousands of photos, which I had flicked through (just for research), but no recurring "someone special." She posed with plenty of men but also plenty of women, and it was impossible to tell anything more.

With their heads leaning in together toward the computer screen, Hally and Heath made an eye-catching couple. I knew nothing about Heath either, but even I could see he had been making eyes at Hally for the last half an hour in his office. Nothing wrong with that. People had to meet each other somewhere, didn't they? Except for some reason it was pissing me off and I found myself wanting the meeting to be over.

"What do you think, Gin?" Hally asked, looking up at me again.

I blinked, caught out. "Er, sorry, I was following a different train of thought," I said. "Can you repeat that?"

Hally frowned. "I was just saying that I thought the bubble writing around *True Likes* was a little too cute and I wondered if you agreed. Could we find a font that's a little edgier?"

I did agree actually, and I was surprised that she had suggested it. I thought she would have loved Heath's cute little bubbly letters. "Can you show it to us with a different font please, Heath?"

"Sure." He made some quick swipes and clicks with his mouse and then said, "How's this?"

"Much better," Hally exclaimed. "Wow, you're so quick."

More puffing of the chest. I worried if he puffed any further he might pop.

"Happy with this, Gin?" Heath asked.

She was right, this was a much better look. A solid, bold font that looked like it had been stamped on the page. Less Barbie, more authoritative. "Yeah, I like this better too. Can you print us a copy? Hally can take it home and—"

"Don't print mine please," Hally interrupted, giving me a stern look. "I don't know how many times I have to tell this one to stop wasting the trees, but I'm fine with a digital copy."

"Ah yes, sorry." I mentally slapped my forehead. "Digital copies all round then, Heath. Give us a few days for final consideration and we'll sign off on it."

"No problem, can do." He did a complicated wrist dance of saving and exporting while Hally and I looked on. "What's your email address, Hally?"

She spelled it out for him and I wandered away from the desk, thinking about what I would have for dinner. There was a great little Vietnamese café that had just opened around the corner from my apartment and I could pick up a banh mi and some cold rolls. I drooled a little at the thought.

Back in my office Hally gathered up her handbag and I threw my laptop into my backpack, slinging it over my shoulder. "I'll walk out with you."

We rode down the lift together in silence, packed in with other people who were, I assumed, as keen as I was to leave work for the day. My stomach grumbled loudly and Hally gave a quick laugh. "Hungry?"

"I'm starving," I moaned, grateful to have finally cracked through her standoffish veneer. "Lunch feels like yesterday."

The lift hit the ground floor and we all piled out, fanning into the lobby like fish released from a net.

"Before you go," I said, touching her arm. She stopped to meet my eyes with a cool look. "I..." I gulped and swallowed hard, determined to right the wrong.

"Yes?"

"I just wanted to say sorry, again, about what happened the other day on the phone. I'm sure you'll love Wine and Spines and you'll fit in just fine. I don't know why I underrated you like that, but I'm sorry for being hurtful. I can see that what I said would have felt like a put-down and it won't happen again. It's clear to me that you are not only intelligent, but more than capable in all that you do, so please accept my sincere apologies."

She took a beat, searching my eyes with her own. I desperately wanted to look away, but I held her gaze, feeling like it was a test. "Okay."

"Okay?"

"Yes. But don't do it again. It *is* bloody hurtful and I don't need it from you. I get that kind of shit enough in my life already."

I shifted the weight of my backpack. "You do?"

"Of course. People assume because I'm attractive and I go to the gym that I'm entirely vacuous. Even though I single-handedly run a multitiered business, which I have built entirely from scratch, I don't qualify to join the smart-people club. It's too annoying."

"I imagine it would be." I placed my hand on my heart. "You won't get that from me again. Promise."

Hally looked solemn. "Pinky swear?"

"Um, yes, pinky swear." I held up my little finger and Hally briefly linked hers to mine. When she smiled at me the lightness was back in her eyes and I felt a rush of relief. "Let me make it up to you?"

She considered me carefully for a moment, her golden eyes taking me in. "What did you have in mind?"

"I was going to try out a new Vietnamese restaurant for dinner. Come with me? My shout."

"You're asking me to dinner?"

"Well, yes, I mean..." I trailed off and looked at my shoes, which were not offering up any inspiration. I shifted my gaze back to Hally, feeling sheepish. "It's the least I can do. As your editor and all."

She watched me squirm for a moment. "Lucky for you, you're quite endearing when you're eating humble pie. Fine. Dinner it is."

My heart inexplicably leapt and I frowned. What on earth was that about? Surely the last thing I wanted was to be saddled with Hally Arlow for any longer than I needed to be. "That would be great," I found myself saying, the words out of my mouth in a flash.

We stepped out onto the pavement, into the frenetic after-work rush. A gust of crisp autumn wind made me appreciate my jacket and I zipped it up to my chin.

"I was going to walk. The restaurant is just around the corner from my place, but..." Unable to help myself I glanced down at her shoes, trying not to appear dubious. They weren't exactly high heels but they didn't look like much good for a long walk. In contrast, my own well-worn lace ups could have seen me through a day hike through the You Yangs quite comfortably.

"You'd be surprised how far I can get in these," Hally said, answering my unspoken question. "Lead the way."

"So, what did you have planned for tonight?" Hally asked as we took off down Collins Street, speaking loudly over the clatter of passing trams and the hum of the traffic.

"Mostly just eating," I said. "Ever since I went to the gym I've had a giant hunger."

"That was last week. You can't possibly still be hungry from that."

I shrugged. "I just tell it how it is. Making all that muscle left me with a burning hunger."

"Well, you must have a pretty good metabolism," Hally remarked. "And you really don't do any exercise at all?"

"Just walking to and from work. That's pretty much the extent of it."

"How long does it take?"

"About fifty minutes, sometimes an hour if I dawdle in the park."

Hally tilted her head. "Not bad. That's good consistent cardio."

"Not as good as going to the gym though. Right?"

"Each has its merits," she said. "And do you cook?"

"Badly. I never really got the knack. I can do cereal and sandwiches. Pasta at a push and I'm excellent at toast. That's about it."

"I love cooking. I find it really relaxing."

I grimaced. "I find it's like juggling with fire. Literally. Oops sorry." I bumped against her as a woman rushed past me, knocking me off balance.

Hally steadied me, a firm hand under my elbow, the other thrown around my waist. "Got you."

I let myself lean against her for a moment, enjoying the feel of her arm around me, the press of her body against mine. Her arm tightened and I looked up, her gaze searching mine.

"Sorry," I stammered, and stepped reflexively out of her embrace. "It's madness out here tonight."

We walked on and I found myself sneaking glances at her as we talked. As she chatted about the poetry book I had sent her, her face was a picture of friendliness. Had there been an invitation in her eyes just now? *As if*, I chided myself. Every man and his dog probably hoped Hally Arlow was making eyes at them. Except for me of course. I wasn't hoping for something like that from her.

We walked slowly through the Carlton Gardens, the sky darkening now winter was coming. The park lanterns switched on, throwing a warm yellow light across the path. The pedestrian traffic had thinned but we still walked closely together, oblivious to the change around us.

"What made you decide to write this book? Lots of people think about writing, but not many actually do it," I mused, watching a flock of sparrows flit through the trees ahead of us.

"I've always wanted to write something," Hally said eventually, causing me to look over at her. Under the light of the lantern, her hair cast a shadow across her face making it impossible for me to see her expression. "I never had the chance to do something really creative. As soon as I was able to earn any money I was out to work with Mum during any spare time I had. And then I married Xi straight out of school and we were working our butts off to get ahead. I've sunk a lot of energy into my business and it's paid off, but I wanted to do something a bit creative and I've always loved reading. I didn't know what the heck to write about. I thought about trying to do a mystery or something, but I heard someone say once, 'Write what you know' and so..." she trailed off and spread her hands. "I do know me."

"You wanted to write a mystery?"

She laughed, husky and quiet in the hastening darkness. "Ridiculous, I know."

"I've enjoyed the odd crime novel. I think if I was ever going to write anything it would be crime fiction. I've actually planned a few out in my time."

"You have? But you haven't actually written any of them down?"

"Oh no, I'd be terrible at it. I'd pick myself to pieces before I'd written a single sentence. No, I'm better at helping other people write. Come to think of it, that sums me up pretty well. I'm not skilled at doing much at all, but I know how to get the best out of other people."

"Which is strange given your lack of tact," Hally said.

"Hey!"

"Well, it's true. I can only imagine you rub people up the wrong way all the time with your truth-telling mission."

"I have been known to upset the odd person," I admitted. "But you'd be surprised how rarely it happens."

"I guess I would be."

"Hey!" I protested again and Hally laughed.

"Actually," she said, her voice serious. "Your honesty is something I really appreciate about you. Growing up with all the lies surrounding my dad, I've found I just can't tolerate dishonesty or subterfuge. As difficult as your brand of truth-telling can be sometimes, I like that I know I can rely on you to be frank. It's refreshing."

I felt warm listening to her praise, and for the first time in weeks, just for a moment, a heaviness I hadn't even known I was carrying lifted from me. It felt like an age since I'd received a compliment.

At the edge of the park Hally hesitated. Had she changed her mind?

"Would you be happy for me to cook us dinner, instead of getting takeaway?"

"Er, at my place?"

"Sure, why not?"

I thought about my tiny kitchen and the contents of my cupboards, which would be likely to give a health freak like Hally Arlow serious pause. "I'm not sure I have any ingredients."

"Is there a shop close by? We could stop in on the way? I don't mind if you'd rather not."

"There is a shop," I said, hesitantly, wondering what I was getting myself into. "We can cook if you like. I don't know how much help I'll be though. Fair warning."

Hally smirked. "Warning received. Lead the way."

We stopped in at the local IGA around the corner from my apartment and Hally chose a selection of vegetables and fresh herbs, inspecting and smelling each item before she put it in the basket.

"Do you have rice noodles at home?"

"Nope."

"Soy sauce? Sesame oil? Rice wine vinegar?"

"I probably have soy," I said, feeling inadequate. "Definitely tomato sauce."

"Ha," Hally said. "Do you know how much sugar is in tomato sauce?"

"Do I want to know?" I asked, knowing I probably sounded defensive. "I like tomato sauce."

She shook her head. "I won't ruin it for you."

We moved to the checkout line and I watched as the teenaged checkout chick asked Hally for her autograph and then printed out a line of paper from the till for Hally to sign. Hally sparkled at her and signed with a flourish and a love heart, writing the girl's name up the top of the paper. They took a selfie together, and I wondered what the girl would do with the autograph at the end of her shift. Stick it in her diary? The photo would undoubtedly go on her social-media page with a bunch of hashtags. Fame was a strange beast. I couldn't understand the desire to connect with someone purely because they were well-known.

CHAPTER TWELVE

"My apartment is pretty small," I said as we entered the building, suddenly anxious about Hally being in my space. "It's really nothing special."

"It's okay, I'm not sizest."

I turned to look at her and she gave me an encouraging smile.

"You probably live in some kind of mansion though, right?" I pressed the button for the lift.

"Why would I?"

"Because you're rich and famous. That's what people like you do."

"Hmm, people like me, hey?"

"You're not rich and famous?"

She dipped her head. "Oh no, I am, but I didn't know I was supposed to live in a particular kind of house because of it."

The lift let us out on my floor just as Thomas and Kevin were coming out of their apartment.

"Ginny," Thomas exclaimed, looking at me and then Hally and then back to me before swooping down on me and kissing my cheeks. He waggled his eyebrows suggestively. "What do we have here?"

I rolled my eyes. "Guys, meet Hally Arlow. Hally, this is Thomas." I gestured to Thomas who was bouncing on his tippy toes in excitement. "And Kevin," who was holding onto Thomas and almost in a swoon.

"Hally," Kevin breathed, as Thomas took Hally's hand, bent over it and kissed it, whispering reverently, "We're big fans."

Hally's mouth twitched and I suspected she was struggling to hold back laughter. "It's lovely to meet you both."

"Well, we'd better press on," I said, ushering Hally across the corridor to my door where I struggled with my key. "Work to do and all that."

Over my shoulder I could hear snickering, which I chose to ignore, keeping my hand on Hally's back as I almost, but not quite, pushed her inside.

"They seem lovely," she said as I slammed the door behind me, forgetting to be worried for a moment about Hally's first impression of my apartment.

"They are," I said. "They're very enthusiastic friends. So, this is where I live."

Hally looked around her, resting her handbag on the countertop where I put the groceries. "I like it," she said simply. "It's very you."

"And that is?"

"Clear cut, no mess, no fuss."

I didn't know whether to be pleased or disappointed. It wasn't exactly a glowing report of me or my apartment, but then it was perfectly accurate. I went with, "Thank you."

There was a thump, followed by a second slightly quieter thump, from the bedroom which I knew to be Asimov and Olive alighting from the bed, but which startled Hally. Right on cue, the two cats padded into the kitchen, Olive giving little chirps of happiness, Asimov keeping his emotions in check.

"Meet my cats, well, one is mine and one is Cathy's. The big grey one is Asimov and he's mine. The littler ginger one is Olive."

"Asimov, as in Isaac?" Hally asked.

I nodded, surprised that she recognised the popular, but niche, science-fiction author.

"Cool name. Nice that they're friends." Hally bent down and offered her hand. Asimov sniffed her suspiciously then pushed his big grey mug against her as Olive wound around her legs.

"We got them from the RSPCA at the same time. They were in the same enclosure and seemed to get on well. Cathy often has to go up to Sydney for work and family stuff so we look after Olive when she's away. Asimov seems to enjoy the company and I feel less guilty for leaving him alone all day."

"I hate that feeling. Xi and I had a dog and I always felt so bad for him, stuck at home."

"What happened to him?"

"I lost him in the divorce," Hally said. She made a face, her mouth pulling down at the edges. "Everyone always talks about how hard it is to split up when you've got children, but it's hard with animals too, you know?"

"Not personally, but I can imagine." The thought of losing Asimov to a faceless future ex-girlfriend filled me with horror. "I'd be pissed."

"I was, but Xi loved him so much and Ari, that was the dog, he just used to follow Xi around everywhere he went, so I couldn't split them up. He died a few years ago, but I still miss him sometimes, even though it's been a hundred years."

"How long has it been?" I asked, my curiosity overcoming my hesitancy to ask such a personal question. "Since you guys split up, I mean."

She looked up at the roof as if mentally counting. "Oh, about ten years or so. I lose track of the years. I'm not much of an anniversaries kind of person. We were married for just under five years. Not that long in the scheme of things but it was amazing it lasted as long as it did. Xi wanted kids—thank god we didn't have them. It would have been a disaster. We could barely look after ourselves."

I tried to imagine myself at eighteen, married and thinking about having kids. It was a far cry from my own experience of meandering through uni while I lived with my dad, both of us quietly doing our own thing until I moved out after graduation.

"Now," Hally said, "that's enough of that. Show me around your kitchen."

"Er." I looked around. "We're standing in it."

She rolled her eyes. "Yes, but pots, pans, knives, chopping board. Where is all that stuff. I tell you what, you can be my sous-chef, and you can start by getting out your kitchenware."

Hally made no bones about bossing me around while she chopped and stirred and assembled something that smelled exceptionally delicious, and I found myself enjoying every minute of it.

"Traditionally this doesn't have coconut milk," she said, as she spooned rice into our bowls and added the fragrant, steaming curry. "But I cheated and added it because I like it creamy."

"You didn't have to tell me. I wouldn't have known it wasn't right."

"But you might, one day, and then I'd always be the woman who cooked you a fake jungle curry."

"True. I appreciate your honesty."

"Now wait," she instructed as she fetched her phone from her bag and arranged the bowls on the kitchen bench. I looked over her shoulder as she took the shot and applied a variety of filters. I was impressed with the glossy, almost professional result and said so.

"The trick is in the filters. Subtle, but effective."

"What will you do with it?"

"I made it a story."

I had no idea what she was talking about and I must have looked blank because she said, "It's a way of giving people updates about what you're doing, but it doesn't hang around on your page forever. You post up a picture, add a little comment, people get to engage with you even when there's nothing particularly momentous happening."

"So, you tell people you're cooking dinner? They want to know that?"

"They do."

"I think it would be weird to expose yourself like that all that time. You don't really have any privacy."

"On the contrary. In this way I get to choose what people see of me. The real invasions of privacy are when people take pictures of you without your consent. That pisses me off no end."

"But why would anyone want to know what you're having for dinner?"

"I don't know, Gin," she said, with an exasperated sigh. "Maybe it inspires them to cook for themselves, or maybe there's not much going on in their world and it makes them feel less lonely, or maybe they want to make healthier choices but they don't know where to start. Or maybe it's just a bit of fun and it provides some connection between people who would otherwise be separate. Do we really need to overthink it?"

It was a strange world. I couldn't understand why people cared what anyone else ate for dinner. For me, the most important thing was what *I* would be eating for dinner.

"But overthinking things is my thing. That's literally what I get paid for."

"I suppose that's true. You're lucky. You're the whole package."

"What kind of package is that?"

"You know, good-looking and intellectual."

I squeaked, "Me? I think you might have me confused with someone else."

She raised her eyebrows. "You don't think you're intellectual?"

"More the good-looking part."

She let her eyes travel over the length of my body and I felt heat rise in me. "I think you've got that covered."

I gulped and looked away, confused by what was happening inside me. Hally was my client. I was her editor. This felt like flirting, but that couldn't be happening here. Problem was, it had been so long since I had flirted with anyone I couldn't really be sure.

"Er, thank you. So, can we eat now or do we need to take more photos?"

She swatted me with the tea towel and said, "Eat, eat."

I took my bowl and looked around. I usually just sat on the couch but that didn't seem right with Hally here. The only other option was my worktable covered in papers and books. Hally solved the problem by taking her bowl to the couch and sitting down. I tucked a bottle of wine under one arm, fetched two glasses and then followed suit.

"Red okay?" I asked, showing her the bottle.

"Perfect."

I poured us both a glass, handed Hally hers, then tucked my legs up under me on the couch and rested my bowl on a cushion on my lap. I was suddenly nervous to look at her, feeling the intimacy of having Hally in my space acutely. I was overly aware of myself, my position on the couch, Hally only thirty centimetres away. In her willowy, grey knit cardigan and figure-hugging black pants she looked ridiculously glamorous, far too much for my couch.

My stomach rumbled and I dragged my attention back to the food, which looked delicious. It tasted even better. "Wow," I mumbled as I swallowed. "This is incredible. I can't believe you made this in my kitchen."

"Technically you made it too but thank you."

We ate in silence for a bit, the cats crunching their way through their kibble.

"You haven't wanted to marry again since Xi?" I asked, surprising myself again with the personal question. I wasn't usually one to pry into other people's personal lives, but Hally was an enigma. I had read a whole book about her but I still felt like I wanted to know more.

She looked at me with a confused expression. "Well, it's only just been legalised in the last year."

"Huh?" It was my turn to look confused.

"Gay marriage," she said slowly, like I was a child. "It only just came in last year in Australia so I couldn't have gotten married."

I choked on my food, coughing as I tried to recover. "You're gay?"

"Yes. You didn't know?"

"How would I have known?"

She waved her hand dismissively. "A lot of people know stuff about me. It comes with the whole public-figure territory. And I'm totally open about it."

"But…" I wanted to say, you had a husband, you were married, but then plenty of women had had husbands and been married before they realised they were gay.

"But there are no pictures of you with…there's nothing on the Internet," I said instead and instantly flushed, embarrassed that I'd looked her up online.

She smirked, her pupils wide. "And how would you know that?"

I peered down at my bowl as if an answer lurked in its spicy depths. "Research," I said, weakly. "For your book, of course."

When she didn't answer I looked up to find her gaze trained on me, her eyes dark in their intensity. I straightened my shoulders, determined to regain my professional footing. "Sorry if I've made a bit of a *faux pas*," I said, sounding prim even to my ears. "You don't mention anything about it in your book and it hasn't come to my attention from any other, uh, source, so I made assumptions, which I shouldn't have. I apologise."

"It's okay. I wasn't trying to hide it in the book, it just didn't seem relevant. You do a lot of that, don't you?"

"Which? Make apologies or *faux pas*."

"Both, I guess."

"I guess I do."

I tried to return casually to my dinner, aware of her eyes on me as I ate. Hally Arlow was gay. Now that was a turn up for the books. Well, that answered one question. It would seem unlikely that she was attracted to hunky Heath from Graphic Design. I cursed Thomas and Kevin for leaving out this piece of information, sure that they would have known. How could they have not told me? In fact, surely Cathy could have, or Alice, or anyone really. Why did nobody tell me such a pertinent piece of information?

"It's ironic, don't you think?"

"What is?"

"That you assumed I was straight, when you're gay."

I paused, my fork hanging over my bowl. "I suppose it is."

I wouldn't ask her how she knew I was gay, even though her eyes seemed to be daring me to ask. I was open about my sexuality. Someone must have said something at work, or perhaps I had mentioned it myself in conversation. My brain whirled. My body felt as if someone had ignited a sparkler in my chest. Was something happening here between us?

"I knew it," she said, indicating that in fact, she hadn't known it definitely.

"And how is that?" I said.

She looked me up and down. "How could I not know?"

"You're saying I look gay? Now who's making a *faux pas*. I would have thought that's not very politically correct."

"Initially, I couldn't decide if you were gay, or just bookish," Hally said, ignoring my comment. "But I went with both."

"Bookish?"

"Sure, bookish. And a bit infuriating with your dark and mysterious ways, but really quite cute when you're earnestly apologising for one of your '*faux pas*'." She made little air quotes with her fingers.

My phone rang in the kitchen and I almost threw my bowl onto the coffee table in my haste to escape the conversation.

"I'd better take this," I said, indicating the phone. "It's my dad."

"Of course."

Dad wanted to chat. As he meandered through a long wandering sentence about carpentry and bedside tables, my eyes met Hally's across the room. Had she just called me cute? Was it supposed to be a compliment or an insult? It took me some time to realise Dad was trying to tell me he had made me a new bedside table. He wanted to bring it around. Would tonight suit? I explained that I was otherwise occupied tonight, as Hally's gaze held mine and my heartbeat raced inexplicably. We made plans for him to visit the on the weekend.

I hung up and stayed where I was, using the kitchen bench as a shield. I didn't know what the hell was going on here.

"My dad," I said again, stupidly.

"Yes." After a long moment Hally tilted her head and said, "Are you coming back over here?"

I bit my lip. "I'm not sure."

Hally smiled softly, tucking a strand of her glossy hair behind her ear. "Should I maybe come to you?"

A thousand butterflies took flight in my stomach. "You could."

Hally slowly made her way from the couch and around the kitchen bench to stand in front of me. She was only ten centimetres or so taller but it was enough that I had to look up a little to meet her gaze. She was so close I could see how smooth her skin was, and a tiny freckle by her left ear. Her eyelashes were long, and she looked at me from under them, reaching out to graze her thumb across my jaw. "Would it be okay if I kiss you?"

My face answered yes before my brain could weigh in and Hally dipped her head, capturing my mouth with her own. Her lips were featherlight, warm, inviting, kissing mine with a heat that left me trembling. My hands gripped the countertop behind me as she took me in her arms and our bodies met. Holy shit. Behind my closed eyes my brain lit up with a series of neurological fireworks that would have made Alice and all her Romance minions proud.

As Hally's tongue met mine I moaned, embarrassment and desire sparring for first place on my emotional podium. Had she heard that?

"You're delicious," she murmured against my lips, kissing her way up my neck to my ear where she nuzzled, sending shivers dancing across my skin. "Hot and delicious."

Did she have me confused with someone else? No one had ever called me hot before, especially not someone as classically hot as Hally. On the hotness scale she was, by public opinion, up there in Scoville Heat Units with the Carolina Reaper chilli, where I would be unlikely to bump the benign bell pepper off its lowly position.

I took a step back, inserting some air between us as my body cried out against my action. "Uh, Hally, do you maybe have me confused with someone else?"

She tightened her grip around my waist, searching my eyes with her own. "No, why would I?"

I shook my head. "Quite obviously you're the hot one."

"Can't we both be hot?" she whispered, leaning in, her mouth hovering tantalisingly close to mine.

Yes, my brain screamed. *We can be whatever you want.* But things were moving very fast and I couldn't quite wrap my mind around the fact that I was kissing Hally Arlow. "I don't know," I said. "This feels confusing."

She pulled back and straightened my shirt, catching my fingers in her own. "I'm sorry. I don't want to confuse you."

"I thought you didn't really like me."

"I've changed my mind. You've grown on me."

"I have?"

"Yes. I mean, you can be a pompous arse sometimes and you were a bit standoffish at first, but apart from that you're actually very likeable. You make me laugh. You're kind and you're generous—you over-tip café staff, you take care of your friend's cat without blinking an eyelid and I see you trying hard to be the best you can be. You sent me wine and poetry when you stuffed up. You didn't have to come to the gym with me but you came and gave it a good crack, even though it clearly nearly killed you." She grinned, obviously pleased with herself. "And you're an exceptionally good kisser. That's something new I've just learned about you."

My fingers flew to my lips. "This is unexpected."

Her brow creased. "Good unexpected? Or not so good?"

"Good," I said, breathing out a breath I didn't know I had been holding. "Very good, but very unexpected."

"Do you need to take a little break? Get your head around things?"

My body ached to press up against her again, to feel the swell of her breasts against mine, to press my palms into her back and feel her mouth hot against mine. I'd been kissing Hally Arlow. In what world did this make sense? My brain made me say, "That's probably not the worst idea."

She stepped back carefully and I immediately wished her closer. She checked her watch. "I should probably get going anyway. I have an early meeting tomorrow and I need to do some preparation tonight."

I watched her gather up her bag and phone, my body vibrating like a violin. "I'll see you next week," I said, feeling like I should say something but not sure what. "We're making such good progress with your book we might even finish the edits next week."

"That would be good."

"Yes. Cathy will be pleased."

Hally raised her eyebrows.

"We all will," I added quickly. "I mean, not pleased that it's finished, pleased that the book is on its way."

"Yes. Well, I'll see you next week then."

At the door, Hally paused. "Call me if you need to talk. If you'd like to talk."

"I will."

She let herself out. I exhaled deeply and slid to the floor, pressing my glasses up my nose. What in the hell had just happened? I had kissed Hally Arlow, is what, and enjoyed it to boot.

"She kissed me," I said to Asimov who had stalked around the corner to find out why I was sitting on the floor. He merely looked at me, disapproval etched in the cut of his whiskers.

"What?" He set about washing himself vigorously. "It's not illegal. People enjoy kissing," I told him. "And that was a very fine example of kissing."

But what business did I have kissing someone like Hally? She wasn't my type in a million years. Not that I had anything against her, but with her wide mouth and perfect looks, her glamorous outfits and public lifestyle, she was entirely the opposite of someone I would ever date.

Asimov finished his washing, stretching out on the floor next to me with a swish of his tail. "It was just a kiss," I assured him. "That kind of thing happens sometimes when people work closely together."

I wasn't sure if he believed me. I wasn't sure if I believed it myself.

CHAPTER THIRTEEN

By the time Friday night rolled around I had replayed "the kiss," as I was thinking of it, in my head too many times to count. I hadn't told anyone else about it, unless you could count Asimov and Olive, and that was weighing heavily on me. I was careful to avoid bumping into Thomas and Kevin, anxious not to have to subject myself to their innuendo and speculation. I had been on the verge of telling Cathy when we spoke but she had sounded so harried about her family issues, that I hadn't been able to bring myself to say the words. Instead, I mumbled them to myself in the shower, reminded the cats about it on an hourly basis and dreamt fitfully that I stood up to give a speech at Wine and Spines and told everyone that I had kissed Hally Arlow. And very much enjoyed it.

But what did it mean? I wasn't the casual-fling type. As much as I loved sex, I didn't enjoy taking all my clothes off with a total stranger, and so had been cautious about falling into bed with people, choosing to wait for women with whom I felt I had developed a real connection. Women with whom I would go on to have a relationship. And surely that was not Hally Arlow. And so it was just a kiss, I told myself. Repeatedly. It didn't mean anything. A one-off, friendly fumble in the kitchen. Except that I didn't do one-off friendly fumbles which was obviously why I was having so much trouble moving on from it.

I even considered telling all to my dad who was bringing my new bedside cabinet over the following morning. We had never shared confidences. I'd introduced him to my past girlfriends once the going got serious, and he had even seemed to like Pam who had bonded with him over the geometry of carpentry, but that was about as personal as we got with each other. I had no idea if he was seeing anyone and couldn't imagine myself asking.

There had been radio silence between Hally and me for the past two days and I had come down with a terrible case of checking disease. I checked my phone, my email, my work messages constantly, just in case. I even had Katie from reception call my work phone a couple of times to make sure my voice mail was working properly. But Hally didn't reach out and neither did I. Because what would I say?

I mulled it over as I poured myself a glass of wine and went to the cat tree to scratch Olive under her chin. What would I say? Perhaps I should have texted her. After all I had all but kicked her out of my apartment after she'd kissed me, so perhaps she was waiting for me to reach out. I should probably have let her know I was okay with everything. How had I not thought of that before?

I fetched my phone and sat on the couch, hovering over the messages. Then, I took a deep breath and quickly keyed in, *Just letting you know I'm all good.* Almost simultaneously a message from Hally popped up on the screen with a ting. Embarrassingly, my heart skipped and I was thankful only the cats were around to witness my shiver when I saw her name. *Sorry I haven't called, work's been mental. Coffee sometime?*

We had messaged each other at the same time. Did that mean something? Suddenly my phone vibrated in my hand,

Hally's name flashing on my screen with a phone call. Shit. Was I ready to speak to her?

"Hiya," I said, trying to sound casual. Hiya! I grimaced. Who said hiya? No one cool, that's who.

"Hiya, yourself," Hally said, a smile in her voice. "We texted at the same time."

"Yes, I think perhaps we did." Ug. I was so nervous. Now I was sounding like an eighteenth-century school marm.

"I'm driving, so I didn't want to text again. I was pulled over at the lights but I thought I'd call instead. Hope that's okay?"

Wait, was she nervous too? "Yes, of course. How are you?"

"Good. It's been a hectic few days. I've basically been in meetings for the last forty-eight hours straight. Such a bore. It's my least favourite part of the job."

"I can imagine. What are you meeting about?"

"Expansions. We're taking the brand international. Soft launch in New Zealand and then we'll push hard into the States. If that goes well will move into Europe, but we'll see. For now we're getting the NZ spaces up and running. I need to get over there in a couple of weeks to set up the regional office."

"Wow. That's huge."

"Sure is. And I love it. I still get a real buzz when I can open a new gym. I love the thought of the community that will spring from it, all the positivity we can bring to peoples' lives. Anyway, I'm rambling. How are you?"

"Same old, for me. Books, words, paper, screens, more books." I could hear traffic through her end of the line, and the beep of a car horn. "Where are you?"

"On my way home from the city. Finally. I'm starving."

"I could meet you for dinner," I said, biting my bottom lip as soon as the words were out. "I pretty much owe you for the incredible meal you made the other night and—"

"Sure." Hally didn't wait for me to finish. "Text me the restaurant and I'll meet you there. Can you be ready in fifteen though? I'm literally ready to eat the steering wheel and I'm not far from your place."

"Absolutely," I said, almost falling over myself as I jumped up from the couch, scaring the cats who scattered from the cat tree in offended haste. "Japanese okay?"

"Love it."

Twenty minutes later I entered my favourite Japanese restaurant and scanned the room, hoping I had beaten Hally there. It had taken me some time to find an appropriate outfit for a casual, last-minute dinner with one of Melbourne's hottest women. After a panicked attempt to find something cool in my wardrobe, which had most of my clothes ending up on the bed, I had gone with all black, from my shoes to the jeans and long-sleeve skivvy. I now feared I looked too much like a stagehand, but couldn't do anything more.

Hally was waiting for me in a private booth at the back of the restaurant, looking painfully ravishing in a simple, cream-coloured, jumpsuit. She stood to greet me, kissing me lightly on the cheek and then slipped back into the booth, leaving me with the faint scent of lilacs. It was hard to believe she had just come from a long day at work.

As I slid into the seat across from her she said, "I ordered a couple of starters, I hope that's okay."

"Absolutely. Sorry if I kept you waiting."

"You haven't. I ordered as the waiter was seating me." She smiled at me across the table, resting her chin on her hand. There was a light in her amber eyes that drew me in and it was all I could do not to rush across the table and fling myself into her arms. "So, you're all good huh?"

"I am." I nodded and then felt myself flush, realising she was referring to my text message. I went on quickly, "I've just been working, like you. Up to my ears in edits and release plans."

"How many authors do you work with at a time?"

"I've got six at the moment, including you."

"And what are they writing?"

I took her through some of the projects as the waitress delivered edamame and a bean-shoot salad, pausing to take our order for main courses. Hally scooped salad into her bowl, using her chopsticks with deft ease, while I popped an edamame into my mouth.

"You really love what you do, don't you."

"One hundred percent," I said emphatically. "This is my dream job. I get to read all day, work with all these amazing authors, I'm around books and people who love books. It's all I could ask for in a job. I don't know what I'd do if I wasn't doing this. I'd probably just sit on the couch with my cats until spiders covered me with webs, or I turned to dust, or something."

"Dramatic?"

I laughed. "Just trying to illustrate my point. It's the perfect job for me."

"What else have you done?"

"Nothing much. A few casual jobs while I was studying. Cafés, restaurants, that kind of thing. Cathy launched the company right out of university and we started off with a large bank loan and a small agenda. We mostly published books for the university, capitalising on our contacts. Over the years she branched out and grew the scope of the company until it became the Red Stone you see today. Now we do crime and YA, romance, nonfiction, general fiction, the whole kit and caboodle."

"And it does well? I thought publishing had taken a real hit since e-books took over."

"We do okay. We publish electronically as well." I didn't feel it was my place to speak about Cathy's business issues. Especially not with one of her star authors. "There are always challenges in any business, as you would know. Not that you have to worry about that in your business. People can hardly exercise online."

"Oh, but they do," Hally said, her face serious. "These days people upload their exercise routines and advice straight to YouTube, you can join online communities where you can exercise in your home, taking instructions from someone over the ether. There are millions of apps devoted to just this. It's very popular. We've developed some 'at home' training modules purely for that reason. People love to stay home. If they can do it from home, with as little effort as possible, it's a win."

"How did you get so business savvy?"

"You mean because I didn't go to university?"

I shrugged. "You seem to really know what you're doing. Most people who are running a business get some training."

"I work hard. I read a lot. I go to seminars and I've had a few mentors over the years. I utilised my community and learned from everything and everyone I could. My first gym started small, a bit like Cathy's story. I promoted it to working mothers, stopping by schools at pick up and drop off times to hand out fliers and special deals. I wanted to focus on women who rarely get to pay attention to themselves."

"I remember reading about that in your book. Actually, speaking of the book—"

Hally waved me away, popping edamame into her mouth. "Please. Let's skip the book tonight. Save it for next week's meeting. I want to talk about you. You know so much about me already, I feel like I hardly know you at all, and there's no autobiography of Ginerva Blake floating around is there?"

"Unless you count my teenage diaries."

"Oh yes." Hally's eyes widened. "What I'd give to read those."

"They're locked. Sealed with a secret code. No one could ever crack them."

Hally's eyes shone. "I'd like to try."

"Actually, I think they're in a box under the house at my dad's. And they're terrible. The worst kind of teenage drivel you can imagine."

"I can't actually imagine you as a teenager."

I pushed my glasses up my nose and sat back as the waitress delivered a platter of sushi and some tempura to our table. Another arrived with a plate of steaming noodles and Hally thanked them and topped up our ceramic mugs with tea.

I watched as Hally spooned wasabi into her soy sauce and swirled it around, then dunked a piece of sushi into it. She chewed with her eyes closed.

"Good?" I asked.

"Heaven. Now, tell me." Her eyes flicked back open. "Why did your parents call you Ginerva? It seems like such an old-fashioned name."

I sighed. I had been ridiculed for that old-fashioned name mercilessly throughout my school years. "Yeah. Apparently my mother liked it and my father and I were left to deal with it."

"Left? Did something happen to your mother?"

"She died, pretty soon after giving birth to me. Stomach cancer. They hadn't picked it up because of the pregnancy."

"Oh gosh, I'm sorry. That must have been so hard for your dad. Do you have siblings?"

"Nope. It's just me and him. The two most ill-equipped people on Earth to be a family to each other."

"Why, what do you mean?"

"I don't know, we just don't really seem to connect that well. He's very quiet. I guess we're both guilty of keeping to ourselves too much."

"But he rang the other night while I was over."

"Yes, we speak. I visit, sometimes he even visits me, but he's more the strong, silent type. Doesn't really say much. He's very good with his hands though. He makes things, beautiful carpentry pieces."

"I'd love to see something he's made."

"Maybe sometime," I said, wondering if it would be true. What was I doing here, sitting across from Hally Arlow having heart-to-hearts about family and growing up? I was baffled. I would never have picked Hally as someone with whom I would enjoy speaking, but here I was, tucking into a delicious dinner and a heartfelt *tête-à-tête*.

Hally used her chopsticks to pile noodles into her bowl. "Where did you grow up?"

"Melbourne, like you. Born here, grew up here, probably going to die here."

"You've got dying on the brain tonight."

I grinned. "Just being practical."

We talked and laughed our way through dinner, chatting with the ease of old friends as we discovered new things about each other. She liked watching table tennis. I liked going to Daylesford for the hot springs. She'd always wanted to live by the ocean. I'd always wanted to take a flight in a light plane. We both liked hot sake, so we ordered some, and then some more. Our feet met a couple of times under the table. Our eyes held like magnets. My heart felt like rising bread—light, fluffy, airborne.

After dinner, and a brief tussle over the bill which we resolved by splitting it equally, we stumbled out of the restaurant into the car park and the cold night air. Hally shivered and it felt like the most natural thing in the world for me to rub my hands on her arms to warm her up. If I'd thought to bring a jacket, I would have offered it to her, but as it was, with my heart beating as if I was preparing for the Stawell Gift, I could barely feel the cold.

"Would you care for a nightcap?" I asked, my hands still running up and down the length of her arms.

Her eyes met mine with a question in them, and I stepped closer, swallowing hard. "I think I have a bottle of sake at my place if you'd like to go there?"

"That would be nice, but just one. Otherwise I won't be able to drive."

"One is fine. Do you remember where I live?"

She said she did.

"I'll walk you to your car," I said.

She laughed, her wide smile lighting up her face infectiously. "It's right here in the car park. Where's yours?"

"Next to yours."

She laughed again and I felt inordinately happy.

She followed me for the short drive back to my apartment. I did all I could to force myself to look straight ahead and not into my rearview mirror where I could see her driving. Was she singing? Talking on the phone? We both parked on the street.

She slipped an arm around me as we waited for the lift. My breath caught in my throat. I couldn't look at her, staring straight at the numbers as the lift made its way down to us.

As we ascended, Hally took my hand in both of hers, pressing it to her lips softly, running a thumb over my knuckles. Her mouth was hot against my skin and my knees nearly buckled.

She followed me down the corridor, my hand still in hers. As I put my key in the lock she wrapped an arm around my waist and dropped a kiss on my neck, spreading through me like a shot of methylated spirits on a campfire.

I closed the door and she kissed my mouth, pressing me up against the door, her hands on my hips. I moaned and slid my hands around her waist, feeling the curve of her slender hips under the silky slip of her jumpsuit.

"Do you want it hot or cold?" I asked, against her mouth as her hands moved slowly, tantalisingly, up my ribs.

She pulled back, her pupils wide, confusion creasing her brow.

"The sake," I reminded her. "Hot or cold?"

"I don't think I want sake anymore," she said, dipping her head and finding my mouth again.

Her tongue ran lightly against mine and all thoughts of sake were forgotten. When her hands crept up under my shirt, grazing over the top of my bra, my knees gave way and I clung to her for a moment, desire rendering me inarticulate.

"Bedroom," I managed, finding both my words and my feet, grasping her hand as I led her away from the front door. We stopped by the couch to kiss some more, and then again in the corridor, my hands tangled in her hair as her tongue met mine.

I stopped short in the doorway. Hally bumped into me, peering over my shoulder at the mound of clothes covering my bed and the baleful stare of two cats who did not appreciate either the mess or the activity.

"What's all this?" Hally asked, her arm wrapped around me from behind. "Did you have a clothing crisis?"

"Maybe." I ducked out of her embrace and quickly gathered up the clothes, throwing them onto the armchair in the corner. The cats took the hint and left with backward glances of disapproval. "Or maybe I was just doing some sorting out."

"Sure you were," Hally teased. "Or maybe you were looking to impress me over dinner with your outfit choice."

I turned to her. "And did I? You can be honest."

Her eyes were serious. "I wouldn't dream of being anything else with you, Gin."

"And I appreciate that, but you're dodging the question."

"You look very suave."

"I was worried I looked like I was the props-moving person, you know, in a play."

"You do also look a little like that." She crossed the room and took me in her arms, whispering into my neck as she peppered my skin with kisses. "But it's a good look on you, and frankly, I'm a bit less interested in the clothes right now, and more about what's underneath them, if that's okay."

My hands found the zipper at the back of her jumpsuit and I edged it down, allowing my hands to play over the bare, warm skin of her back. "That would be more than okay," I said.

We made it onto the bed, my top discarded, her zipper down, her shoulders exposed. I ran my hand over the top of her breasts as she lay beneath me, and kissed her, marvelling at the way her skin goose pimpled under my touch. She groaned lazily and I slipped a hand around her, unhooking her bra, freeing her perfect round breasts. Her hands found the clasp of my bra and pulled it free, her thumbs raking over my nipples.

"I want to be naked with you," I said and lowered my head to kiss first one nipple and then the other, feeling them harden under the probe of my tongue.

She slipped out of her jumpsuit, kicking off her shoes and I helped her slide it down over her legs, pausing for a moment to run my hand over the top of her smooth, tanned thighs.

"You're so fit," I said. "Do you work out or something?"

She grinned and undid my jeans, pushing them down over my hips, taking my underpants with them. I gasped and bent to kiss her belly as I removed her underwear. I kissed down over her soft hair and she opened her legs, moaning as my mouth found her centre, my tongue flicking gently against her as I tasted and explored.

"Gin," she cried as her hips bucked against me. Her hands found my hair, pulling me into her as my tongue increased its rhythm, kissing, sucking, probing. I slid a finger inside her and she ground against me. "Oh my god."

I caught her nipple in my fingers as her movements became more urgent and, sliding another finger inside, increased the pressure of my tongue. With a sudden quiver she was calling my name over and over again, hips riding the high wave of orgasm.

"Holy shit," she whispered as I slid back up her body, trailing kisses over her slick skin. "Holy fucking shit."

I grinned at her. "Good holy fucking shit?"

Her pupils were magnificently dilated, with only the barest rim of the golden irises visible. "The best."

She pulled me down beside her, kissing me as her hand found my wetness. "You are too beautiful," she said, sliding her fingers in and out of me in a lazy rhythm.

I tensed for a moment, not sure what to do with the compliment.

"Are you okay?" Her eyes searched mine.

"I'm not used to being called beautiful," I replied through gasps, as she stroked the length of me, slowly, insistently.

She shook her head, lowering her mouth to mine. "You should be."

She kissed me as she dipped into me, filling me, sliding against me, her thumb providing sweet pressure as I lost my ability to think and could only cling on for the ride. When orgasm tore through me, she kissed me hard and I surrendered to the flood of pleasure, shuddering against her with broken moans.

I didn't say anything afterward, just pulled her close to me, her arm wrapped around my body as we floated somewhere above the bed, somewhere below the roof, somewhere in the realm of the previously undiscovered.

"Hally," I croaked, as her breathing slowed.

She gave a little jolt in my arms. "Yes?"

"That was...unexpected."

"You say that a lot."

"Only with you."

CHAPTER FOURTEEN

Somewhere in my mind's dark recesses I became aware of a distant ringing. I tugged at the covers, pulling them up to my chin as I tried to roll over and couldn't, a slumbering, naked Hally pinning my arm to the bed. I struggled from sleep, wincing as I opened my eyes and morning light streamed into the room. In all the impromptu happenings I had forgotten to shut the curtains before we had fallen asleep. The ringing continued and I realised it was my doorbell. I slid my arm out from underneath Hally, trying not to wake her, fumbled on my glasses and threw on some clothes from the pile on my chair.

"Coming," I called quietly from the corridor as I stumbled to the door.

"Jesus, I'm coming," I repeated as the ringer sounded again. Whoever was at my door at this hour had better have a damned good explanation. Only the thought that it had to be something disastrous and needing my help propelled me forward to find out.

I peered through the peephole and recoiled in horror. Dad. What the hell was he doing here?

I ran a hand through my hair and straightened my top, realising I had chosen a very dressy evening shirt. It looked strange with the accompanying tracksuit pants but there was no time to change so I opened the door, hoping Dad wouldn't notice my disarray.

"Dad."

"Thought you might have forgotten," he said. "Took you a while to answer the door."

"No, I must have slept in a bit, that's all. Come in."

I stepped away from the door and he disappeared back into the corridor, returning with a trolley upon which sat a gorgeous, squat little dark wood bedside table with a single white drawer.

"Oh my god, Dad, it's so beautiful. You made this?"

He grunted in affirmative. "Pop it in the bedroom for you?"

"Oh, no, no it's a terrible mess in there. Let's just leave it out here and I'll move it in later when I've tidied up. Coffee?"

"Sure."

As I boiled the kettle and filled the plunger with coffee I sent fervent prayers up to the gods of awkward parent-child relationships, requesting that Hally not wake up and join us. She had certainly seemed to be deeply asleep as I had crept out of the room, but I had no idea if she woke up to strange noises or would happily sleep through. I had a vague idea that she was an early riser, but given the kitchen clock was showing ten a.m., this seemed in dispute.

That said, we had had broken sleep at best, finding each other through the night to discover new pleasures. God. A jolt of desire burned through me. *Easy, tiger*, I told myself. I couldn't think about Hally right now with my dad propped on a kitchen stool, looking at me expectantly.

"Here we go," I said as I brought the plunger over and fetched the milk and two mugs. We both gazed at the plunger for a minute or two, and then I carefully depressed it and poured the coffee into our mugs. I gave Dad a generous slug of milk, dropped a little in my own cup and leaned against the bench.

"How long did that take you to make?" I asked, genuinely impressed with his craftsmanship. "It's so lovely, Dad, thank you."

"Not a worry. I worked on it this week. You mentioned you didn't have one the other day."

"That was very thoughtful of you. I love the handle on the drawer," I said, noticing the glassy, emerald knob for the first time.

"Pulled it off a door I found at the tip shop. All the wood is reclaimed stuff I found there. An old oak bookshelf that was falling apart so I stripped it and repurposed it."

"That's very cool. One day you'll have to show me the process."

He nodded and took a sip of his coffee, looking around my apartment.

"Here's Astro." He wrinkled his forehead like he was trying to remember something. "Aseem? Astrid?"

"Asimov," I supplied, as Asimov sauntered into the room, followed closely by Olive.

"Right. How is he?"

"He's very good, thanks. And this is Cathy's cat, Olive. She's staying with us while Cathy's in Sydney with her mum."

I shook some crunchies into the cats' bowls and returned to the bench where my dad sat running his thumb over the handle of his mug. I compared our hands, wondering if they looked the same. His were large, tough-looking, well-worn from all his manual work. My own, by contrast, were slim and entirely unscuffed. Did I have my mother's hands? I certainly had her colouring. From my few photos, she was dark-haired like me, only hers was long and straight and hung down her back. She had worn it out loose, looking every bit a woman of the seventies with her flared jeans and flowery blouses. My dad had always kept his light blond hair, now completely grey, closely cropped. I assumed it was something to do with his stint in the army as a younger man. I supposed we didn't look much alike.

"Is that coffee I smell?" Hally's voice called from the hallway.

Oh shit, shit, shit. Please let this not be happening. "Yes, of course," I said brightly, praying Hally had at least put some clothes on. "Stay there if you like, I can bring it to you."

She poked her head around the doorway. "I'll have it out here with you if that's okay."

"Of course, of course." I breathed a sigh of relief as she entered the room, dressed in the previous evening's outfit. It was a little crumpled, but she held her own, looking her usual ravishing self. In fact, if I hadn't been in my tracksuit pants, we would have looked the part for an evening show at the Malthouse.

"Dad, this is Hally. Hally, this is my dad, Steven."

"Nice to meet you, Steven." Hally offered her hand and he took it shyly, giving it a quick shake.

"You too," he said.

I fetched Hally a mug and she settled herself on a stool next to him.

"Dad just dropped around this bedside table he made for me," I explained as I poured her a coffee.

She turned to look at the table and oohed appropriately, exclaiming over its construction. "It's a real beauty," she said, giving my dad a wide smile.

He dipped his head at the compliment and studied his coffee.

We sat together in silence for a few moments before Hally began to gently question my dad about his carpentry projects and they fell into an easy discussion on different kinds of woods and how to source and upcycle materials. She was clearly impressed and with growing relief I watched them chat, my initial embarrassment slowly receding. Nothing like your dad meeting your…well, now what was Hally? My work colleague? That didn't sound right, given the night we had just spent together. Lover? Girlfriend? Both of those implied an ongoing relationship, which was a presumption I wasn't willing to make. Acquaintance sounded cold, and friend felt like both an over and understatement.

"What?" Hally asked, and I looked away, realising too late that I had been staring.

"Nothing." I smiled. "Just didn't know you knew so much about wood."

"My dad, for all his shortcomings, used to be pretty good with his hands. I went with him to the tip shop a few times to scavenge for wood. He never really showed me what he was doing but I enjoyed watching him in his workshop."

"I could show you a few things," my dad offered. "If you're interested."

"Oh, Dad, I'm sure Hally's just being polite."

"No, I'm not," Hally replied, giving me a stern look. "I'd love to come and have a lesson. It would be fantastic to learn how to make something simple. Where would you start?"

"You could make a serving tray, or a cheeseboard pretty easily," he said, his eyes lighting up. "Even a little stool wouldn't be too tricky if I showed you how. Come by anytime. Bring Gin. She could use a lesson in practicality herself."

"Dad!" I protested. "We both know I'm no good at that kind of thing."

He tipped back the last of his coffee and stood up. "Thank you for the coffee, girls. I'll leave you all to your day."

"Would you like another cup?"

"No, I'd better push on. I've got a few half-finished projects to tackle today and I'd better be getting at them. Lovely to meet you, Hally." He gave her a shy smile, ran a hand over his head and fetched his trolley.

I waved him goodbye as the trolley rattled behind him along the corridor.

Back in my apartment I grimaced at Hally. "Sorry about that. Bit of a shock to the system first thing in the morning."

"He seems really lovely."

"He is. But I suppose no one really expects to have coffee with, uh, well, someone else's parent first thing on a Saturday morning."

She grinned. "No, I don't suppose they do."

"Seeing as we're up, would you like some breakfast? Or do you need to get going?"

She checked her watch, eyebrows rising in surprise. "I'm taking my nephews to the indoor wave pool today. I didn't realise it was this late. I really should go home and change."

"I could make you a piece of toast to take with you?"

"Well, I do remember you telling me you're excellent at toast, so how could I say no?"

She smiled at me in a way that made me want to forget about toast and parents and nephews and take her back to the bedroom for the day, but I pulled myself together and set about turning the bread into toast. Hally watched me, leaning her elbows on the kitchen counter.

"The trick is to get the butter on while it's warm," I said, forcing myself to focus on the task at hand. "That way the toast absorbs the butter and the spread, rather than having everything just sitting on top of a cold, hardened piece of bread."

"I see."

I looked up to find Hally gazing at me, her eyes brimming with amusement.

"What?"

"You're cute when you make toast. Very intense."

I put down the knife, butter dropping onto the bench. "Cute? That's the second time you've called me cute. I don't think I do cute."

She spread her hands, indicating that I had little choice in the matter.

"Cute is for My Little Ponies and puppies. I'm…not cute."

"Except that you are."

I picked the knife back up, determined to press on. "I'm going to pretend you didn't say that. Vegemite? Or peanut butter?"

"What kind of peanut butter do you have?"

"Just the normal kind. I didn't know there was more than one kind." I fetched it from the cupboard and showed it to her.

"I'll go with Vegemite, thanks."

"What's wrong with this peanut butter?"

"It's full of added sugar and salt."

"Sounds good to me."

"I prefer to eat my sugar and salt on purpose, rather than having it mixed into things it doesn't need to be in."

"Vegemite it is then," I said.

I spread it onto her toast and put it into a takeaway container, snapping the lid shut and handing it over. "Here you go, for your drive home."

"Thank you. I'll bring you the container next week when I come in."

"Excellent." Why did I feel a little deflated at that? Had I been hoping to see her before we returned to work? Shit. *Ease up, Gin*, I told myself.

At the door, Hally slung her bag over her shoulder and reached out, smoothing the hair away from my forehead. "Thanks for dinner, and breakfast."

"Thank you." I repeated back to her. I wanted to say something more, but I couldn't decide on what would sound best. Anytime? My pleasure? They were too suggestive. See you soon? Too casual.

She leaned in and kissed me lightly on the lips, setting off a delicious fizzle of nerves in my already well-spent body, waving to me as she walked away, hips swinging jauntily, down the corridor.

Far out. I closed my door and looked around. Nothing was different, except for the new bedside table sitting in the middle of the room. But everything seemed foreign, like I was seeing it all for the first time. There was my couch, where we had shared a searing kiss, our coffee cups on the bench. Hally had obviously made the bed before she left the room, smoothing out the covers and fluffing the pillows, but I could smell her perfume as I lay down, pressing my palms against my eyes.

Asimov jumped up with a chirp, settling himself against my arm. If it wasn't for the perfume I could almost imagine that last night had been some kind of insane, erotic dream. That and the fact that my body felt like I was some kind of sex kitten. Would this be weird at work? Would we need to talk about it? I pressed harder on my eyes, creating a pattern of neon fireworks behind my eyelids. What would I tell Cathy? Perhaps I could just keep it to myself for now. I shivered as I thought back to Hally's skin against mine as we moved together in the bed.

I was drifting off to sleep when my doorbell rang again and I jumped, startled by the sound. The last few days had seen a significant increase in traffic through my normally quiet apartment and I was starting to find it a little tiring.

"Who is it?" I called as I made my way through the door, hoping it wasn't Thomas or Kevin come for a gossip.

"It's me," came a voice I knew too well but was definitely not expecting.

"Cathy!" I cried and threw open the door. "What are you doing here?"

"I missed my cat," she said, giving me a hug, "and maybe you too."

She followed me into the apartment. "Nice outfit."

"Huh? Oh." I looked down at myself. "I'm trying out different combinations," I said lamely.

She took in the coffee mugs on my kitchen bench and looked me over. "What have you been up to?"

"Me?" I feigned innocence. "Nothing much really. Um, Dad came around, the cats and I have been catching up on some weekend sleep. Same old story."

She peered at me, resting her bag on the bench in the same place Hally's had been, just half an hour before. "Gin. What's up with you?"

"What's up with *you*?" I parried. "You're supposed to be in Sydney."

"I needed to meet with the printer on Monday morning and I decided to come and have a weekend at home. I booked a carer to help Rachel with Mum, much to her disgust, but it just didn't feel right to leave her high and dry. Mum's been so..." She waved her hand around. "All over the place. Can we make some coffee? I'm dying for a coffee."

"Coming right up," I said, busying myself in the kitchen.

"Olive," she cried, picking up the meowing cat. She buried her face in Olive's fur and kissed the top of her head. "Mummy missed you."

"She missed you too"

"Shame. Poor darling. So, your dad's been round? Did he bring you that?" She gestured at the bedside table. "It's beautiful."

"Yes, isn't it fabulous? He made it. I mentioned that I needed one, and the next thing you know he's bringing one round for me."

"I suppose what he doesn't say with words he makes up for in action."

I knew my dad loved me, but it certainly wasn't something we ever said to each other. He'd told me he loved me when, as an eight-year-old, I'd gotten lost at the Lunar Park Fair on a visit for a schoolmate's birthday party. When they hadn't managed to locate me for over an hour the child's mother had called my dad. They found me across the road at the beach, sitting on the sand making a castle. I hadn't wanted to go to the party, let alone the fair with its treacherous roller coasters and terrifying house of horrors, so I had taken myself off on a naturalist adventure instead. My dad had held me tightly in his arms and whispered many times that he loved me. I had felt terribly guilty as he had swiped at his eyes, wet with tears.

"Are you free today?" Cathy asked, changing the subject. "I thought we could hang out, if you're not busy."

"Sounds good to me. Have you had breakfast? I'm starving, I'll make us something?"

Cathy looked at the plate on the bench with toast crumbs and the buttery knife and open Vegemite jar.

"You haven't eaten?"

"No, I..."

"What *have* you been up to, Ginerva?"

I squirmed under her steely gaze, reminding myself that we weren't at work and I did not need to succumb to her interrogation.

"Gin, it's me, your best friend," she wheedled. "I can tell there's something going on with you and I want to know what it is. Please don't punish me for being away by keeping me in the dark about your life."

"Oh my god, Cathy, I'm not punishing you. It's nothing. Well, not nothing. I don't know how to...I, er, well, I slept with Hally." I fumbled with the bread, not looking up as I jammed it into the toaster.

There was such a long silence that I was forced to look up at her. Her face was such a picture of surprise it was almost comical. "You what?"

"I slept with Hally."

"As in Hally Arlow?"

"That's the one."

"I thought you despised Hally Arlow."

"I thought so too. But I don't know, it just kind of happened. She's actually not that bad."

"What a glowing report. I'll be sure to pass it on to her. In fact, why don't we just print that as a review on the jacket cover of her book. Three stars, Ginerva Blake. She's actually not that bad. Are you fucking mental, Gin? You can't be sleeping with Hally, you're supposed to be publishing her book, not getting her in the sack."

"I know, I know." I held up my hands. "It just happened, I'm sorry. I don't even know how it happened. We went out for dinner and the next thing we were back here, and the next thing—"

"Oh my god. This is so unlike you."

I hung my head. "Is this really bad?"

"I suppose there's no law about it but it's definitely unprofessional. I certainly wouldn't be encouraging any staff to sleep with their authors."

"No, of course not. Can we just keep this between us?"

Cathy sighed. "I think maybe we should."

The toast popped, breaking our silence and I jumped. Jesus. I needed some more sleep. I was wreck.

"Was it good?"

"Sorry?"

"Sleeping with Hally? Did you, was it, you know?" She grinned suddenly, back to being best-friend Cathy that I had grown up with and shared all my deepest darkest thoughts. "Good?"

I took a deep breath and let it out slowly. "It was actually pretty fucking amazing."

"Now *that* we could put that on the jacket cover," Cathy said, with a giggle. "But seriously, can you try not to sleep with her again, at least until you finish working together? Is that going to be a problem?"

"No, of course not. It won't be an issue. It's not a thing."

"You're going to need to talk to her about it, make sure you're on the same page."

"It won't be a problem," I said, confident that by now Hally was probably chalking the whole episode up to an embarrassing sake-induced slipup. People like Hally Arlow did not make a habit of sleeping with people like me.

Cathy looked dubious, her brow crinkled with worry. "If you say so."

CHAPTER FIFTEEN

As if by some unspoken understanding Hally and I had let the weekend roll through without communicating. I figured she was busy doing Hally things—Snapchatting, Twittering, exercising and making green smoothies—and I enjoyed a couple of days with Cathy, catching up with some of our favourite activities.

We spent Saturday afternoon in the art gallery, walking slowly through the new Indigenous exhibition, powerfully moved by the experiences reflected by our First Nations people. We took notes and got excited by the idea of a Red Stone *First Nations' Modern Art* book. Saturday night found us perched on stools in the window of a pasta restaurant in the city, watching people go about their evening, as we caught up on weeks of rushed telephone calls and video chats. And by Sunday afternoon we were indulging in wine and cheese at the Italian film festival, losing our hearts to cinematography that makes you want to rush home and pack a bag to go grape picking in Tuscany. When I crawled into bed on Sunday night I felt more like myself than I had done in weeks.

As I walked to work on Monday morning, I realised all this confusion with Hally was most probably Cathy's fault. If she hadn't been away so much lately I would have been spending my time with her, rather than going to the gym, or falling into bed with one of my authors. Cathy was right. This behaviour really wasn't me.

As I walked the streets I found myself rehearsing what I would say to Hally. April was doing its best to hold on to autumn, but May was just around the corner and winter would be upon us in a heartbeat. I walked quickly to keep out the cold. What had started out as exercise had become a routine I was really enjoying.

The basic structure of Hally's book was all but nailed down. One last session would do it, and then it would be on to the serious edits. And those could mostly be done by email. We wouldn't need to be spending so much time together, and that was probably for the best.

Apart from the obvious issue of sleeping with one of Red Stone's authors, I honestly didn't think my heart could make it away scot-free if I continued spending this much time with Hally. She was a bit too alluring and far too glamorous. We lived in different worlds, were excited by different things. I was a cerebral person, spending most of my time in the thought-driven universe of art, books, music, words. Hally was all about the body.

We were chalk and cheese and the attraction that had flared between us would likely fade out as quickly as it had started. Like potassium and oxygen, I thought, as I walked, congratulating myself on the analogy. These quick attractions most often burned hard and bright, like a supernova, but had the power to leave a black hole in their wake. I was smart enough to see that it would be me, not Hally, who ended up a casualty of the affair.

We were scheduled to meet on Wednesday, but I wanted to have this conversation before we came face-to-face, not trusting myself to articulate the words as clearly as they were in my mind.

I plugged in my hands-free headphones and called Hally as I walked, hoping she wasn't already in a meeting.

"Morning," she said, her voice husky in my ear.

I suppressed a shiver and the desire to melt into a puddle right there and then on the street and forced myself to concentrate. "Got a sec?" I said, all business.

She matched her tone to mine. "Sure."

"What happened between us on the weekend," I started, and then floundered, wishing I'd written it down before I called. "What happened was…"

"Lovely," Hally supplied.

"Yes," I agreed before I could help myself. "And thank you for that." God, where was I going with this?

"No problem."

"The thing is, we have to work together, and it's a bit unprofessional for me to be behaving in this way. I think it would be better if we could just focus on getting your book done and go from there. I can't really do my best work for you if I'm, well, compromised."

"Compromised?"

"I might not ask you to change something for fear of hurting your feelings."

"I find that highly unlikely, but okay, yes, I take your point."

"Good. So, can we go back to that?"

Hally paused. "I don't really believe in going backward."

"Well, not backward, more like forward, forward to what we were before."

"Which before? The time at the beginning when you didn't like me much and I *really* didn't like you? Or sometime after that?" Was she teasing me? I couldn't really tell over the phone.

"Okay, well, how about friends. Work friends, sort of thing, with a job to do. Can we do that?"

"Of course," Hally replied, her voice sounding distant. "Absolutely."

"Great." I blew out a sigh of relief. "That's great. So, I'll see you Wednesday?"

"You will. Hey, I'd better go. I've got people waiting for me."

"No problem, thanks for the chat. Have a great day."

"And you." And she rang off.

I stopped outside the building to grab a coffee before heading upstairs to my office, reflecting that the conversation had gone well. Sure, the words hadn't exactly rolled off my tongue, but the general feeling had been positive, and Hally had seemed fine with the whole thing. And of course she would have been. If I'd asked her how she felt about things I'm sure she would have said something like, "What things?" She was probably used to casual sex. She could take this kind of thing in her stride. It was me that had been making a mountain out of a nonexistent molehill, but I was glad we had had the conversation and could now move on.

With renewed energy, I made my way up to my office, eager to start my day and immerse myself in work. There might even be time to start a conversation with the gallery about connecting with some of their Indigenous artists, and that filled me with excitement.

"And what were you and Ms. Arlow up to the other evening?" a voice said behind me as I made my way down the corridor to my apartment that evening.

I spun around to find Thomas walking behind me. "Hey, are you following me?"

"Well, it's the only way to find out what's going on in your life these days." I waited for him and we kissed hello, his rough cheek grazing mine. "Where have you been all my life?"

I laughed and swatted him on the arm. "Just here. Nowhere special."

"So, since when did you bring authors home to your apartment? I've never seen you do that before."

"I do lots of things you don't see."

He waggled his eyebrows, thick furry lines dancing about on his forehead. "Really?"

"Oi." I swatted him again. "Actually, I do have a bone to pick with you and Kevin. How come you never mentioned that Hally was gay? When we talked about her the other night, neither of you said anything."

Thomas frowned and pursed his lips. "I thought everyone knew. You didn't know?"

"No."

"How did you find out?"

"She told me."

"Really. And what else did she tell you? Was that while she was in your apartment?"

"Nothing, and yes."

Thomas leaned against his door, crossing his arms. "What are you not telling me? What's going on here?"

"There's nothing going on here, I promise." Would I be struck down? It wasn't exactly a lie but it also wasn't exactly the truth. I just didn't have it in me to pick apart my encounter with Hally and serve it up to Kevin and Thomas for dessert. "We just had a bunch of work to do and it went over time so we grabbed some dinner."

He studied me with watchful eyes. "If you say so."

"I do."

"Come over on Friday night? We're having a Trivial Pursuit dinner."

"Sure, sounds good."

"And let me know when you're ready to tell me all about it," Thomas said, winking at me and letting himself into his apartment.

"We're just friendly," I called after him. "Friendly friends."

When Hally appeared in my office on Wednesday afternoon it felt a little less like friendly friends, and a bit more like strained acquaintances who had seen each other naked and completely come apart. But by the time we had knuckled down to work, any initial awkwardness had pretty much dissipated. We made our way through the last chapter and prepared a list of final edits for her to address.

"And I think that's it," I said, leaning back in my chair. "Once you've done those, we read through the book and check it line by line, tightening up sentences, fixing grammar, making sure it all reads well."

"How do we do that? Do I come in and we go through it together?"

"No, that would take too long. Basically I'll read it, one chapter at a time, and send them through with notes and comments as they're done. Then you send them back with your changes tracked and I reread them."

"My god." Hally sniffed. "That sounds like it will take forever."

I pushed my glasses up my nose and smiled. "It's a lot quicker than you'd think. You've done most of the hard part. Think of it like sewing, you've made the quilt, now you just have to go around and tidy up the stitching and cut off the loose ends."

"Have you ever made a quilt?"

"No, have you?"

Hally's mouth twitched into a smile and she shook her head. "No."

"Okay, well—"

She cut me off. "I get the principle. So, we just email each other from here on?"

"That's the idea. When that's done I get a couple of proofreaders to go over it and then we print a few proof copies. I'll hand them round to people, you can have a copy, and we'll do a last check over of everything before we get the final print run. Also, if it's okay with you, Alice offered to read over the book and provide a fresh set of eyes. I think now would be the time for her to do that, before we get really bogged down in the finicky edits. Are you happy for me to send it to her?"

Hally seemed distracted, tapping her pen on her diary. "Sure, that's fine with me."

"Great. Well." I stood up and stretched, trying to stifle a yawn. "I think we're done for today. You off to the gym?"

"I went already this morning. You?"

"Ha. Everything okay?"

Hally looked startled, her eyes flicking over me. "Yes, of course." She gathered up her bag and tucked away her diary. "I'll hear from you soon then."

"You first."

"What?"

"You do those last changes and send them back to me, and then we start the chapter by chapter."

"Right, yes, of course."

"You're sure you're okay?"

"Gin." Hally frowned. "I'm fine. I have a lot going on at the moment. Apologies if I'm a tiny bit distracted."

I held up my hands. "Absolutely."

She sighed and rubbed her temples. "Sorry. I didn't mean to be short with you. It's just…"

"What is it?" I asked, genuinely concerned. I hadn't ever seen her look so ruffled.

She shook her head. "Sometimes the work I do leaves me exposed to…undesirables."

"What do you mean undesirables?"

"Crazy people, stalkers, people with bad intentions."

It was my turn to frown. "Has something happened?"

"Some idiot is sending me threats. I'm getting these constant creepy emails, which normally wouldn't bother me so much, but this guy is really persistent and he's mentioned my sister's name, which really freaks me out. Delphi keeps a low profile. It's just her and the kids, since she split with her husband, and she's no party animal. Her life revolves around the boys and I feel incredibly protective of her, of all three of them. I can handle it if a lunatic decides to fixate on me, but bringing my sister into things…" She shook her head. "It's just not on."

"Have you been to the police?"

"I have. They have very little to go on. Of course it's all fake names on the Internet. It's not hard to use technology to hide where and who you are."

"So they can't do anything?"

"I don't know. It's early days, but it's worrying me."

"I'm sorry to hear that," I said, wishing I had something a bit more substantial to offer. Why didn't I know a detective in cybercrimes, or a whizz-bang techno freak who could help track down this stalker? For a moment I lamented my small world of books and words.

"I'm sure it will all be okay. Like I said, it's not the first time and unfortunately I suspect it won't be the last."

"Well, if there's anything we can do to support you in this time, please let me know."

She held my eyes for a moment and I felt how stilted my words had sounded. I wanted to offer more. I wanted to say, come and hide out at my place until this all blows over, bring your sister too, bring the boys if that will make things better, but I knew that would just be too weird.

She gave me a smile that didn't quite reach her eyes. "Thanks, Gin. I guess I'll see you at the wine thing then."

"Oh yes." I had forgotten Wine and Spines but the event was Friday fortnight. "See you then."

"How did it go with Hally?" Cathy asked via video chat from the Sydney office.

"Fine, we're all good. I think she's pretty keen to just get the book done as soon as possible now."

"Are you sure that's not you, Gin?"

"We probably both are," I conceded.

"So, it's not going to be awkward between you?"

I thought back to our meeting that afternoon. Things had felt a little off. Hally had been a bit distant, but then, as she had explained, she had a lot on her plate right now. I certainly hadn't gotten the vibe that she was pining away for me. "No, she's very professional." I took off my glasses and rubbed my eyes, squinting and stretching. I felt tired. Strangely heavy. A bit achy in my chest. "I think I'm coming down with something."

"Really? Like what."

"I don't know. Flu, maybe? I feel kind of shitty."

Cathy pixelated on the screen, froze and then came back into focus. "That's no goooooooo—" The word paused and stuck like she was a robot, and then she was back. "You should go home, get an early night."

"Yeah." But I didn't feel like going home. I felt restless and hot.

I walked home through the gardens, stopping to sit on a bench and stare up at a large Moreton Bay fig tree with its long hanging branches and wide, dark leaves. The cold of the metal bench penetrated my thin trousers and made me shiver, but I ignored it. I was irritatingly out of sorts and I couldn't put my finger on why. Everything was going so well at work. I was out of the woods with the Hally edits and on the home straight. I had already had a few nibbles for the new *First Nations' Modern Art* project and my other authors were all behaving themselves, dotting all their I's and crossing all their T's.

A spatter of rain hit my face and I noticed droplets darkening the pavement. Damn. I hadn't brought an umbrella. I pulled my jacket tighter around me and legged it to stand under the fig tree as the rain grew heavier, great wet drops hurling themselves out of the sky. The fig provided me with some protection but I was still getting wet. I turned my face up to the sky, enjoying the icy cold of the rain on my cheeks as it slid down to my chin and dripped off. My glasses blurred and I leaned back against the tree, feeling myself as one with its trunk. The branches dipped and swayed in the wind and thunder broke overhead.

"Are you okay?" someone called, but I couldn't see him clearly because my glasses were wet. He seemed to be waving an umbrella at me. "You can come under if you like."

"I'm fine," I called back. "Enjoying it."

And I was. It felt like relief—all the noise, the wind tearing at my jacket, the rain soaking me to the skin. My frustration ebbed and I laughed, and then shivered, realising I was freezing. I ran-walked the rest of the way home, throwing off my wet clothes and thawing out in a hot shower while the cats sat on the bathmat.

"It's raining," I told them with a giggle. "I got wet."

As the heat permeated my frozen skin I started to shake and then surprised myself by breaking into deep, chest-wracking sobs.

"I don't know why I'm crying," I told the cats as I sat down on the shower floor and hugged my knees to my chest. The water rained over my head, washing my tears away faster than they could fall. "But don't worry, I think it's okay."

CHAPTER SIXTEEN

The ballroom at the Grand Hyatt was impressive, dripping with ostentatious chandeliers, stiff white tablecloths hanging like ghosts over the tables. I was glad I had chosen to wear my fancy black smoking jacket with its maroon paisley cuffs. With a freshly ironed white shirt and my standard black trousers I felt almost dapper.

The room was busy, swimming with colour and perfume as Australia's who's who of the publishing world rubbed shoulders. I studied the map at the doorway, locating the Red Stone tables off to one side and made my way over, smiling and nodding at anyone who looked my way, as per Cathy's instructions. She had been adamant that not only must we all show up but to parry and dally with the best of them. Ever the dutiful employee, still working under the assumption that HR had me on notice, I would need to grin and bear my way through the event.

John, Alice, Frank and Lara were gathered at one table already, and if we hadn't been in the middle of the Grand Hyatt Ballroom you could have mistaken this for one of Cathy's Round The Table sessions.

"Do we sit anywhere?" I asked, pulling out a chair next to Frank.

John held up a pudgy hand and pointed to the next table. "You're over there."

I stopped and glanced over at the empty table. "What? Why?"

John shrugged. "There are place cards on the tables."

"And you guys are all sitting together, but I'm over there." I huffed, and narrowed my eyes, wondering if someone had done a quickie and swapped me out for someone else.

"Don't worry, Gin," Lara said. "I'm actually not at this table either. I just sat here for a moment to speak with Alice."

"Fine, fine. Well, enjoy your evening," I said and scoped the next-door table for my name. Alongside Heath, I saw the foodie Jess Silverman's place card, and then Hally's. I would be sitting directly across from her and found myself suppressing a little shiver of nervousness. I was in between Massimoto (excellent) and Jeremy Durge (not so excellent).

Durge was a tedious, uppity and horrendously snarky reviewer from NONFICLIT, a publication that focused on ways to tear apart most of the books I edited. The only thing that gave me joy about Durge and NONFICLIT, was that the name of his publication had the word "clit" in it. I doubt he'd realised that when he'd come up with the name, but I'd buy tickets and stand in line overnight to see his face when someone alerted him to it. Durge always dressed in the same greasy brown suit, his dark oily hair combed over to one side to hide his balding. I couldn't imagine what had inspired Cathy to invite Durge, let alone seat him next to me.

A quick look at the last Red Stone table showed it to be upper-level management—Cathy, our HR manager and the CFO, as well as a couple of senior people from Sydney I recognised from our email list but hadn't met.

I shook out my napkin and took my seat, trying to decide if Cathy had done me a favour, and sitting next to Durge was the lesser evil of the three tables, or if I was in purgatory for an unknown indiscretion.

"Ginerva," a voice said from behind me, and I turned to see Massimoto pulling out the chair next to mine.

"Good evening," I said, giving her a warm smile. She was one of my favourite authors on Earth. It would certainly be no hardship to sit next to her for an evening, and I could just pretend Durge didn't exist.

We immediately launched into a discussion of the difficulties linking Precambrian fossils with their Cambrian counterparts and I became so engrossed that it was some time before I looked up and noticed that our table had begun to fill up. Durge had planted himself next to me and was studying his rodent-like teeth in his knife, while Heath and Jess Silverman were deep in conversation on the other side of Durge. I introduced Massimoto and Jess to the table and let the chat wash over me as more people arrived. A night like this could go on for a while, and I would need to conserve my energy to make it through.

A waitress took our drink orders, and I caught Cathy's eye at the next table. She gave me a make-sure-I-don't-have-to-mop-you-up-at-the-end-of-the-night look, and I took the cue to go easy on the alcohol, giving her an understanding nod as I ordered a gin and tonic. When the first of the speeches began Hally had still not arrived.

There was much talk about celebrating the diversity of our community, embracing the new digital world unfolding around us, publishing houses being the engineers of their own destinies and authors plumbing hereto unseen depths. I sipped my drink politely and tuned out, hoping the food would arrive soon.

I perked up as the speaker began a diatribe on digital piracy and intellectual copyright, enjoying the way she pounded the podium as she expounded on what was clearly a deep passion.

Hally arrived as the speaker was in full flight, spittle catching the light and flying across the front tables. I was glad we were seated further back.

"Sorry I'm late," she said in a stage whisper. We all smiled and shuffled in our chairs as she sat down.

"Everyone," I whispered loudly to the table, "this Hally Arlow. Hally, this is Jess Silverman, and Heath you know—" I caught a glare from the next table and saw Cathy frowning and shaking her head. "I can catch you up after."

I watched her out of the corner of my eye as another couple of jovial speakers took to the podium to hand out industry awards. Hally wore her hair out in loose chestnut waves that fell softly around her shoulders. A simple halter-neck black dress, rimmed with silver edging, showed off her slender shoulders and toned arms. She had long silver danglies swinging from her ears and silver cuffs on each wrist. She looked red-carpet ready, the picture of glamour. Perhaps sensing my gaze, her eyes flicked to mine and held. I had the feeling of being a fly caught in the amber. My pulse roared in my ears, jumping around in my neck. *It's just a biological reaction*, I intoned, *just biology*. Nothing to see here.

I pushed my glasses up my nose and smiled. Hally held my eyes for a moment longer before smiling briefly and looking away. I swallowed hard and reached for my drink, taking a sip, and then another. Throwing caution to the wind I polished it off and caught the eye of a passing waitress.

"Another, please," I mouthed. She nodded.

"...and the award goes to...Cathy Belayme, Red Stone Publishing." The tables around me erupted with applause and I snapped back to attention, joining in the clapping vigorously. Okay, this was unexpected. What had I missed?

Cathy made her way up to the podium, smiling brightly, as she accepted the award. She held it up high for a moment and then stepped up to the microphone.

"Friends," she started, and then paused as if collecting her thoughts. She cradled the award and looked out at the audience, our eyes meeting for a moment. I grinned at her encouragingly and gave her a thumbs up. "I'm absolutely thrilled to receive this award on behalf of the Red Stone family. An award like this, an award for innovation and excellence, means a lot to a small publishing house like ours. With limited resources, the team has to rely on its instincts, on its acumen and its ingenuity to do what we do. We love what we do, every one of us, and I think that shows in the work we produce. Congratulations to my people." She broke off and held the award up to us. "This is all of ours."

We all applauded and watched her make her way from the podium, smiling and shaking hands with friends and colleagues as she made her way back to her chair.

There were more awards after that, and I clapped and cheered dutifully while I snuck glances at Hally, hoping our eyes would meet again. The waitress brought around the drinks and I swallowed mine quickly, thirsty in the growing heat of the room.

When the speeches were done and the awards all handed out, the waiters finally brought around the starters, depositing small plates of tomato soup and crusty rolls in front of each setting. The table broke off into small groups to chat and I was pleased to see Hally enjoying a conversation with Jess Silverman. With their shared love of food and cooking they would find some common ground, even if Jess's forte was ancient ceremonial religious fare. Surely she also enjoyed a good laksa?

Dinner was an elaborate onion tart with an array of sauces in dots around the plate and a huddle of pickled vegetables. Shared plates of mash and beans were also delivered and I added liberal portions of each to my plate. The alcohol was running freely and I was feeling loose, if not easy.

"Wait, wait," I said, halting the table before people could tuck in. "Hally will want to take a picture. For her Snapchat," I explained to Massimoto whose knife and fork were already hovering above her plate. "She likes to share all her experiences with her fans. Hashtag team Hally, right, Hally?"

Hally smiled, but it was strangely brittle and didn't quite reach her eyes. "I'm fine," she said, with a laugh that sounded forced.

I gave her a "What's up?" look and she answered me with a tiny shake of the head, before looking away. Why was everyone shaking their heads at me tonight?

Durge turned to me, locking me in his sights. He sneered. "You'd be *au fait* with that world now, Ginerva."

"I'm sorry? What world is that?"

"Food photos and hashtags."

"Me? And why is that?"

"Well, surely you must know something about it if you're publishing Hally's book."

He smelled of mothballs and I had to resist the urge to lean away from him. "Yes, but that's not my specialty. I don't go in for the hashtags myself."

Durge pursed his ratty little lips. "Well, neither do I, but I imagine you've had to immerse yourself in that world to some degree."

"Just because we're bringing out the book doesn't mean I'm suddenly an Instagram guru. I don't live my life that way. Superficial pop culture is hardly my thing, and I mean, if it had been up to me..." I trailed off, suddenly aware that the table had gone quiet.

"You were saying," Hally said, coldly. "If it had been up to you?"

I gulped and gripped my glass.

"Please, enlighten us, Gin."

"No, it's okay, I...I was just saying I'm not much of a hashtags kind of person."

Jess Silverman gave me a baleful look and I tried to smile back, attempting a laugh. She looked away.

Hally pushed back her chair. "I think I'll go and freshen up."

I watched her walk away from the table, my cheeks hot with embarrassment. Across the way Cathy was glaring at me, her eyes suspicious and worried. She raised her eyebrows. It was my turn to shake my head.

"Shall I see if she's okay?" Massimoto whispered. The darling.

"No, I'll go. I'll just..." I pushed my own chair out. "Take a walk," I finished, and did my best not to run away from the table. I could see Hally leaving the ballroom and I jogged through the room to follow her.

"Hally, wait up," I called as I entered the hotel foyer and saw her disappearing toward the street door.

She turned around, stared at me for a moment and then kept walking.

I dashed after her, calling her name as I ran.

I caught up with her on the street. "Hey, come on, please wait a moment," I said, putting my hand on her bare arm. Her skin was cold and she wrenched it away quickly.

"What for, Gin? So you can put me down and embarrass me some more? Not done yet?"

"No, god, I'm sorry, I didn't mean anything by it. You know I'm just not much of a hashtag person."

She bit her lip, her eyes hard to read. "You're not much of a hashtag person," she repeated, but there was an edge to her voice.

I spread my hands helplessly. "You know that."

"And you think that's what this is about?" She almost spat the words, and I took a step backward.

"It's not?"

"Jesus Christ, Gin. You fucking embarrassed me. You basically told that whole table that I was some superficial, pop-culture loser that you would have preferred not to waste your time over."

"I didn't, I…"

"You said some of those actual words."

"Yes, but…" What could I say? She was right, except that I truly hadn't meant to hurt her. I'd just been needled by Durge's superior sneer and let my tongue run away with me.

"If it had been up to you, what, Gin? You never finished your sentence."

"It doesn't matter."

"It does to me. You're supposed to be the honest one, she who values the truth above all else, so tell me. What would have happened if it had been up to you, Gin?"

I took a shaky breath and exhaled. I felt like I owed her the truth. "I wouldn't have published your book."

"So why the hell were you pushing me so hard to get back on board with it? You rang me, basically begging me to do the book with you. I knew you didn't think highly of me, but I thought you had revised your opinion somewhat. Tell me what was really going on, little miss truth-teller. Why didn't you just stick to your guns and leave me to find another publisher when we both would probably have been better off for it."

I rubbed the bridge of my nose, stress and frustration chewing up my brain space. "I'm on probation at work. If I lost your book for Red Stone there was a chance I could get fired."

Hally shook her head, a tear escaping down her cheek. She swiped at it angrily with the back of her hand. "So you used me? Well." She swiped again. "Fuck you."

"What? No, I didn't."

"You didn't believe in me, or my story, you just used me for personal gain, to keep your job." She spoke as if the words were just dawning on her. "You don't care about anything but yourself, and certainly not me. Bloody hell, Gin. Thanks for everything. You sure know how to make a person feel like crap."

"Hally, it wasn't like that," I protested.

"Save it. Do you know, I actually respected you and I thought it was mutual. I thought we had become friends, more even. I confided in you, I opened up to you." She looked away, a muscle in her jaw working hard. "But that whole time you were just up there on your lonely old high horse, going through the motions so you didn't lose your job."

She turned and walked away and I watched her go, my heart cracking. Was she right? My head screamed no, but my heart fired off flares of doubt.

I couldn't go back to the ballroom. I knew Cathy would be mad, perhaps HR would even convince her to finally give me the flick right there and then, but I couldn't bring myself to go back inside. Instead, I turned the opposite direction to Hally and walked. The city was crowded with Friday-night drinkers spilling out onto the streets in front of clubs and restaurants, so I headed down to the Yarra to watch the boats and walk by the water. A crew of rowers had their racing shell out, oars dipping into the water in sync as they powered through the still, inky black. I leaned on the railings to watch them, my heart aching with regret. I had been such an arsehole.

I took out my phone, ignored the seven messages from Cathy and quickly fired off a text to Hally. *I'm sorry. I fucked up. I'm so sorry for hurting your feelings. Can we talk?* I didn't expect her to answer immediately, but by the time I eventually made my way home and flopped into bed, she hadn't called or responded to my text. Maybe tomorrow, I thought, as I curled up and hugged my spare pillow. I imagined I could still smell Hally's perfume on it, breathing deeply as tears leaked out of my eyes. I was an awful human being. I had been prideful and superior, and I had caused hurt to others with my actions. I had hurt Hally, but she was wrong about one thing. I did care about her. I cared a whole damn lot.

CHAPTER SEVENTEEN

"Knock, knock?" Alice tapped on my open door. "Got a sec?"

"Sure," I said, resigning myself to half an hour of inane conversation. "What can I do for you?"

Alice held up a stack of paper and I peered at it, realising it was the copy of Hally's manuscript I'd given her a few weeks ago and all but forgotten about. "You've done an amazing job."

My heart beat heavily. "You think?"

"Definitely." She sat herself down in the chair opposite me and crossed one leg over the other, flipping her blond hair over her shoulder. "It reads really well, and I love the little snippets of advice at the end of each chapter. It's got great flow and I was really engaged the whole way through."

"Well, that's great, thanks, Alice."

"I read the original."

"You did? How did you get it?"

"Cathy gave it to me."

"She did, did she?" I was starting to suspect Cathy of foul play here.

"Yeah, she said she thought you might refuse to do it but she really wanted the book for Red Stone so she asked for my opinion on it."

"And what did you tell her?"

"I told her that I could see merit in the idea but that I thought it would take a hell of a lot of work to get it off the ground. Hally's idea was solid, but having never written anything before, let alone a book, the execution was lacking some finesse."

"That was very diplomatic of you." I narrowed my eyes. Alice was sounding so…unromantic. What was going on here?

"When you took it on, I knew you'd have your work cut out and I didn't expect you to get this result. Hally must be really pleased."

I sighed. "Hopefully."

"You haven't spoken?"

I didn't see much point in trying to hide the truth. Everyone at my table had heard my giant gaff and the whole team had watched Hally and me leave in the middle of the event. Words moved fast in this business. "Not since Wine and Spines. We've emailed edits back and forth, but I haven't spoken to her."

"I have."

I sat upright at that. "When did you speak to her? Why?"

"She rang me, said she didn't want to continue working with you and asked if I'd take over the editing process."

"Shit." I ran a hand through my hair, aware that it was probably sticking up all over the place. "What did you say?"

"I advised her to stay with you. I told her that from what I'd seen, what you'd already achieved together was amazing, that the book was a wonderful reflection of what she had intended and she should be very proud. I also told her that the editing process was nearly finished and it would be hard for her to start over with someone new at this late stage."

"And what did she say?"

"She said she'd think it over."

I blew out a breath I didn't realise I'd been holding. "I guess she decided to stick it out with me then. We finished the last edit a few days ago and I've done my final read. We'll have proof copies through next week."

Alice nodded. "I'm glad. Like I said, you've done a good job."

"Er, thank you. Why are you telling me this?"

"Because I can see you're struggling and I think you deserve to know that even though you've been an idiot, you've still actually done a good job."

I think my mouth actually fell open. "Thank you, Alice."

She stood up and left the manuscript on my desk. "No problem."

"Mum's finally starting to settle down a bit," Cathy said, her voice crackling over my car stereo as I honked my way through rain-fuelled, peak-hour-traffic hell to Dad's house that afternoon. I had promised to drop over for dinner and was already regretting it as I thought of my warm apartment, the cats and the couch waiting for me.

"That's great, must be a big relief."

"It is. I'm looking forward to coming home. I think I can be back this weekend."

"Excellent."

"I'll come and pick up Olive on Saturday if that suits."

"Sure, fine, no problem." Would Asimov be heartbroken? Thankfully we still had each other. That was all that mattered. Just me and him, alone in the world, together.

"You okay, Gin?"

"Fine," I croaked, yanking the steering wheel hard to avoid a pedestrian who stepped out in front of my car. With his headphones on, he barely heard me as I leaned on the horn to alert him to his mistake. "Just stuck in crazy traffic with a bunch of arseholes."

"Melbourne's still the same then?"

"Nothing's changed."

"Spoken to Hally yet?"

"As I said, nothing's changed."

"You'll have to speak to her at some point, Gin. You've got a book launch to organise."

"You might need to tell her. I've left messages, I've emailed, I've texted. She only responds to questions about work, so I'm sure the launch will be fine."

"Do I need to assign someone else to her?"

I thought of Alice's conversation. "You can try. If she wants to work with someone else that's okay with me."

"Leave it with me. Listen, Gin, there's something I need to tell you."

I experienced a twinge of anxiety at her tone. "What is it?"

"I need to give you a heads-up. You're going to receive a formal caution at work tomorrow. HR are going to send you a letter and you'll be officially on probation. After what happened at Wine and Spines, Rory and Vanessa were insistent that you stop receiving special treatment."

I had been expecting this but it still hit me like a kick in the guts. "Right."

"I'm sorry, I really am. I know you didn't mean to be hurtful. And it's only probation. If you put your head down and work hard it'll be over in a couple of months and everything will be back to normal."

There was a roaring in my ears and I heard Cathy as if she were speaking to me from far away. My voice felt stuck in my throat.

"Gin?"

"Yes, I understand, it's really okay," I finally managed to say. "It's no more than I deserve."

"Do you want to call me when you get home? We could video chat over dinner."

"Thanks, but I'm on my way to Dad's for dinner. Another time." I took a deep breath and sat up straight, forcing myself to sound cheery. "Please don't worry, it's not like this is coming out of left field. I fucked up, I know it, I'll do my time and hopefully we can all just move on. Surely even I can't make it worse from here."

"Okay." Cathy didn't sound sure. "If you're sure you're all right?"

"Look, it's best to just have it all out in the open. It's better this way. I'm better this way. I swear. You can stop asking."

"I'll stop asking when you actually seem fine."

"As you wish."

Dad answered the door in his flip-flops, shorts and a T-shirt. If it wasn't for the beanie perched on his head you could have been forgiven for thinking he was just off to the beach.

"Brr, Dad, aren't you cold?" I asked, rushing in through his doorway to escape the rain.

"Not really," he said. "Been in the workshop. It gets warm in there."

I screwed up my face. "No, it doesn't. You should put a jumper on, you'll freeze to death."

We both looked at each other for a moment, and I wondered if he was imagining himself freezing to death. At the frequency with which we spoke on the phone, it could be a couple of weeks before anyone found him. I immediately resolved to call him more often. He disappeared into his bedroom and came out pulling on a thick woollen jumper.

"Beer?"

"How about tea? It's too cold for beer."

"Coming right up."

We sat in the kitchen where I had grown up, taking our places at the little brown table that had served as our dining table for as long as I could remember. There were still three chairs. As a young child I had gone through a stage of putting one of my dolls in the spare chair and calling it "Mummy's chair." As a teenager I had been silently enraged by it and moved it into the workshop. Dad hadn't said a word, just made space for it. When my rage finally abated, as a young adult I had rescued the chair and brought it back out, and I wondered if it felt lonely to Dad now, all on his own.

The tea was strong and hot and we didn't say much as we drank. I asked Dad what he was working on, he asked me about work, and by the time the pizza arrived we were scraping the bottom of the barrel for conversation.

I organised plates and napkins for us at the table and opened a beer for Dad while he paid for the pizza. I was mid-chew when Dad suddenly said, "Did you still want to bring Hally round to the workshop sometime?"

I blinked, pizza paused in midair. "We're not really hanging out so much anymore, Dad. Most of the work we had to do together is finished."

He nodded. "That's a shame."

"It's really fine," I breezed. "That's how it goes in publishing."

Dad reached over and covered my hand with his. I looked down at his hand, weathered and rough, much bigger than mine, and hot tears rose in me like a geyser. I swallowed at the lump in my throat and sniffed as my nose began to run. Tears slipped down my cheeks.

"Damn it," I said and lifted my glasses to press a napkin against my eyes.

"Sorry, mate," he said simply.

The meeting room was already full and in session for Round The Table when I slid into an empty seat next to Frank, catching a mid-strength glare from Cathy. Ever since delivering my official warning she had been softer than usual. I'd tried to explain to her that I knew the whole thing was entirely my own fault and I had no one to blame for the mess I was in but myself, but I could tell she was worried about me.

"Sorry," I mouthed and opened my notebook, trying to look inconspicuous.

There was the usual too-ing and fro-ing around the table. Lara from YA had received a submission with a young trans protagonist that had the team excited. Alice's Next Big Thing was shaping up to take Australia by storm, the world even, and John and Frank had no less than their usual full plates on the boil. I caught everyone up to speed quickly on my work and sat back to let the rest of the meeting wash over me.

The twist in my guts when I spoke about Hally had distilled to a manageable dull ache, but I still looked forward to having this all behind me. Hally hadn't returned any of my calls and would only answer work-related emails. I had eventually sent her a long and detailed apology, attached to a bunch of flowers delivered to her home, hoping that she would find it within herself to forgive me. The flowers arrived back at my house with a note that simply said, "Let's just get the book done." After that I stuck purely to the professional, only contacting her via email when I had something essential to communicate. But it burned.

With the editing done and the proofs on my desk, we would have very little to do with each other in the coming months. Marketing would organise her book launches and the promotional work. I'd be kept in the loop of course, but it wouldn't really need any input from me. With many of my niche books, Marketing relied on my contacts at universities and magazines like Durge's for promotion, but this wouldn't be the case for Hally's book. They would have a commercially viable book and I could sense them salivating at the thought. I could feel my relationship with Hally slipping through my fingers, but what could I do about it?

"Gin, hang back for a second would you?" Cathy said, interrupting my thoughts.

My colleagues were packing up their laptops and notebooks and heading out of the room. I sat up with a start and said, "Sure, of course," hoping my mental absence hadn't been too obvious.

I packed up my notebook, mentally scanning to think what I could have done to warrant the one-on-one time. With my formal warning in hand I hoped nothing else I'd inadvertently done was about to tip me over the edge. When the room cleared I glanced at Cathy, waiting for her to speak, anxiety clawing at my stomach.

"I just wanted to give you a heads-up that Hally is coming in today. Didn't want you to get a shock if you bumped into her in the hallway."

"Thank you." She was right to warn me. I would have been startled and god knows what my bumbling, fumbling mouth would have come out with. At least this way I had time to be prepared, just in case. "What's she coming in for?"

"She needs to lock in her launch dates and promotional visits so that she can organise her business trips around them. Marketing will go through the plan with her. If there's anything in particular you'd like them to consider make sure you have a word with them this morning."

"Okay. I don't think there's anything I need to add. I'm sure they know what they're doing with this one."

Cathy gave me a sympathetic look. "I'm sure they do too. Hey, you want to grab lunch today?"

I shook my head. "I've got a meeting with the gallery. For the new Indigenous art book," I explained. "Thanks though."

"Another time."

My meeting went well and I didn't even mind that we ran over time, pleased at the thought that I would be out of the building while Hally was in it, grateful not to have to try to make small talk with her in front of the team. The gallery had a host of portfolios of up-and-coming Indigenous artists for me to look over, alongside the more established and well-recognised artists like Albert Namatjira and Emily Kame Kngwarreye. I spent a glorious couple of hours with Anna, the gallery's Indigenous art curator, gazing at artworks and discussing the path ahead for the book.

I made my way back to the office with a head full of ideas. For the first time in a while I felt a buzz of excitement, my notebook crammed with contacts. I barely noticed my surroundings, walking on autopilot while I thought about the project. It could be bigger than Ben-Hur. I entered the lift and pressed the floor for our office, watching absentmindedly as the doors slid closed. My thoughts were so focused on the project that I almost didn't notice when a hand stopped the doors just as they were closing and Hally slipped in. My surprise appeared to be mirrored in her face.

"I thought you were coming in earlier," I said, as she took her place next to me and the doors closed.

Her back was straight, her shoulders stiff and she looked straight ahead as she said, "I was waylaid."

My mind scrambled, my tongue glued to the roof of my mouth. I should say something, anything really. I scanned frantically for something neutral. "How are...your nephews?" I asked as we rose.

She glanced at me, a suspicious frown creasing her brow. "They're fine, thank you."

"Good, that's great."

We rode the rest of the short trip in silence. I cursed myself. It had been a poor opener. I should have gone with something more engaging. Perhaps another apology even.

"Hally, I'm sorry—"

"I think it's best—"

We said at the same time.

Hally reached out and pulled the emergency stop. The lift jolted to a halt.

"Woah," I said. "I thought they only did that on movies. I didn't know that was an actual thing."

"Gin," Hally said, turning to look at me. Her eyes searched mine. My pulse quickened, breathing shallow.

"Yes," I breathed.

"We have to work together for another few months. You'll be at my book launch and we may cross paths a few times at various events in the future. I want, no I *need* us to act normally around each other. I'm embarrassed enough by all this as is, and I don't like playing it out in public. I'd appreciate it if we could just move on now. I want to put it all behind me and get on with getting the book out. I've got enough going on without having to worry about this. So you can stop apologising now, okay? Consider it done and dusted. Apology accepted."

"Okay, great," I said, feeling strangely wounded by her words. I should have been relieved. This was what I wanted to hear from her, but the reservation in her eyes, the way she held herself slightly away from me, even when she was looking straight at me, were sobering. I wanted to ask her if they'd caught the stalker guy yet, if she was still having problems with the creepy letter writer, but the expression on her face was not inviting. "That's great," I repeated.

She gave me one last scrutinising glance and then popped the emergency stop back in. The lift heaved and I clutched the rail, stumbling a little. Hally caught my arm and let me go just as quickly, her touch burning into my skin.

Moments later the doors opened and Hally strode out into our reception area with a warm greeting for Katie, who practically threw herself over the desk and into Hally's arms with her eyes. Did Katie know Hally was gay? Was Katie gay for that matter? I realised I knew very little about the people around me.

"See you later, Gin," Hally called as she made her way down the hallway, I presumed to meet with Marketing.

"Yep, bye," I said to her retreating back. "Good to see you." I wasn't sure if she heard. She didn't turn around. I slunk back into my office, the high from my lunchtime meeting barely a memory. *Come on, Gin,* I rallied. *This is good. Hally's happy to move on, you're out of the doghouse.* I prowled around my office, picking up knick-knacks and putting them back down again. I couldn't understand why I felt so bad. Wasn't this exactly what I had been wanting? I had been upset with myself for hurting Hally's feelings and now she was saying she was over it, happy to move on. So why the hell did that feel like a sucker punch?

CHAPTER EIGHTEEN

Winter came and went in a long, icy blur. People often think of Australia as hot, but Melbourne winter can pack an Antarctic blast, and this year was no exception. I had plenty to focus on at work and threw myself into it, barely coming up for air. I worked from home a fair bit in the evenings, just me and Asimov and the oil heater, huddled together in the lounge room. In the mornings, I hauled out the car and fought my way into the office through the worst of the rainy traffic with the rest of the Melbourne.

"You're in a funk," Cathy declared as she dunked a teabag in her cup and parked her bum on my heater. The first few days of spring had sprung but my apartment was still cool. "You've been inside here for too long. You need air."

"I get plenty of air. I get air every time I come into the office."

"Fresh air."

"Technically, if this air we're breathing right now wasn't fresh, we'd both know about it."

She rolled her eyes. "Gin, don't be annoying. You know what I'm saying."

"Well, what do you want me to do?" I asked.

"I want you to stop working so much and get out of here."

"That's a weird thing for one's boss to say."

"I'm not speaking as your boss right now. This is a best-friend lecture. We haven't been anywhere or done anything in forever. You're just always working."

"Fine. Where do you want to go?"

Cathy blew on her tea and took a sip. "We could go to the theatre? Or wait, Ronaldo Skiffler is hosting a panel discussion at the Writers' Centre on Friday night. We could go to that? Someone sent me tickets the other day."

"I don't know, I thought you meant just getting a coffee or something. I really wanted to lock down the text for the Indigenous art book this week. I might not have time to go to a panel discussion."

"You have time. As your boss, I forbid you working this Friday night."

"I thought you were talking to me as best-friend Cathy."

She glared at me. "Don't be a shit. Come on, I want to *do* something. All we do is sit in your apartment and drink things and eat pizza. I need to remember what the rest of the world looks like and I won't take no for an answer. I'll pick you up on Friday at six thirty."

I sighed. "Fine, fine."

When Cathy buzzed my phone to say she was waiting downstairs I considered telling her I wasn't in the mood to go out, but I had a feeling she would come up and drag me out by the armpits. I preferred to exit the building in a more dignified fashion so I threw on my jacket, patted Asimov goodbye, assuring him that a little space was probably good for both of us and left.

The days were finally lengthening, and the sun had just gone down, the warm glow of dusk softening the streets as we drove to the Writers' Centre. Pink and white blossoms were bursting on the trees and I felt my mood lift. Cathy was right. It was nice to get out and do something different.

"Who's on the panel?" I asked as Cathy pulled into the car park.

"I actually don't know. I think it's something about women authors."

"I do like Ronaldo Skiffler," I said. He was renowned for his humorous but penetrating interviewing style and always had a great selection of diverse authors.

Cathy smiled at me and we made our way into the building. We secured ourselves a couple of overpriced wines in disposable glasscs (the waitress assured me they were made from biodegradable corn starch) and found our seats. The woman sitting next to me studied her program and I looked over her shoulder, trying to glean a little about the evening before it began.

"Shit," Cathy whispered, just as I saw a photo of Hally's face in the program. *No, no, no.*

"May I borrow that?" I said, reaching over and gently lifting the program out of the woman's hand before she had a chance to answer.

"Women authors in a man's world?" I hissed at Cathy and handed the program back. "Hally is on this panel. What the actual fuck?"

"Oh my god, Gin, I'm sorry, I had no idea." Cathy had the grace to look contrite. "Do you want to leave?"

"Yes." I made to get up just as Ronaldo Skiffler took to the stage in a blaze of flashing lights and applause more fitting for a Justin Bieber concert than a writers' event. Cathy tugged on my arm and pulled me back into my seat.

"We can't leave now," she whispered. "Sorry."

For the next hour and a half, I watched Hally interact with a panel of other female authors, eloquently discussing the trials and tribulations of navigating the heavily gendered landscape of publishing. She spoke with grace and acuity. She was witty and charming, and she totally held her own on a panel I would have considered her intellectual superior only a few short months before.

I had been such an idiot. I had underestimated her from the word go, choosing only to see the Lycra and the hashtags while I overlooked the business acumen and her inherent intelligence. I shrank low in my seat, heart squeezing tighter than a vacuum-sealed jam jar. So what if her first draft had been rubbish? Whose first-ever book wasn't a bit rubbish? It went with the territory. And coming from me, who had never even attempted to write a paragraph of my own, let alone an entire book, it was shameful.

I clutched at my shirt, fanning myself. It was hot in the room and I suddenly felt as if I couldn't get enough air. Standing abruptly, I stumbled my way down the row and out of the theatre, mumbling apologies. I didn't stop in the foyer, pushing open the doors and running to the car where I bent over, catching my breath in the cool night air. Foolish tears slipped down my cheeks and I brushed them away angrily.

"Gin," Cathy called, and I heard her hurried footsteps approaching the car.

I stood up quickly, taking a long slow breath.

She rubbed my shoulders. "Are you okay?"

"Fine. It was just hot in there." My voice sounded shaky and I was grateful that she didn't press me harder. We drove home in silence.

"Sorry about that," she said when we arrived at my apartment. "Unlucky."

I opened a bottle of wine and found some cheese and crackers. "Not your fault. I'm glad I saw that. She was pretty great, don't you think?"

"She was."

"You were right about her, Cathy, and about the book. I was such a stuck-up snob. It's going to be a success and she'll probably have a crack at another one and Red Stone will benefit from the relationship. If only I haven't messed it up for you all."

Cathy smiled at me kindly. "Let's just get the first one out, hey?"

We nibbled on the crackers and drank our wine, my thoughts consumed by images of Hally on the stage, her engaging smile, her easy laughter, her effortless beauty.

"You really fell for her," Cathy said, interrupting my thoughts.

"Who? What? I don't know what you're talking about." I sat up, gulping at my wine.

"Hally, I can tell. You're all moony. I mean, you've been out of sorts and all in a funk ever since Wine and Spines, and I knew you liked her, but I just thought you were embarrassed by what happened. I didn't realise you had fallen in love with her."

I inhaled sharply, wine catching in my throat as I coughed and spluttered in protest. "I'm not. I just..."

"You just what?"

"I think," I said slowly, recovering my equilibrium, "I think I miss her or something."

"Or something?"

"No, I do, I miss her. We spent quite a lot of time together over this book. Sure, there was the kissing, and the sex, and that was pretty incredible, but we also talked a lot and she was easy to talk to. We had fun. I don't know." I waved my hand in front of my face. "It's all so unexpected and unlike me. Maybe I'm having a midlife crisis."

"It's too early for that, I'm afraid."

"Menopause?"

"Again, not for at least another ten to twenty years."

"Christ."

"I honestly think you might be in love with her, Gin."

I gazed at Cathy with baleful eyes. "How can I be? She won't even talk to me."

"Unfortunately it doesn't work like that. Just because she won't talk to you doesn't mean you're not in love with her."

"She's so not my type."

"And people can only fall in love with people who are exactly their type. That's totally the way it works."

I blew out a sigh and ran a hand through my hair. "Your sarcasm is not appreciated. Let's talk about something else. How's your mum?"

Cathy gave me a searching look and then seemed to give up. "She's good. I'm heading back to Sydney next week to check on her properly but Rachel seems much calmer on the phone. She said Mum seems to be really settled at the moment which is great. She goes up and down I guess."

"I'm sure. What are you going to Sydney for this time?"

Cathy blushed and looked away. With her dark skin I could almost have missed it but I knew her too well.

"Cathy," I exclaimed, my interest piqued. I nudged her with my foot. "Spill it."

"I've got a date," she said finally, wrinkling up her nose.

"Who with? How have you managed to get to date stage with someone that I haven't even heard about yet?" I asked, peeved.

"Actually, she's one of the community nurses who was doing home visits for Mum. We struck up a friendship and after she stopped coming I tracked her down on Facebook and we started chatting."

"But that was months ago, how are you only telling me about this now?"

"It was nothing, at least, I didn't think it was anything. But last time I was in Sydney we caught up for a coffee and—"

"You caught up for a coffee!"

"Yes, Gin, please calm down."

"I just can't believe you didn't tell me."

"You had a lot going on, I didn't want to distract you."

"Cathy, these are the kinds of distractions I need," I instructed her. "From now on, do not keep any of these distractions away from me please."

"Fine." She laughed and looked embarrassed. "Anyway, she's really cute and I'm a bit nervous."

"Name?"

"Darleen."

"Ooo, nice name."

"I know right."

"Makes me think of—"

"*Rosanne*," we both said simultaneously.

"So," I said, "where are you and the delightful Darleen going on your date?"

"We're going to see a film at the Openair Cinemas."

I sighed. "That sounds perfect. Hopefully it's a scary film so you can snuggle."

Cathy laughed and whacked me on the arm and then said, "Hopefully. I'll keep you posted."

"I'll be checking my phone every five minutes, so make sure you do."

"Hey, I know we said we'd change the subject, but are you going to come up to Sydney for Hally's launch?"

I pursed my lips. It was expected that I would attend both the Melbourne and the Sydney launches and I would need to decide soon, with the events only a month away. "Not sure yet."

"Just come. You're going to have to see her at the Melbourne launch and it will be good for you to be seen doing the right thing by the Sydney office."

"I thought that whole probation thing was done and dusted."

"It is, but it never hurts to keep trying to make a good impression."

"Can you book me a room at that nice hotel where you stay?"

Cathy grinned. "I can."

"What about the cats? I can't leave them."

"Thomas and Kevin can feed the cats. It's not like they never have before."

"True. I'll think about it."

"Don't think too hard. It will be good for you to get away. We'll have fun. We can go to Bondi Beach and get that frozen yoghurt you like."

I narrowed my eyes at her. "Will I get to meet Darleen?"

"Gin! We've only had one date. Who knows if she even likes me?"

"As if she doesn't. What's not to like?"

"I don't know." Cathy shrugged. "It feels like it all gets so much harder as you get older. In my twenties we would have just fallen into bed and had it all sorted by morning. Now there's so much emotional baggage floating around, it's way harder."

"You don't have to tell me," I said, nodding vigorously. "I have no intention of getting back into the dating world."

"Oh please, as if you're giving up for life. This is just a little hiccup."

"More like acid reflux."

CHAPTER NINETEEN

Marketing had arranged the Melbourne launch of Hally Arlow's *True Likes* at Mon Ami, one of Melbourne's bespoke penthouse bars. The floor-to-ceiling windows showed off panoramic views of the city, the buildings lit up like thousands of Christmas trees. Waiters and waitresses in soft denim overalls swung through the crowd with trays of champagne saucers and intricate little canapés that made me glad I had eaten earlier.

The room was packed, but there appeared to be an invisible line down the middle. On one side there were the excessively muscular fit people who had to be related to SweatHard, and on the other were the bookish types, the bookshop proprietors, reviewers, bloggers, writers, and of course most of the Red Stone crew. I wondered how much champagne it would take for the two sides to mingle.

A makeshift stage had been set up opposite the bar at the end of the room, with a banner showcasing the front cover of Hally's book. Copies of the book were arranged artfully next to the microphone.

Cathy stepped up onto the stage and tapped the microphone. "May I have your attention please?" For such a large group, the room quietened down surprisingly quickly. "This evening's celebrations are being held on the lands of the Wurundjeri People and I wish to acknowledge them as Traditional Owners. I would also like to pay my respects to their Elders, past and present, and Aboriginal Elders of other communities who may be here today.

We're so excited to have you all here tonight to celebrate the launch of Hally Arlow's book *True Likes.*" The crowd applauded enthusiastically and Cathy went on to describe how much all the Red Stone staff had enjoyed working on the book with Hally and how she just knew it was going to be big hit. "And now I'd like you to join me in welcoming Hally Arlow to the microphone."

The crowd twisted and turned to catch a glimpse of Hally, applauding and cat-calling as she made her way to the stage. She kissed Cathy on the cheek and stood in front of the microphone, smiling widely at the crowd. She was the definition of glitter and glamour, in a floor-length, gold-coloured suit with an open-necked white shirt that plunged at the neckline, displaying the fine cut of her collarbone. She wore her hair out, straightened and tucked discreetly behind her ears. She was so electric, a sexy bolt of lightning. I gripped my drink tightly, forcing myself not to fall down in a flat-out swoon.

"Thank you all so much for coming," she started and the muscled side of the audience broke into more raucous applause. The bookish side politely followed. When the applause died down, Hally described what had inspired her to write the book, how she hoped to show others coming after her, especially young women, that their dreams too could be realised through the combination of hard work and of course, a good dose of sweat. More cheering. She thanked her family, her SweatHard family, her social-media communities, the people at Red Stone, and then, her eyes found mine and she was thanking me while my heart tried to break out of my chest. I raised my glass to her and took a quick sip, hoping my hands weren't shaking.

"Man, she is so hot," a voice whispered in my ear and I jumped as Thomas slid an arm around my waist. I had invited him and Kevin as my wingmen, and because I knew they would love the evening. "You were so lucky to work with her."

"Mmm," I murmured, thinking he didn't quite know the half of it.

With her speech over, Hally raised her glass and toasted, to family and friends, new and old and then made the whole room pose for a selfie with her, which I imagined she would upload straight to Instagram or something. In a fit of insanity I had signed up to the service one night, and spent hours feeling like a voycur as I scrolled through photos of Hally and peered into her life. In the morning I cursed myself, knowing I had uncorked a genie that would be extremely hard to coax back into the bottle. I now had an absolutely strict policy of not checking Hally's page for updates, which I regularly broke. From what I knew of her, I was aware that the page was carefully curated, but it still felt like I had crossed a line, knowing for example that she had had tacos for dinner with friends at Jiminy Crickets.

I did get a window into how she inspired others. Her photos attracted hundreds of comments, many from shared stories of how they were achieving their fitness goals through her gyms, changing their lifestyles because of her health messages, starting their own businesses because of her influence. She clearly knew how to resonate and connect with people and she championed quite a few philanthropic causes.

"When is she coming over next?" Kevin asked, joining me on the other side. We watched as Hally left the stage and the music started up again.

"Yes, this time we expect to meet her properly," Thomas said, elbowing me. "None of this whizzing past in the hallway. We need to be more prepared."

"Sorry, guys, but that was a one-time thing. We barely see each other anymore."

"Really?" Thomas looked puzzled. "You seemed so friendly with each other."

"Just business," I breezed. "Another drink?"

"I'll get them," Kevin offered and sashayed off in search of a waiter.

"So, you're not even friends?" Thomas asked.

"Not really. Not, not friends," I clarified, "just not anything really."

"So why did she look at you like that?"

My head snapped around and I glared at him. "Like what?"

"When she looked over at you, during her speech, she went all funny, like she checked out of the building for a moment or something."

"She didn't."

"She totally did."

"Well, I don't know, maybe she was thinking about something else. Ah, drinks."

Kevin handed them out.

"Well, I still want to meet Hally properly," he said. "Can you introduce us?"

I thought about it. It would be rude of me not to say something to Hally at the launch. It was my duty to go and congratulate her. If I took the boys with me it could potentially be less awkward. "Sure," I said. "Let's go find her and then we can head off."

"What?" Kevin pouted. "I don't want to leave. The party's only just warming up."

"Yeah," Thomas agreed, "we should stay longer."

"You guys stay. I think I'll head off. It's all a bit much for me and I've still got another one to get through in Sydney."

"Party pooper," Kevin said.

"Look, she's over there." Thomas was craning his neck and pointing through the crowd toward the stage area. Hally hadn't made it far through the room.

Hoping I wouldn't make a fool of myself I followed behind the boys as they shimmied their way through the crowd. It would be fine. I'd congratulate her on a job well done, introduce her to Kevin and Thomas, then hightail it out of there, and no one would probably be more relieved to see me go than Hally.

We waited patiently while group after group kissed Hally and told her how fabulous everything was. When we were finally propelled to the front of the line I found all the things I had mentally rehearsed had slipped clean out of my brain and I was left standing there like a nervous teenager, rubbing my hands on my pants. Up close, the dazzle of her suit, the excitement in her eyes, her wide smile stung in a way I wasn't prepared for.

Thomas elbowed me hard, connecting with my ribs. I jumped but it was the push I needed to find my tongue. "What a great night, Hally, you must be so happy. I just wanted to introduce you, well, reintroduce you I suppose because you met that time, I don't know if you remember—"

"Thomas and Kevin," Kevin said hurriedly, leaning in to take Hally's hand. He pressed it fervently to his own heart. "We're such big fans, Ms. Arlow. We absolutely love everything you do. We adored your post about that group building washrooms in African primary schools. We donated and so have all our friends. Do you remember us from the hallway? We're Gin's neighbours."

"I'm so glad," Hally said, laughing and letting Kevin hang on to her hand. "And yes, of course I remember you both. Thank you for coming tonight."

"We wouldn't have missed it for the world," Thomas said, nudging me out of the way to take her other hand. "We're also SweatHard members."

I raised my eyebrows. I had known they were gym junkies but I didn't realise they were team-Hally.

"I'm surprised you haven't dragged Gin along with you," Hally said.

Thomas threw back his head and barked out a laugh. "Not this one. She wouldn't be seen dead in a gym."

"Is that right?"

"Oh yes, she'd rather cut off her own arms than lift weights."

Hally caught my eye and winked, the hint of a smile playing around her lips. Words deserted me. Had she really forgiven me? Was she ready to be friends? Or was this all part of the Hally Arlow public persona that everyone was so in love with? It would make sense. She would hardly be likely to give me the cold shoulder on a night like tonight, when all eyes were on her and she wanted to sparkle and shine.

"It's lovely to meet you guys," Hally was saying as I came back down to earth. "Will I see you in Sydney, Gin?"

"Yes of course, wouldn't miss it."

And with that Hally gently extracted herself and turned to the next group of waiting well-wishers, immediately swallowed up by the crowd.

"Well, that's it then," I said. "Home time."

"Gin," Thomas said, narrowing his eyes as he stared at me. "What the hell was that?"

"What was what?" I asked, genuinely baffled.

"That *look* she gave you. That flirty little wink. That's the second weird look she's given you tonight. Is something happening between you two?"

"No," I replied, a little too emphatically. "There is nothing happening between us."

"If I didn't know better, I'd say she's into you, but that can't be right." Kevin announced, grabbing our hands and pulling us toward the bar. "People like Hally don't go for people like Gin."

"You mean people like Gin don't go for people like Hally," Thomas corrected.

Their words pained me more than either of them could ever know. "Sorry, guys, I'm really the worst kind of party pooper but I'm absolutely exhausted so I'm going to pass on this one." I just couldn't bear to spend an evening watching Hally light up the room and everyone in it, knowing how badly I had messed up whatever chance we had of a friendship, let alone anything more. "I'll see you guys back home later. If it's not too late we could sneak in a game of Scrabble?"

"Oh lord." Kevin shook his head. "There is genuinely something wrong with you, Ginny-poo. You're passing up free drinks and a fun party for your PJs and a possible late-night game of Scrabble. Have you seen your psychologist lately?"

Asimov seemed to be asking me the same question. My apartment was overly quiet and I flopped on the couch, gazing into space. What are you doing here? Asimov's eyes asked me, with a reproachful stare.

"I don't know," I replied. "But don't you start. I'm tired, okay?"

He held my gaze for a moment and then stretched out his hind leg and licked it vigorously. Conversation over.

I was tired, in that inside-your-bones way, but my head had Hally in her gold suit, winking at me, playing on a loop.

I rubbed my temples and closed my eyes, sinking back into the couch. My head was doing a number on me and I really needed to be done with all of this. I just had to get through the Sydney launch next weekend and I would be free of the whole thing. Hally would do her publicity tour, I would knuckle down to work and forget she ever existed (after I deleted my Instagram account) and life would go back to normal. And that was a good thing. I was pretty sure that would be a good thing.

I woke up on the couch sometime later with a bleary start. My watch read two a.m. Ug. My head felt woolly from the champagne and my mouth was dry. I had a crick in my neck and the lights were all still on. I stumbled to the kitchen and gulped back a glass of water, resolving to turn over a new leaf. It was time to clean up my act. My phone chimed and I rummaged through my bag for it. I hoped it wasn't Kevin and Thomas hitting me up for that Scrabble game.

My heart flip-flopped. It was from Hally. *Sorry I didn't get to see you to say goodbye. Thanks for all you did to make this happen.*

I stared at the message, wondering what it meant. Was it just the regular, thanks-so-much-for-being-my-editor-and-wasn't-that-a great-launch message? I had never received a text message like that from any of my authors so that seemed unlikely.

I turned off all the lights, took the phone to bed and stared at the message, cradling it in my hand as I lay on my side.

Congratulations, I eventually wrote. *You deserve all the accolades. It was a great night.*

Three little dots under my message showed me that she was writing back. I held my breath and released it with a hiss when her message arrived. It simply read, *Good night, Gin. Sleep tight.*

I hugged the phone to my chest. Surely that meant she had forgiven me. This was not a display for her adoring fans. This was just her and me, texting late at night. Asimov jumped on the bed and I showed him the screen. He seemed more interested in tucking himself into the crevice at the back of my knees.

You too. Good night, Hally. I typed.

I waited, in case she was going to type more, and eventually fell asleep with the phone in my hand.

CHAPTER TWENTY

Sydney was hectic. The airport was crowded. The baggage handlers were on strike and angry mobs gathered around the luggage carousels to wait as whoever had been coerced into doing the job sent one bag down the chute every twenty minutes or so. I happily dodged the line, my carry-on bag slung over my shoulder and made for the taxi line.

I gave the taxi driver the address of the hotel and sat back, leaning my head against the leather seat as I watched the Sydney suburbs crawl past. The Friday-afternoon traffic was thick and my driver beeped his horn angrily at every chance, but my mood stayed up. I was strangely excited for this trip. Cathy and I would go to the launch tonight and I would have tomorrow free to stroll along the cliff tops by the beach at Bronte, one of my favourite walks.

Then on Saturday night Cathy had arranged for us to have dinner with Darleen, who had been featuring heavily in our conversations of late. Cathy was smitten and I was keen to establish that Darleen was too. I planned an early morning breakfast at Bondi markets on Sunday morning before my afternoon flight home. All in all it was shaping up to be a fun weekend.

The skip in my step barely faltered when I entered the hotel lobby and found myself standing side by side with Hally, who was also checking in.

"Here's a coincidence," I said.

"Probably not so much," she replied. "Cathy organised it. I assume she did for you too."

"That she did."

We were called up to the reception desk by separate clerks and I waited for her to finish checking in when I was done.

"Which floor are you?" I asked, showing her my key-card folder. "I'm on six."

"I'm ten."

We walked together to the lift. As we waited, I read about the jazz band on the rooftop that evening, and daily aqua yoga at seven a.m. sharp.

"Apparently breakfast is spectacular here. I love a buffet breakfast, do you?"

Hally smiled. "Always thinking with your stomach."

I dipped my head. "True. But I just love the little tubs of yoghurt, and the fruit and the eggs! Why are buffet eggs so much better than normal breakfast eggs? I don't usually even like scrambled eggs but give me buffet scrambled eggs and I'm all yours."

She raised her eyebrows at me and I felt myself blush. I tapped a tattoo on the lift button, sinking into silence.

I got out at six and told her I'd see her later at the launch party.

She stopped the doors closing with her foot. Did I want to share a taxi with her to the venue? Yes, I really did.

This time she was in a red dress with gold cuffs, and I wanted to tell her she looked like Wonder Woman but I didn't know if she'd find that insulting. To me it was a good thing. I, on the other hand, was wearing the same black pants I had worn to the

Melbourne launch the previous weekend, but this time I had swapped my go-to white shirt out for a silver satin shirt, in an attempt to avoid being mistaken for a waiter. If the Melbourne launch was anything to go by, the wait staff would be dressed far more glamorously than me.

"You look lovely," she said as I joined her in the foyer.

I barely knew how to answer her. It was a generous comment.

"As do you," I said finally.

I followed her into a cab and we sat side by side in the back seat for the short ride. Tonight's affair would be just as large, just as glamorous, and I wondered what it would be like to create such a stir everywhere you went.

"How long are you in Sydney?" I asked.

"A week. I've got a bunch of gyms to catch up with and I'm guest lecturer on a panel for business students at Sydney University."

"Wow, that's great."

"You're surprised?"

I shook my head. Clearly, I had underestimated her too many times in the past. "Not surprised, impressed. Sydney Uni's business school has an excellent reputation."

We lapsed into silence, both of us taking in the sights as the taxi edged its way up a bumper-to-bumper Oxford Street. It seemed like Sydney was already in party mode, big groups spilling out on the streets, snatches of laughter and high energy filtering into the cab.

Hally checked her watch. "We could probably just walk it from here. Are you happy to?"

"Absolutely."

After a small argument over who would pay the driver, I convinced her that it was the publisher's job to cover this cost and handed over my work credit card. We jumped out of the cab, finding ourselves amongst the throngs of restaurant and party goers on the busy street.

"It's up this way," Hally said, looking at the map on her phone. In line with Hally's brand, Marketing had secured another hip and chichi venue for the evening's festivities.

It was a warm night and I rolled up my sleeves, wondering if Hally was feeling the heat in her ensemble. Heads turned as we walked, eyes caught on Hally, some in recognition, others with just plain admiration.

"My sister and nephews will be here tonight," Hally said. "They flew up from Melbourne this morning for a day of sightseeing."

"That's exciting. Are they staying the whole weekend?"

"Unfortunately not. The boys have their basketball comp on Saturday afternoon so they're flying out straight after breakfast tomorrow morning. I was hoping to get up here earlier today and spend the day all together but I couldn't manage it. Work is flat out at the moment."

"That's a shame. Still, it's great they could be here tonight."

"I know. My sister had a big work do and couldn't make it to the Melbourne launch so she decided to bring the boys up to Sydney as a special treat and come to this one instead. It'll be good to have family here, you know?"

I didn't really know. I couldn't imagine what it would be like if my dad came to one of my work functions. I tried to picture him in a shirt and tie, champagne glass in hand, and came up empty. He just wasn't that kind of guy. But I was glad Hally was chatting with me so easily and I didn't want to do anything to derail our conversation, so I agreed with her.

The venue was already filling up when we arrived. The now-familiar mix of Red Stone staff, gym goers and literary types mingled, perhaps a little more easily in this room than in Melbourne. I decided that the literary types looked fitter, and the gym junkies looked a little more intellectual. Perhaps the divisions weren't quite so apparent up here.

Two boys, who looked to me to be somewhere just under ten, ran up to Hally, trailed by a woman who looked so much like Hally I nearly did a double take.

"There's an ice sculpture here," the older of the boys exclaimed.

"And you can get an actual drink from it," the other one shouted, excitement shining in his eyes. The good-looks gene was ridiculously strong in this family. Both boys had wide grins, tousled dark hair and the same arresting, amber eyes as Hally. Her sister's eyes were brown, and up close I could see she was just as beautiful in her own right.

"Hush," Delphi said, admonishing them. "Remember I said we have to behave ourselves here."

"Boys, where's my squeeze?" Hally asked, throwing her arms open and they tumbled in. She hugged them tightly and made a little growling sound, releasing them as they squealed. She leaned over and kissed her sister on the cheek.

"Gin, this is Delphi, Cameron and Scott," Hally said, pointed a finger at each as she made the introduction. "Guys, this is my editor, Gin."

"Hi," Delphi said, her smile not quite reaching her eyes, making me wonder what Hally might have told her about me. The boys considered me briefly and I reached out my hand to shake theirs, which they seemed to enjoy, pumping my hand enthusiastically. Whatever message was out there about Editor Gin thankfully didn't seem to have trickled down to the kids.

"It's so great that you could all make it," I said, trying for warm and sincere, but the music stopped as I spoke and my voice was too loud. Delphi took a step back and gave me another cool smile.

She hated me. I could tell. I looked to Hally but she was concentrating on the boys and didn't appear to notice any awkwardness. Feeling sweaty I smoothed my hands on my pants. "Well, if any of you need anything, just sing out. I'll go and check in with Cathy."

I backed away and left them to their family catch-up, wishing I could find some place to hide away. Hally might have forgiven me, to ease our working relationship, but I suddenly realised it didn't amount to us being friends, and her family had no need to follow in her footsteps. I looked for Cathy, feeling gauche amongst the sophisticated and good-looking Sydney crowd. I was rarely involved in glitzy events like this—they just weren't part of my usual brief. I tended to end up at university bookshops or museums and botanical gardens, and I could quickly feel my earlier jaunty mood evaporating.

I spied Cathy by the book arrangement at the back of the room. She was deep in conversation with Red Stone's head of HR and I immediately stopped in my tracks, not keen to renew that connection. Since my probation I had kept my head down, happy not to attract any further heat. The little stand-up tables were full and the bar crowded. I couldn't decide where to put myself.

I eventually took refuge in the toilets, sitting on the seat in a cubicle until I noticed the music had stopped and I could hear the speeches, at which point I snuck back out to insert myself in the crowd. The sentiment was similar to the previous week's launch, but this time I slipped away at the end without saying goodbye.

Back in my hotel room, I took off my shoes, enjoying the feel of the plush carpet on my bare feet, and sat on the floor with my laptop. I surfed BestReads and uploaded some reviews I had written on the plane. I got into an argument with Easy_Reads_ Jeff about the merits of the latest anthology of mythological Norse gods, and enjoyed the cascade of comments that poured in as others on the site joined in.

When I closed my laptop it was after midnight and I felt better, the awkwardness of the party mostly forgotten. The cool look in Delphi's eyes still haunted me, but I pushed it out of my mind as I crawled between the starched hotel sheets and snapped off the light. It wasn't as if I would have to see her again.

I woke up early, keen to get a head start on the hotel's buffet breakfast spread. After a quick shower and a scroll through the comments that had come in to my BestReads feed overnight, I headed down to the dining room.

I'm not usually an overeater, but I make an exception for buffet breakfast. I took a little of everything, my plate a smorgasbord of scrambled eggs, Asian noodles, yoghurt and fruit, Indian rice, pancake with chocolate sauce, fried tomatoes, tiny croissants and toast. Balancing my plate in one hand and a coffee in the other I scanned the room for a free table, almost dropping the lot when my eyes met Hally's at a table across the room. She smiled politely and waved me over, indicating the free seat at her table, where she was sitting with her sister and nephews. Shit. It was too late to pretend I hadn't seen her, and despite the early hour, the room was already full, with few available alternatives. It was either sit with strangers or sit with Hally.

I smiled back and crossed the room, heart hammering in my throat.

"Morning," I said, hovering near the table.

"Morning," Hally replied, eyeing my plate. "Have a seat."

"Thanks." They were seated at a large round table with a spare seat next to Delphi. I sat down quickly.

"Wow, look at your plate," one of the boys exclaimed. "What a guts."

"Cameron!" Delphi admonished. "Don't be rude."

"No, it's okay," I waved a hand. "I know it's probably overkill but I don't get to do this very often."

"Neither do we," said the older of the two boys who I remembered was called Scott. "Mum, can we go back for seconds?"

Delphi looked over at my plate again and looked unconvinced.

"Please, Mum," Cameron wheedled.

"Go on, Delph. It's a special treat," Hally said.

"I suppose. Go easy though. We've got to leave for the plane soon and I don't want you to upset your stomachs."

"Yes." Cameron pumped his fist in the air and shot out of his chair. "More pancakes."

"I want those pastry things," Scott said, following him away from the table.

"Gin has a healthy appetite," Hally said to Delphi, who was still eyeing my plate suspiciously.

"You must be lucky," Delphi said.

I really wanted to tuck in, my mouth salivating copiously, but I said, "Why's that?"

"To be able to eat like that and look like you do."

I looked down at myself. "I guess so."

Unable to wait any longer I spread the eggs across the toast and took a bite, almost groaning with pleasure. I was glad I had booked in for two nights. I would be sure to get down to breakfast much earlier on Sunday to enjoy my meal in peace and quiet.

The boys arrived back with their plates of seconds and tucked into pancakes and pastries.

"So good," Cameron said, through a mouthful.

"Drink lots of water," Delphi instructed them. "Otherwise the sugar might make you feel sick on the plane."

"Cameron still gets a bit motion sick," Hally explained, tousling the boy's hair as he opened his mouth wider than I would have thought possible and shovelled in a mouthful of pancake.

"Yes, and who will have to deal with it on a plane by themselves if something happens?"

"Mum, I'll be fine. Don't worry."

Delphi huffed and folded her napkin, placing it carefully on her plate. I continued my work around my plate, moving on to the pancake. Cameron was right, they really were delicious. Tomorrow I would possibly start with the pancakes.

Hally sipped her coffee, her own plate empty. "What did you have?" I asked her.

"Fruit and yoghurt."

I nodded. The yoghurt was good. A perfect blend of tart and creamy, but it wouldn't have been enough for me. Somehow, staying in a hotel gave me the appetite of a body builder.

"Okay, boys, you need to finish up now," Delphi said. "We need to get moving if we're going to make it to the plane on time."

I watched the boys scoop up their last mouthfuls, Scott brushing his hand across his mouth to wipe away crumbs.

"Scott, napkin, please," Delphi reminded him.

Scott looked around him and Hally handed him a fresh napkin from the centre of the table. "Don't say I never give you anything," she said, with a grin.

I watched as the family hugged each other, Hally whispering something to Cameron that made him giggle. "I'll walk you out."

The boys waved at me and Delphi gave me a polite nod and I watched them wind their way through the dining room, wheely bags in tow. Hally had left her purse and phone on the table so I assumed she was coming back. I dipped my croissant into my coffee and focused my attention back on my breakfast, glad to be free from the critical eye of Delphi.

"Will you go back for seconds?" Hally asked, sliding into the chair Delphi had vacated and reaching across the table for her coffee.

"Would you think badly of me?"

"Not that it matters what I think of you, but no, why would I?"

"It's probably not a very healthy choice. You're all about the healthy eating. Without pointing out the obvious, you just walked past all those pancakes and had yoghurt for breakfast."

"That's my choice. I don't judge you for yours."

I glanced at her thoughtfully, as I finished the last of my scrambled eggs. Did she really believe that? I had assumed she would think everyone should approach life in the same way she did, but now that I thought about it, she had never behaved that way.

"What?" she asked. I could see she was wearing a little mascara, but apart from that she was makeup-free, her skin fresh and smooth, her eyes bright.

"I'm surprised you think that way. I would have thought you couldn't help but judge people a bit more, given the industry you're in."

"Since when did judging people ever help them change their lives?"

"Touché."

Hally toyed with her coffee cup. "So, how are you planning to spend your day in Sydney?"

I told her about my plan to do the Bondi to Bronte coastal walk, waxing lyrical about the picturesque views and the possibility of whale sighting. "We're right at the end of their seasonal migration back down to Antarctica, but I'm still hopeful. There is a fantastic view from the cemetery at Bronte, with some really old graves dating back to the eighteen hundreds. It's incredible really, almost like a history book of colonial Australia."

"Sounds amazing."

I felt I had been rambling and quickly said, "And what are you up to today? Business meetings?"

"Actually, I don't have plans today. I have the whole weekend off. I don't start my meetings until Monday morning."

"Oh wow."

We lapsed into silence.

"That walk sounds interesting," Hally said, and finished off her coffee.

I didn't want our breakfast to be over. If she left now, I had no idea when I'd see her again. There were no more events. She'd do a bunch of book signings, but Marketing would organise that. "Would you like to come with me?" The words popped out of my mouth unfettered.

Hally put her cup down and studied me.

"I mean, no pressure, just a thought, don't worry if you're not up for it—"

"Actually, I think a walk would be great," Hally said.

"Well, all right then."

CHAPTER TWENTY-ONE

We caught a cab down to Bondi Beach. It was a warm morning and the beach was already thick with locals and tourists, indistinguishable from each other, playing paddle ball and swimming. The lifesavers were on guard and the waves were rolling in, blue as blue. I had done the walk before and led Hally away to the beginning of the walkway that topped the large basalt rocks on the south side of the little bay.

"We start here," I said, and we stopped for a moment to lean on the railing and admire the view. The ocean was spread out before us, a blanket of deep cobalt, crests of waves breaking out to sea catching the sun. As she gazed out to sea I snuck a glance at Hally, admiring the shape of her long brown arms on the rail. She looked a million bucks in a pair of simple denim cut-offs and a loose white tank top.

"I love the ocean," Hally said. I couldn't see her eyes behind her sunglasses, but her voice sounded almost wistful. "I don't do enough of this kind of thing."

"Neither do I."

Hally turned to me. "Thanks for letting me come along today. I think I really need this."

"It's my pleasure. Shall we get started?"

We set off along the boardwalk, Hally taking the initial steep ascent with barely a break in her stride while I huffed and puffed next to her.

"I suppose there's something to be said for keeping up a general level of fitness," I said, trying not to sound like I was panting. Thankfully the pathway evened out.

Hally smiled at me. "You're not doing too badly. All that walking to work must be good for your health."

"I suppose it is."

"Oh my gosh, look at those surfers all the way out there." Hally pointed to a spot far below us where a small group of little black dots bobbed on large white surfboards. "They must be so brave." She stopped to snap a picture and I waited while she fiddled about with her phone for a minute and then continued walking.

"Do you ever find it weird that people know what you're doing all the time?"

"Not really, it's sort of par for the course these days. Your phone is pretty much recording your every move, you get tracked every time you go online so that advertising agencies can serve you up targeted ads. I just figure you're either all in, or all out. Anyone who thinks they're able to maintain privacy whilst having an online presence is either working extremely hard or deluding themselves."

"That's kind of cynical isn't it?"

She concentrated on the path. "Why?"

"I don't know." I hesitated, choosing my words carefully so as not to come across as rude or pompous. "It seems like you're actually inviting people into your world. You're letting people look at your life and comment on it, to get to know you and the people in your life. You're actively forgoing your privacy and exposing yourself online. I do go online but I feel like I don't give much away about myself."

"What do you do online?" Hally asked, her voice curious. "What's your go-to? I remember you said you don't do Facebook or Instagram. Do you tweet?"

I had a momentary twinge of guilt thinking about the Instagram account I had created to check out Hally's pictures and then pushed it away. I hadn't touched it for months now. "I like to look at book reviews."

"Really? Do you ever write any yourself?"

I told her all about the BestReads site. "We can comment on each other's reviews and there's usually a healthy exchange."

"By healthy you mean…"

"Robust conversation."

"So, your thing is arguing with people about books online."

"I wouldn't say arguing."

"Disagreeing politely?"

I thought back to Easy_Reads_Jeff and his stinging reply to my latest review and the exchange that followed. "Sometimes it's not so polite."

"So, let me get this right. You go on to this site, tell everyone you've read this book and what you think about it, and then you all get into a mini fight about whether or not your views were valid?"

It sounded a little superficial when she put it like that, but I had to agree.

"And how is that different from Facebook or Instagram?"

"What do mean?" I asked, genuinely confused. "It's a whole different thing. We don't post photos or say anything about our lives."

"But you're putting your thoughts on there, and you're telling people how you feel about something, and you're engaging with an online community."

"True." The trail dipped sharply down the side of the cliff face and I held on to the rail as we trotted down the steps. "I suppose I hadn't thought of it like that."

At the bottom we found ourselves in the sheltered confines of Tamarama beach, surrounded by hollowed-out sandstone cliffs and brilliant white sand.

"Perhaps we're not that different after all," Hally said, kicking off her shoes. "Want to walk across the sand?"

I followed suit and I followed her across the beach, the sand warm beneath my toes. Was she right? Was my beloved BestReads just a form of Facebook for geeks?

"People just want to connect," Hally said, as we reached the end of the short beach and made our way back onto the path, brushing off our feet and slipping our shoes back on. "That's what all this online stuff is about. Surely you can see that? It doesn't matter which forum it is, people are just trying to find common ground to engage with each other and find deeper meaning in their lives."

"And you think online mediums can provide deeper meaning?"

"Sometimes, yes. Sometimes it's just a bit of light relief. Isn't it like that on BestReads?"

I had to admit that it was.

"It can obviously all get out of hand though," I said. "Any news on the creepy letter writer? Did they catch him yet?"

Her jaw tensed and she stopped walking, turning to look out to the ocean. "Not yet. This one is really disturbing. I've had plenty of weird letters and strange gifts but I think this is the first time I've felt truly threatened. He left a dead bird on my doorstep the other day. A magpie, broken neck."

"Oh my god, Hally, that's awful. How did you know it was from him?"

She blew out a breath. "There was a note with the bird."

"And the police have no idea who he is?"

"They said they're following some leads but so far..." She shrugged. "Nothing."

We both looked out at the ocean for a moment in silence, watching the frothy white tips of waves break far out in the distance.

"Hey," Hally broke in, her tone suddenly light. "Where's all the ice cream? I thought for sure we'd get an ice cream on this walk."

I laughed. "The next beach is Bronte. I'm sure we can get something there."

"Good. All this deep and meaningful conversation is making me crave ice cream."

Thankfully there was an ice cream van at Bronte and we both ordered gelati.

"Chocolate," we both said at the same time and shared a grin.

"If we walk on a bit further we'll get to the cemetery," I said, catching a drip of my ice cream with my tongue. "This is officially Bronte Beach so we can stop here, but I'd love to show you this cemetery. It's pretty incredible."

We walked on, sticking to less-loaded topics as if by unstated mutual agreement. Hally told me about her nephews, regaling me with funny stories of their quirky ways. I told her about my new projects at Red Stone.

At the cemetery we stopped to take in the view. In front of us, the ocean took up one hundred and eighty degrees, a great open vista of blue water and sky. Behind us, nestled into the cliff, were hundreds of old ornate crumbling headstones.

"Holy shit," Hally breathed. "This is incredible. What a view."

"I know. It's supposed to be one of the most beautiful cemeteries in the world. Want to go look around?"

We spent the next hour rambling through the graves. I showed her the grave of the great Aussie bush poet, Henry Lawson. She snapped pictures and I enjoyed just watching her.

It was almost lunch time when we settled under a tree to rest our weary legs, overlooking the ocean far below. Hally lay down on the grass next to me, tucking her arms under her head, while I sat cross-legged and gazed out at the sea.

"The sky is such an incredible colour today. There are literally no clouds," she said, sighing deeply. "I'm just going to close my eyes for a moment, it's so peaceful here. Wake me if I fall asleep, okay?"

"You can rest your head on my legs if you like? Might be more comfortable."

"Thanks." Hally wriggled around until her head was in my lap.

"Better?"

"Better."

With her eyes closed I was free to study her face. Her eyes were framed by soft brown lashes and perfectly sculpted eyebrows. Her forehead was wide and clear, her nose perfectly straight. Her lips, rose-coloured and plump, curved upward with the hint of a smile. It was all I could do not to reach out and touch the lines of her face, follow the contour of her cheek bones, fix the lock of hair that fell across her forehead.

"See any whales yet?" she murmured, her voice husky, eyes still closed.

"Not yet."

"Let me know if you do."

"I will."

"Gin?"

"Yes?"

Her eyes fluttered open and held mine in her lazy gaze. "This is nice."

My breath stilled. "Yeah. It is."

She closed her eyes again and this time I couldn't resist, reaching out and running a finger along the edge of her hairline, gently smoothing the curl away from her forehead.

She sighed quietly.

I let myself trace the shape of her ear and brushed the back of my fingers against her cheek. She turned her head slightly and her lips were on my hand. I ran my knuckles over her lips which parted slightly, her breath warm on my hand. My thumb traced the line of her bottom lip and grazed the tip of her tongue. I could see the pulse in her neck, my own heartbeat thudding crazily in my ears.

Eyes still closed, Hally reached up and took my hand in hers, pressing it quickly to her lips where she kissed it and then pressed it loosely against her chest, fingers intertwined. She ran her thumb over my own, desire skidding through my veins. Her chest rose and fell quickly.

I don't know for how long we sat like that. I forgot about the whales, watching her breath settle as she slipped into sleep. When she woke she looked momentarily startled, as if she hadn't expected to find herself here. She let go of my hand and sat up stretching. I tried to stretch out my own legs but found they were too numb to move. I groaned and lay back, trying to shake out my legs as pins and needles flooded my feet.

"Oh, ow," I cried, laughing and wriggling.

"What is it?" Her face creased with concern.

"Pins and needles."

She grinned and tapped the side of her forehead. "Sorry, my heavy head. Must be all these brains. Here, let me help you up."

She stood and looped her arms under my armpits, half lifting, half dragging me up to a stand. I stamped my feet and gradually the numbness receded as she held me up, her breasts pressed into my back.

"Thanks, I think I'm okay now."

She held me for a moment longer, then released me and I stumbled forward. Hally reached out and grabbed my arm and I laughed as I found my feet.

"Feels like you're always catching me, thank you. Sorry, I've got jelly legs."

"That's what friends are for, no? Think you can make it back or should we call a taxi?"

Friends. She had called us friends. Well, that was certainly better than being nothing at all to each other. "No way," I said, quickly. I didn't want our day to be over. It was quite clear within myself that I would drag myself back to Bondi on my elbows if it meant spending more time with Hally. "I'll be fine once we get going."

The way back seemed shorter somehow, and over too quickly. We stopped for lunch by the beach, sharing a couple of packets of egg and lettuce, and cheese and Vegemite sandwiches as we wriggled our toes in the sand.

"How are you feeling about the book?" I asked, as I tossed back the last crust and brushed the crumbs away.

"I'm pretty pleased with it, actually. When I think back to how it all began, to find the idea has become an actual living and breathing reality is super exciting."

"You worked hard."

She gave me a gentle nudge with her elbow. "We both did."

"We should probably celebrate."

"Isn't that what all these launches have been about?"

"I suppose so, but that's not really us celebrating is it. It's more about everyone else. I tell you what, I'm going out for dinner tonight with Cathy and her new girlfriend. Would you like to join us? We could toast to our awesome achievements. I'm sure they wouldn't mind humouring us."

Hally looked out to sea for a moment, her face an unreadable mask, and then turned back to me. "Wouldn't that be crashing your dinner?"

"Definitely not. If anyone's crashing dinner, it's me."

"And how's that?"

"It's Cathy's date and I was tagging along to meet the new girlfriend, Darleen," I said.

"I like that name."

"Same, it reminds me of—"

"*Rosanne*," she said, with a smile. "Well...I was going to order in and get stuck into a pile of work tonight."

I shook my head, thinking of all the nights over the last few months I had done the very same thing. "We can't have that. Red Stone prides itself on treating its authors well, so I simply must insist that you come."

"How about I see how much I get done this afternoon? If I can crank through some emails and finish my presentation for the business students I'd love to come."

"Great." I reached over and grabbed her hand, hauling her up from the sand. "My turn to help you up. Quicker we get you back, quicker you can get your work done."

We agreed that Hally would send me a message around five about coming to dinner. After seeing Hally back to the hotel I had headed out again to make the most of the day, taking myself off to explore Brett Whiteley's Studio in Surry Hills, stopping for a coffee and cake in a nearby Hungarian patisserie. On my way back I found myself staring in a shop window at a lovely, short-sleeved, maroon shirt, with epaulettes and little silver clamps on the end of the collar. My wardrobe had not had a new edition for so long, I decided to splash out, swinging the bag happily as I walked back to the hotel.

As five o'clock drew closer, I wouldn't say I paced around my hotel room so much as mooched, telling myself all the different reasons why she wouldn't come. She would be tied up with work, she would regret saying we were friends and back out of the engagement, she would find something far better and more exciting to do. I decided that the last one was the most likely. She was Hally Arlow for god's sake. She could do whatever, whenever with whoever. The last thing she would choose to do on a Saturday night in Sydney was go out for dinner with her publisher and the dorky editor who had repeatedly pissed her off.

But a few minutes before five my phone pinged. I snatched it up, clicking open a message from Hally which told me she would love to come to dinner, if I would just tell her what time and where.

We're meeting at six thirty at Suzos, I replied. *Share a cab?*
I'm not at the hotel so I'll meet you there.

Cathy was coming to dinner from her sister's place in Surry Hills, so I left early and hopped on a bus, happy to see some more of Sydney on my way. Cathy was already *in situ*, sitting with a slight, blond-haired woman at a table for four. Their heads were bent in closely together and they were holding hands over the table.

"Hi there," I said as I approached.

"Gin," Cathy said, waving me over.

As I sat down next to Cathy, she said, "Darleen, this is Gin, Gin, this Darleen."

"Pleased to meet you," I said, and Darleen laughed. It was a nice, warm laugh that instantly made me feel happy that Cathy had found her.

"And I am pleased to meet you too," Darleen said.

"I ordered a bottle of wine," Cathy said, reaching over and pouring me a glass of white.

"Thanks. I should also mention that Hally is coming."

Cathy stopped pouring and put the bottle down, fixing me with a wide-eyed stare. "Hally's coming here? To dinner? With us?"

"Yes," I tried to sound nonchalant. "Hope that's not a problem?"

"No, it's not a *problem*," Cathy said, mimicking my voice.

"Feels like I might be missing something here," Darleen said, cocking her head at us.

"Gin has invited one of our authors to dinner."

"And that's bad because?"

"Oh, it's not bad. It's not bad at all. It just so happens that Gin has an enormous crush on said author."

"Cathy!" I exclaimed.

"Say it isn't so," she challenged me.

"It isn't so," I said in my most pompous voice. "We have simply re-established a friendship and she was without plans for the evening so I invited her along. I may have had a crush on her in the past, but we are friends now and that's important to me, so don't you go ruining it with your innuendo."

Cathy rolled her eyes and took a sip of her wine. Darleen smiled and nodded at me approvingly. "You tell her," she said and I liked her even more. As irritating as Cathy was right now, I was also inordinately pleased for her. It had only been a few moments but I could already tell that Darleen was a good one.

"Whatever," Cathy muttered.

"Just please behave yourself when Hally arrives. Don't mention anything about crushes, please," I said.

"Me behave myself? *Me?* Because I'm the one who usually puts my foot in it and causes social disasters wherever I go."

"True," I said. "Let's just try to be...chill."

Cathy grinned. "Chill, hey? Sure, Gin. Let's all be chill."

I needn't have worried. Cathy, ever the consummate professional, was friendly and charming with Hally, and didn't tease me once. Darleen and Hally also seemed to get along well, and if our table was guilty of anything, it was possibly a little too much raucous laughter in the quiet of the restaurant.

"That was delicious," Hally said. "I've actually been wanting to try out this restaurant for ages. It just seems silly to go here by myself when I'm in town."

"Why would you have to go by yourself?" I asked. "Surely you've got plenty of people to go out with in Sydney."

"Not really, I don't know that many people here socially."

"But I've seen pictures of you in Sydney at parties with people..." I trailed off, realising I was outing myself as having stalked her online.

Hally arched an eyebrow. "Online?"

"Instagram," I mumbled, busying myself with a forkful of cheesecake.

"I thought you weren't on Instagram," Cathy said, spearing her own forkful.

I sat up straight. "I needed to get an account for research purposes."

"Of course you did," Hally said, but her tone said she didn't quite believe me. "Anyway, just because I go to parties here, doesn't mean I know anyone well enough to want to go out for dinner with them."

It struck me then that Hally, for all her social-media activity and high public profile was quite a private person. "Fair enough. Well, we're glad you could come to dinner with us then."

"That we are," Cathy agreed and raised her glass in a toast. "To friends," she said, pointedly looking at me. I felt myself blush hard and focused my attention on the glasses.

"To friends," we all said after her.

Hally and I shared a taxi back to the hotel after dinner. Cathy and Darleen were headed back to Darleen's house for some alone time.

"Plans for tomorrow?" I asked, as we waited for the lift, hopeful that Hally might like to join me on another day out while we were both here. "I was thinking of heading to Bondi markets in the morning, if you'd like to join me."

"I love those markets. Actually, that would be great. I need to get a birthday present for my mum."

My spirits immediately lifted. "Excellent, it's best to go early so we can avoid the crowds. We could have breakfast together and then go."

"Another breakfast of champions for you?"

I grinned, feeling sheepish. "Of course. Got to make the most of it."

"Did you know there's a rooftop bar at this hotel?" Hally asked as we stepped into the lift.

I said I did, looking for the buttons for both of our floors.

"Should we check it out? Maybe grab a nightcap?"

My fingers hovered over the buttons as I glanced at Hally. She was leaning against the wood panelling at the back of the lift, her arms crossed over her chest. "Tonight?" I asked, unsure of myself.

"Why not?"

Unable and unwilling to think of any reason why not, I simply asked, "Which floor?"

"I guess it's the top floor."

I scanned the numbers and pushed the highest number as the doors slid shut.

There was a piano player picking out jazzy sounds in the corner, and for the second time in a fortnight I found myself in a room with three-hundred-and-sixty-degree views of a city at night. With Hally. The bar wasn't crowded and we easily found a table near the window. Trying to find landmarks I recognised in the darkness I pressed my forehead against the glass while Hally went to get us drinks.

"There's the Harbour Bridge," I said when she came back to the table, two glasses with ice and a generous pour of amber liquid in each hand. She deposited the glasses on the table and leaned over my shoulder to peer through the glass. Her body pressed against mine and I could feel her breath against my ear. I willed myself to remain still but couldn't help leaning back a little against her.

"It's so pretty," she murmured and then withdrew to sit across the table from me.

"Cheers," I said, picking up a one of the tumblers and sniffing it.

She clinked her glass to mine and we both took a sip. I shuddered, whiskey blazing a hot trail down my throat.

"Hope you're okay with scotch," she said.

"I like it. I don't have it too often, but I enjoy it when I do."

She tipped her glass back and took another sip, exposing the soft lines of her throat. "You're so beautiful," I said, the words popping out of my mouth before I could help myself.

"And that's what you like about me," she said, matter-of-factly as she placed her glass carefully on the table.

I started, certain I must have looked as confused as I felt. "You think I only like you because you're beautiful?"

She shrugged, turning her face away to the window. "Am I wrong?"

"Hally, look at me," I said, reaching out to touch her hand. "I like you in spite of the fact that you're beautiful."

It was her turn to frown. "What's that supposed to mean?"

"It means that beautiful socialites are really not my type, but I seem to have…" I chose my words carefully. "I've developed feelings for you anyway."

She gave me a half smile. "That's the weirdest compliment I've ever received."

"I like you," I said again. "You're intriguing and you challenge me and you're so easy to talk to. The fact that you're so good-looking is just an element that takes me by surprise sometimes."

She tipped back her drink and pushed back her chair. "Let's get out of here."

I couldn't read her mood. Had I said too much? Was she insulted? I took one last sip and left it there, ice cubes melting into the remains, and followed Hally out of the bar. She didn't say anything as we waited for the lift and unable to decide if she was offended by my words or mildly pleased, I decided I had said enough. I followed her into the lift and she pressed just the one button. For her floor. And looked at me, her face a question.

CHAPTER TWENTY-TWO

I stepped toward her and took her in my arms, pressing my lips to hers, melting as she pulled me tightly against her. Heat coursed through my body. We almost didn't notice the elevator had stopped, and we stumbled out just as the doors were closing. She took my hand and we walked down the corridor, our footsteps muted by the thick dark carpet and fabric-lined hallway.

I took a moment to look around her room. She kept it neat, suitcase tucked under the desk, a book on the nightstand. I wondered if she put her clothes away in the cupboard and had to resist the urge to check. I could see her towel hanging in the bathroom and a scatter of small bottles around the bathroom sink.

"What are you looking at?" Hally asked, following my gaze around the room.

"I've never been in your space before. You've been to my place, but this is the first time I've been to yours."

Hally laughed. "This is nothing like my place."

"Maybe you could invite me over sometime."

She cocked her head. "Maybe I could."

"This is good too though," I said, taking a step toward her. She met me halfway, and we kissed, slowly, heat rising. The tip of her tongue met mine and the kiss deepened, my hands finding their way up her back to her hair.

"I missed you," I whispered.

She pulled back. "You did?"

"I did."

"A lot, or just a little?"

"A whole lot actually."

"Maybe you'd like to show me how much?"

I said I would like to do exactly that and wrapped an arm around her, kissing her as I backed her up slowly toward the bed and lowered her down carefully as her knees buckled. She wrapped her legs around me, and I pressed against her, kissing her neck, her collarbone, hands pushing up under her shirt.

She caught my hand and held it still for a moment. "Gin?"

"Yes?"

"This doesn't have to be complicated, right?"

I paused, my mouth hovering over the dip at her throat. Complicated? My heart was screaming *yes it does, it really, really does*, but my body, afraid that all this would go away if I tried to address that, said, "It does not."

"Good." She released my hand and stroked the back of my neck, sending a cascade of shivers down my skin. "Now, where were we?"

We slept in a tangle, finding each other in the night with the kind of urgency you would expect from lovers who were saying goodbye. I didn't know what to think of it but decided that thinking had no real place in this exchange and let my body ask for what I needed.

I was woken from a fitful sleep when Hally said suddenly, "Gin," and snapped the light on next to me.

"Sorry," she said, her voice tense.

I struggled to open my eyes, squinting against the glare from the light and my inability to focus. "My glasses," I said. "Could you please pass them to me?"

I blinked the room into focus, noting with surprise that she was standing by the bed, fully dressed, with her suitcase next to her. How long had I slept?

"What's happening?" I asked, pulling the sheet up over me and sitting up.

"I need to leave."

"What? Why? What time is it?"

"It's five thirty."

"In the morning?"

I shifted my glasses and rubbed my eyes. "Can you fill in the gaps for me? Is it Monday? Did I sleep through Sunday?"

"I've got a family emergency. I need to fly back to Melbourne."

I snapped to attention. "What's happened?" I asked, sliding out of the bed and retrieving my clothes from the floor where we had discarded them the night before. I pulled my shirt over my head and struggled into my underpants, trying not to fall over.

Her voice was tense. "It's my sister, my nephews—" she broke off and looked away. "They've received a threat."

I tried to process what she was saying. "From whom?"

She swallowed, her jaw tense. "From that guy I was telling you about. Up until now he's only being bothering me, but last night—" she broke off.

I rubbed her back and she took a shaky breath. "My sister's been texting me all night but my phone was on silent. Apparently an email came in last night with a picture of the boys at breakfast with us yesterday. This fucking psycho is threatening to kidnap them if I don't contact him. I've been ignoring his emails for months and I guess he's just stepped it up a notch. I need to get home and get this sorted out."

"Jesus. What do the police say?"

"I don't know yet. Delphi was in a state when we spoke. She didn't give me many details. I just need to get home and get things sorted out. Make sure they're safe. Don't feel you have to leave the room just because I am."

"It's fine. I can go back to my room," I said, jamming my feet into my shoes and looking around for my phone. I spied it on the floor and slipped it back into my pocket. "I'm ready."

I followed her out and we walked to the lift in silence, Hally's face a picture of distress. Her eyes, usually light, were heavy and hooded, her mouth pulled into a grim line.

"I can come with you to Melbourne," I said, as we waited for the elevator. "If you give me five minutes to run downstairs and grab my bag we can go together."

"No," she shook her head. "You don't need to do that. This is my mess. I made it. I'll fix it."

"What do you mean, you made it?"

The elevator arrived and Hally strode inside. I scurried in after her. She pressed ground.

"You've said it yourself, I invite this kind of attention through my social media. And now I've put my family in the line of fire."

I frowned and grabbed the rails as the lift lurched to a stop. "I don't think that's what I've said."

She turned to me, her eyes blazing. "You said, and I quote, I invite people in to look at my world, to comment on it. You said I *expose* myself online."

The doors slid open and Hally strode out into the foyer. I jogged after her and put my hand on her arm. "Hey, Hally, wait."

She shook off my arm. "I don't have time to wait. I need to go and be with my family. I need to fix it."

I waited with her as a taxi pulled up and opened its boot for her bag. I caught her hand and stopped her once more. "Hally, it's not your fault that a psychopathic arsehole is sending threatening emails to your family. You didn't post anything about the boys. You're always so careful about that kind of thing."

Her face cracked and she shook her head. "Everyone knew I'd be in Sydney though. I'll never forgive myself if something happens to them. I've got to go." She let go of my hand and slid into the back of the taxi, closing the door firmly after her.

I watched as the taxi pulled away from the curb and rolled off down the street. At this hour there was hardly any traffic, the street still in darkness except for the puddles of light from the streetlamps. I smoothed down my shirt and patted my pockets for my room key.

Uh oh. No room key. I must have left it in Hally's room. I wondered how they would take it back at the front desk when I told them that I had left my room key in another guest's room, a guest who had departed so hastily, leaving me stranded. Surely, I wouldn't be the first?

An awkward exchange with the front desk secured me another key, and some knowing looks from the front desk clerk. I made my way back to my room where I showered and changed. I felt at a loss, anxious to find out if Hally was okay, so I went downstairs for an early breakfast, but with my head racing I didn't enjoy the feast as planned. I had never meant to imply that something like this could possibly be Hally's fault. As terrifying as it was, stalking was nothing new, and I suspected the crazy who was going after Hally would have done so regardless of her posts. I hoped the police would help her see this.

I rang Cathy as I meandered through the Bondi markets that morning, filling her in on Hally's situation.

"Have you spoken to her this morning?"

"No, I don't want to interrupt her. I figure she'll have enough to deal with when she gets home, what with her family and the police. I've sent her a message and told her to call me anytime."

"And I'll send her an email," Cathy said. "Let her know we're here if she needs anything."

"Good idea. She seems to be blaming herself for this. She's got it into her head that all her online activity has caused this."

"You wouldn't have had anything to do with that now, would you?"

I gulped, a queasy feeling in the pit of my stomach. "I might have. I guess I've been pretty judgmental of her."

"Oh, my fine friend. When will you learn?"

"I don't know," I admitted. "Maybe one day, when the vultures are picking over my bleached bones."

"Ouch."

"Anyway, Darleen seems great."

"Isn't she?" Cathy sighed down the phone, her voice turning to instant goo. "I really like her."

"I couldn't tell," I said, my tone dry.

"If you tease me I won't ever let you see her again."

I smirked. "I wouldn't dream of it."

When I finally heard from Hally the following weekend, I was going out of my mind with worry, having almost paced a hole in the carpet. Cathy had found out that the man threatening her family had previous convictions for stalking and had been remanded in custody without bail, but for some reason I still hadn't heard from her.

Her text simply read, *Do you want to meet up today?*

I told her to name the time and place.

We met at the Penny Kettle, sitting at what was clearly Hally's favourite table in the back of the café. The waitress set our coffees before us with a little flourish. The barista had managed to swirl two love hearts into the foam on my coffee. I flicked the waitress a suspicious glance, waiting for Hally to snap the obligatory #latteart pic before I sipped it. Instead she reached for a teaspoon, dragging it straight through the magnificent sunset swirl the barista had in scripted in hers.

"Hally, wait," I cried, holding out my hand. "The photo."

"It's fine," she said, her voice hollow as she stared down, the sunset disappearing under her merciless hand. I could almost feel the barista crying. I wasn't sure whether to laugh or cry myself.

"Your followers," I started, then corrected myself. "Your community would want to see these. He's done a pretty great job."

"I'm not doing that anymore."

"But Cathy told me they got the guy. You really don't have to worry now."

There was silence while she carefully removed the teaspoon and licked off the froth. "Do you know how many followers I have?"

"Followers? I thought—"

She cut me off. "Do you know how many?"

I racked my brain, trying to think back to her bio. "Roughly nine hundred thousand."

"Actually, it's over a million now."

"That's good," I said, nodding encouragingly.

"No, that's roughly one million other possible psychopaths who might try to kill my family at any given moment. I'm done, Gin."

"Done? As in, no more social media?"

"Exactly. I've had enough of that superficial crap, as you so aptly put it."

I had to hand it to her. She did social-media hater better than I could ever have expected. But I couldn't find it in my heart to celebrate.

"Let's not be hasty, here." I reached out and put my hand on hers, but she immediately slipped it away.

"I'm rethinking my life," she said, her tone flat.

My heart lurched and I took back my hand. Did she mean me? I figured she wasn't lining up to have a relationship with me, but I had hoped something had changed between us. I had told myself I would be happy with just a friendship but I knew I was kidding myself.

"Look, I get this was scary but—"

"Scary? You're damn right it was *scary*. It was fucking terrifying. He threatened to kidnap Scott and Cameron. They're only seven and nine years old. Completely defenceless. The whole world is fucking terrifying and I'm done with it."

"Come on, Hally, I think you're blowing things out of proportion here. Yes it was scary, yes it was terrifying in fact, but the police *caught* him. It's dealt with now. You can go back to being you."

"You just don't get it, do you. You told me yourself my activity online was basically an invitation for people to feel like they know me. And from there, it's not a far stretch to feel like they're owed something from me. Look, I'm sorry." She pushed back her chair and stood up, her eyes skidding away from mine. "I'm actually not really in the mood for talking. This was a mistake. I'll see you around, Gin."

"Gin." Cathy buzzed my desk phone and I picked it up.

"Hi."

"I want you in on the meeting with Hally this afternoon."

I sat up. "What meeting?"

"She's coming in to talk with me and the team about her book."

I grimaced and shook my head. "No thanks. I haven't heard a word from her in three weeks." My heart was still smarting at the way she'd walked out on me at the café. "I'm clearly the last person she wants to see, and quite frankly, my heart would be better off not seeing her either."

"She'll listen to you, I know she will."

"What about?" I asked, curious.

"She wants to pull it, the book. She's saying it's too much exposure for her family."

Guilt gnawed at my stomach. "Cathy, I was the one who encouraged her to talk about her family in the book. She's hardly going to want me at the meeting."

"I know. And the fact that you convinced her to put it in there in the first place means you're the one to convince her to keep the book on the shelves. I know she's afraid but it's a good book."

"I just don't get it. They caught they guy, didn't they?"

"They did and he's locked up until his trial. He'll go to jail this time."

"So why is she freaking out about the book now?"

"I don't know. My guess is, it's set off a whole chain reaction of fear for her."

I sighed. "I really don't think I'm the right person for this. I also seem to set off chain reactions in Hally, mostly of anger and frustration it would seem."

"Just be in my office at three p.m. please. She's agreed to come in and I want to see if we can salvage this situation."

"Fine."

At three o'clock I resisted the urge to go to the bathroom and throw up, and instead packed up my notebook and a pen and made my way to Cathy's office. Hally was there already, seated at the table in the corner with James, the head of Marketing, one of our lawyers, an officious-looking woman in an expensive suit and Cathy, of course. There was one seat left at the table, opposite Hally, and I slid into it, giving Hally a brief smile of acknowledgement.

"Gin, this is Sophia Lorenzo," Cathy said, indicating the woman sitting next to Hally. "Hally's lawyer."

"Right. Nice to meet you," I said, even though it certainly didn't feel that nice. The atmosphere in the room was tense. I resisted a sudden urge to jump up and down and break through the strain.

"Now that we're all here, let's get started," Cathy said. "Hally, we totally respect that you're having second thoughts about the book, given your recent experience but we're really hoping we can find a way to keep it on the shelves."

"No, my client has instructed me to negotiate the terms of a break of contract," Sophia said, her voice cold.

"The terms are clear in the contract your client signed," our lawyer replied, flicking through a bulky document. "A break of contract has a strong financial penalty."

I tuned out, letting the lawyers haggle with each other, my eyes straying to Hally. She was looking even more gaunt than when I'd seen her last, her cheeks pale, eyes haunted.

"Hally," I said, breaking into the conversation and causing her to look up at me in surprise. "Please don't do this. We really don't want you to do this."

She looked down at her hands. "You just want me to keep the book out there to make money for Red Stone."

I pressed my hand to my heart, stung. "That's what you think of me? I'm that person? Hally, please look at me."

Hally raised her eyes and met my gaze.

"Tell me I'm wrong," she challenged. "Remember now, you're supposed to be the truthful one."

"You're wrong," I said promptly. "I'll admit, in the beginning I only agreed to work on your book with you because it was good for Red Stone's bottom line."

"And because they said they'd fire you if you didn't."

I pushed my glasses up my nose, grimacing at the team around the table. "Thank you, yes. And because they said they'd fire me if I didn't. But somewhere along the line it all changed for me, Hally. I can see the positive aspects of your world. I see what you bring to people, the inspiration, the encouragement, the belief, the motivation to change, to do better, to help others, to come together. It's all there and you'd have to be blind not to realise that's a good thing. I was blind, I admit it, but I see it all now. And I can also see that by putting yourself out there it's a risk and it's exposing, but it's also rewarding, and it allows you to help people. You lead by example, showing people how they can live better lives, not just telling them, and it's a good thing. We need strong leaders in this world. Women who can *show* us how to be our best, not just tell us.

"It wouldn't be the end of the world for Red Stone if you pull the book, but it would be for you. You've worked hard for this and people want to read it. Women want to learn from you, they want to see how they can take the reins in their own lives and go full steam ahead. Your book contains your story. There's nothing in there that endangers your nephews, or your sister or mother for that matter. It's simply the story of how you came to be you. And tell me this. What are you going to do with yourself if you can't be Hally Arlow?"

She blinked, apparently fighting back tears.

"Hally," I said gently. She looked up, meeting my eyes. "I get that what happened to you was terrifying, but you are very careful. You've said it yourself—you vet what you put online and you never expose your family. Surely you can't let one person take away everything you've worked so hard for."

Hally blew out a shaky sigh. "Thank you," she said, her tone gruff. "I'll think about what you've said."

"I must advise you, Hally, that the longer we wait the harder it will be to retract copy," Sophia said pompously. I wanted to reach out and slap her. I settled for glaring at her. "We really should move on this."

Hally looked at me and I tried to look as encouraging as I could.

"I want to think about it all some more. Thank you all for taking the time to meet with me. I'm sorry for the inconvenience I'm causing you. I'm sure you can all understand the predicament I'm in here."

"Take the time you need, Hally," Cathy said, her voice warm with understanding. "We'll support whatever decision you make. Obviously we want to keep the book, but ultimately, only if you're happy about it."

Hally thanked us all again and left the room with her lawyer. James and our lawyer looked seriously concerned. I picked up my notebook. "Anything else from me?"

Cathy shook her head and I scuttled out. Suddenly I knew I had to catch Hally before she left the building and I jogged to the lift, catching her just as it arrived.

"Wait, Hally, just one more thing."

She turned to face me, her hand stopping the automatic sensor from closing the doors. "I'm sorry if I pushed you to do something you regret. I really am."

She looked confused. "What do you mean?"

"I encouraged you to go deeper, to write about yourself, your family, your experiences. It was my fault the book exposes you, and I'm sorry for putting you in an awkward position. I was only trying to get the best for you."

"I know you were," she said. She held my eyes for a moment longer and then took away her hand, letting the doors slide closed.

CHAPTER TWENTY-THREE

I walked home from work slowly. Since our meeting with Hally the week before I had begun to resign myself to a certain fate. We were going to lose the book, and I had clearly lost Hally. I scuffed my shoe on the ground as I waited at the lights to cross into Carlton Gardens, staring at a crack on the footpath. I felt like a fissure had opened up in my life and it was threatening to swallow me whole. I cursed Cathy, soundly blaming her for making me read Hally Arlow's book in the first place but knew I wouldn't change it now for the world. No matter my heartache, I was still glad to have met Hally, glad to have had the opportunity to know her and share some special times with her.

The lights buzzed and I allowed myself to be swept along with the city's pedestrians. Working with Hally had changed me, I could see that now. I was better off for it, even without her continued presence in my life. I knew my despair would eventually subside, but I also knew I wouldn't be quite as cynical, quite as quick to judge. I had climbed down from my high horse and was seeing the world from an entirely different angle these days.

It was cooler in the park and I walked in the shade, lost in my thoughts.

"Gin?" a familiar voice said, causing my head to snap around.

My heart leapt as I stopped to find Hally sitting by the path on a park bench. I looked at her in confusion. "What are you doing here?"

"Waiting for you."

"You are?"

"I wanted to ask you a question." She patted the seat next to her and I sat down, resting my bag at my feet.

"Fire away."

"Before I do, I wanted to thank you, for what you said in the meeting last week."

I bit my lip. "I hope it helped."

"You made a lot of sense."

"Well, that's good."

"Yes, I've decided I'm not going to withdraw the book."

Relief flooded through me. "That's excellent news." Cathy would be thrilled.

"I feel like you see me for who I am now," Hally said, her fingers worrying the zip on her bag. "I wondered if that was right? That's the question I wanted to ask you. Do you think you see me for who I am?" Uncertainty showed in her amber eyes.

"I think I do," I said.

"When we first met you didn't think much of me."

"No, I—"

She held up a hand to silence me. "I didn't think much of you either. But that all changed, didn't it?"

My heart skipped. "It did."

"How did it change for you?"

I stared at her, my throat dry. "Actually," I let my gaze wander over the trees, taking in the variegated greens, the dark woody trunks. "I fell in love with you."

"You did?"

I nodded, keeping my gaze trained away from her, following the movements of a sparrow as it flittered on the pathway.

"Gin?"

"Yes?"

She put her hand on mine and I looked at it, noting her slender fingers. I turned my hand over, palm up, and intertwined our fingers and then looked up at her, unable to ask my question.

"Have dinner with me tonight?"

"It would be my pleasure."

Hally picked me up at eight p.m., giving me just enough time to get home, shower and stress over what I would wear. I was just throwing on my third outfit choice when she texted to say she was outside.

"Where are we headed?" I asked, as she pulled away from the curb.

"I made a reservation for us at my favourite restaurant up in the Dandenongs, if you don't mind a bit of a drive."

"I'm happy," I said, settling back into the seat. I wound down my window and let the warm evening air flow over my body as we drove, gazing up to look at the stars. Sitting next to her like this, in easy silence as the night rushed by—I really was happy.

It was cooler in the hills, but still balmy enough that I didn't need a jacket. The restaurant Hally had chosen was set on wooden stilts against a hillside, the dining room high among the treetops, almost like a tree house. We were shown to a table by a young waiter, who greeted Hally by name, and slid into our seats. The heady scent of cooling eucalypts wafted in through the open windows and I gazed around me in delight.

"Never been here before?" Hally asked.

"Never. I love it."

"I'm glad."

We didn't talk much as we perused the menu and Hally seemed intent on keeping the conversation light through dinner. I didn't complain, happy to be sitting across from her, as we made our way through plates of handmade pasta and a loaf of crusty bread.

When our stomachs were full and our plates clean, the waiter cleared them away, and returned with tiny cups of espresso and a plate of chocolates.

"Mum made these today," he said with a grin. "She wants you to try them. On the house."

"Oh, Jimmy, your mum is the best. Please tell her the food is divine as always."

"Will do. Can I get you anything else?"

Hally raised her eyebrows at me and I shook my head, rubbing a hand over my stomach. "I'm done. In the best possible way."

"I think we're good thanks," Hally told him and we both watched as he whipped away, clearing other tables and laughing and joking with the customers.

"I fell in love with you too," Hally said suddenly, so quietly I almost missed it.

"You did?" My eyes found hers, heart thumping around in my chest like a drunk timpani player. "But you...you barely spoke to me after Sydney."

She sighed. "Everything was so stressful and messy. And I was mad with you."

"Why?"

"I thought you were judging me. You had already judged me for my lifestyle, my work, my everything basically. I felt defensive in case you were judging me again. I felt like I had exposed my family to risk and you had already pointed out that it was a possibility so even though you didn't say it, I felt like you had to think it was all my own fault."

"I'm sorry, I never should have said those things. It wasn't fair."

"No, it's okay. It's a complicated world. Things are never totally black and white and I think it's possible that we're both right. I've been thinking things through all week and I feel like I've finally found my perspective again. The online stuff is definitely about community. I didn't make that up, but community can also have its dark spots, just like any physical community."

I nodded. "I think you're right."

She blew out a sigh. "I was pretty confused by it all. And when you add in the fear and the threat against my family... well, I just wanted to run away from everything."

"I get it."

"You do?"

"Yes. Hally, I've been such an idiot so many times with you, and you've held up a mirror and shown me myself, behaving like an arse. I get wanting to run away."

"But you don't want to run away now?" She reached across the table and took my hand in hers.

"No. Actually." I took a deep breath. "The opposite. I was hoping things *could* get complicated. In Sydney you said you didn't want things to be complicated between us. Do you still feel that way?"

"I wasn't sure I was ready to let you back in."

"Are you now?"

She leaned forward, her thumb tracing my palm. "Let's get the bill."

Outside, the night was well and truly in situ and the stars were brilliant above us. My hand slipped into Hally's and she pulled me close to her as we walked to the car. She blipped it open but before I could get in, she turned me to her and brushed her lips over mine. My stomach fluttered, my body melting into hers.

"Complicated sounds...complicated," she murmured, her mouth against mine.

"I think I like complicated," I replied, winding an arm around her and pulling her in close. "But it's up to you."

"If this is complicated, I think I like it too."

"This is unexpected," I said.

I felt her smile against mine and she laughed. "Do you never consider the possibilities in advance? Life does always seem to be creeping up on you."

"You never do what I imagine you'll do. I honestly thought I'd never hear from you again."

She kissed me again, her mouth warm against mine. "I couldn't stay away from you."

"I'm glad," I said, surrendering myself to the kiss.

"I don't want to lose you," I murmured when we came up for air. "Can we lock in this complicated thing?"

"Are you saying you want to go steady with me?" she teased. Her eyes were light, shining with what I could only hope was happiness.

"Would you?" I asked. "Is that a thing you'd do? You know, with me?"

"I would," she said, solemnly, brushing my lips with hers. "And then, would you take me back to your place?"

"Oh, yes," I said. "I definitely would."

Bella Books, Inc.

Women. Books. Even Better Together.

P.O. Box 10543
Tallahassee, FL 32302

Phone: 800-729-4992
www.bellabooks.com